King Goshawk and the Birds

T0161441

Eimar O'Duffy

KING GOSHAWK AND THE BIRDS

DALKEY ARCHIVE PRESS

Originally published by the Macmillan Company in 1926.
First Dalkey Archive edition, 2017.

Library of Congress Cataloging-in-Publication Data
Names: O'Duffy, Eimar, 1893-1935, author.
Title: King Goshawk and the birds / by Eimar O'Duffy.
Description: First Dalkey Archive edition. | Victoria, TX : Dalkey
Archive Press, 2017. | Series: Cuanduine trilogy : 1
Identifiers: LCCN 2017014905 | ISBN 9781943150205 (softcover :
acid-free paper)
Subjects: LCSH: Ireland--Fiction. | GSAFD: Dystopias.
Classification: LCC PR6029.D76 K56 2017 | DDC 823/.912--dc23
LC record available at https://lccn.loc.gov/2017014905

www.dalkeyarchive.com
Victoria, TX / McLean, IL / Dublin

Dalkey Archive Press publications are, in part, made possible through
the support of the University of Houston-Victoria and its programs in
creative writing, publishing, and translation.

Printed on permanent/durable acid-free paper

BOOK I
A CORNER IN MELODY

BOOK II
THE COMING OF CUANDUINE

BOOK III
THE TRAVELS OF CUANDUINE

BOOK I

A CORNER IN MELODY

CHAPTER I

The Pillow-chat of Goshawk and Guzzelinda

GOSHAWK THE WHEAT KING and Guzzelinda his Queen, sitting up in the royal bed in the Palace of Manhattan, held conversation thus:

Said Goshawk: "You did well in marrying me, my dear; for it was well said by someone or other: 'Happy is the wife of a Successful Man'; and am I not the world's greatest success, and the Biggest Man that ever was in all time? The Wheat of the world is mine. Tea, Sugar, and Milk are my vassals. Coal and Oil are my tributaries. As my Laureate sang yesterday:

Under my ukase sun and rain
May shine for naught and fall in vain—

and if there's poetic license in the couplet, why, there's truth in it too. Big is your husband, my dear, and big are his interests. Aren't you happy?"

"That's all very well," Guzzelinda answered. "But it was a wise man who said: 'Call no man a success until he's dead and has carried out all he promised.'"

"Well," said Goshawk, "I'm not dead yet, nor anything near it. But, short of that, what have I failed in, and what promise have I not performed? All that I ever coveted I own. I cannot count my riches. I do not know the limits of my power. There is not a human ear that has not heard the sound of my name. I hold the governments of the world in pawn. Parliaments dare

3

not offend me. What ships on the sea that are not mine are of no account. I own all the airways of the world. I have set up Notre Dame de Paris here as my private chapel, and carried the Sphinx out of Egypt to adorn my gardens. The world's best pictures clutter my galleries, and I have a lien on the remainder. My advertisements are graven on every landscape, from the Rockies to the Himalayas, from the Riviera to the Vale of Avoca, from the oases of the Sahara to the ice-cliffs of the Antarctic. There is wealth and power and publicity such as never were known before. What more could a man do? What on earth have I left undone?"

Said Guzzelinda: "You have not written your advertisement on the face of the Moon; and you have not performed the prom with which you won my girlish heart to love you."

King Goshawk knit his brows in some annoyance. He said: "The Moon shall bear my stamp before very long: my scientists are seeing to it. But what is this other promise you speak of? You must forgive me if, after the lapse of so many busy years, I have grown forgetful."

Said his Queen: "It's a good saying my people have: 'Memory falls to the bottom of a long purse.' Have you forgotten that evening long ago in my father's garden, when we sat and listened, hand in hand, to the song of the nightingales? and I said: 'How sad to think how many birds are singing all over the world that I can never hear'; and you answered: 'Darling, when I have come into my kingdom you shall have all the song-birds in the world for your very own.'"

"By the Buck!" cried King Goshawk. "I remember it now. I was young and foolish then. However, only a big man could make such a promise, and only a man as big as I am now could perform it. You shall have your birds, my dear, if they cost me a hundred million."

"My dear," said his Queen, "there was never one like you for assimilating a proposition and making it right over."

Thus far the pillow-chat of Goshawk and Guzzelinda. Now shift we our ground to the city of Dublin, between the sea and the mountains, by the bright waters of Liffey; where our feet tread more easily than on the shores of Manhattan or in the palaces of kings.

CHAPTER II

By the Ford of Hurdles

THERE WAS A PHILOSOPHER once who lived in a little room in a tumbledown house in a back lane off Stoneybatter; which is not a place prolific in philosophers, for the reason that the folk there are too busy picking up half a living to have time for the cultivation of wisdom. The Philosopher himself could only make time for it by giving up the food-scramble entirely; which he was able to do because he had been left a share of money by his father, who had been left it before by his grandfather, a man of exceeding wealth and wickedness—not the kind of wickedness that would give any one a thrill in the reading: I wish it had been, for I would like well to entertain you with the clink and chatter of banquets, or to drape alluring phrases round the limbs of dancing girls. But the truth is that the Philosopher's grandfather was a water-drinker, and a water-drinker of the worst kind: that is say, he drank it between meals for his health, not at meals for his pleasure. Moreover, he cared nothing for women; and it is not on record that he ever missed a Mass. His wickedness was none of this sort; which indeed the gods readily forgive, knowing the weakness of man. His sins were those that cry to heaven for vengeance: not murder, for he feared the rope; nor the sin of the cursed cities, for nature had not treated him so unkindly; but the other two, on which no god could have mercy, but which are none the less so commonly committed that if they were legally punishable there would not be enough free men to be gaolers to the others; and yet are so universally denounced that if I were to take up testimony against them I should be called a mere speaker of platitudes. I must be original at all costs, for my livelihood depends on it: therefore, I dismiss the wickedness of the Philosopher's grandfather without further comment. Peace to his ashes: for his spirit shall have none. The room inhabited by the Philosopher was at the top of the house, but that was all the good that could be said for it. It was neither large nor lofty, and had but one window, which was so close to the floor that the Philosopher had to stoop as low as to his waist to look out of it: not that there was much to see: only the tenement opposite: and even that was not visible unless he opened the window; for the glass was encrusted with the dirt of civilised ages, and, though the Philosopher had frequently rubbed it off the inside, it never occurred to him to clean the outside, his mind being so occupied with other matters that he overlooked that solution to the difficulty. In this room the Philosopher kept all his worldly goods, namely, a bedstead, a chair, a table, a cooking stove, some crockery, an old trunk full of spare clothes, and a heap of books; and for it he paid five shillings and sixpence a week to his landlord, an excellent man and a patriot, who, if the girls in his employment were sometimes driven to supplement their wages with what they could earn on the street, made ample atonement for it by valiant assaults upon any book or play that denied the superhuman chastity of the women of Ireland.

The Philosopher was not very old: only about sixty: but he looked more, because in his search for wisdom he had been forced to deny himself much air and sunshine; which is the same reason why most of the people in the streets look older than their years. For in a progressive age man wants so much, and wants that much so quick (time being valuable, though why I know not, when it is so equitably distributed, each of us having his twenty-four hours a day of it) that fellow-man must stay out of the sunshine to accommodate him. This is a clumsy sentence; but a man who has a long tale to tell, and has little leisure and no patience, must use language as best he can, and the reader must act as he would if someone were to pour him a pint of wine into a gill measure: lap up what's spilt if he thinks it worthwhile, and if not let it go and nothing lost. As it is, I let a thought go when I found the parenthesis getting overweighted, as the waiter might have held back a finger or so of the wine, and it concerns this matter of the distribution of time. It seems to me a most unjust, unwise, and altogether reprehensible course to apportion this with rigid equality when the needs of men are so manifestly unequal. Surely the captain needs more than the cabin boy? the head clerk more than his junior? the ministers of State more than the teachers of children? Surely the director of a large business needs more for his plans and combinations than those whose sole function is to work for him and serve him? Surely the man who has three houses needs more than the man who has only one room? And surely the man who owns yachts and motors and deer forests needs more time for their enjoyment than he who is limited to a tram-ride on Sunday to the seaside? Consider, too, the effects of this soul-killing equality upon the enterprise and initiative of the individual. Where is the incentive to speed and punctuality when every body, whether slothful or energetic, can command his twenty-four hours a day? And by what means can we prevent the lazy and the unscrupulous from wasting the precious commodity so lavishly bestowed on them? When one realises the temptation to idleness offered by this unnatural apportionment of award without regard to desert, one marvels that any work is ever done by anybody, and that the world has not long since lapsed into chaos.

But to return to our Philosopher. Was he happy? Was he sad? Wisdom brings neither happiness nor sadness but a remarkable lack of both: for happiness is possible only where there is a sense of finality, and the wise man knows there is finality in nothing; by which knowledge also he escapes sadness. Mundane things worried the Philosopher not at all. He never noticed whether he was comfortable or not, and he never cared what he ate. He did not even lament his lack of books, believing that there was more to be learnt from the talk of a child, the smile of a woman, or the folly of men than from all the books that ever were written. His wisdom had not been gained in the way which, if it were efficacious, would make Croagh Patrick wiser than the saint who prayed on its summit: to wit, by experience. If experience were necessary to wisdom he would have been a fool, for he never had been out of Dublin in his life, his father having dissipated in folly what his grandfather had accumulated in sin, so that the Philosopher never had more than a tram-fare to travel with, and no way of getting it without dropping the search for wisdom and going down to fight for money amongst those who were far better equipped for the struggle than he was. "What matter anyway?" he said. "There are four hundred thousand people in Dublin, and if I went round the world itself I wouldn't be able to talk with half that number. And when you come to think of it, the people of Dublin are as much different from one another as any one of them from a person of Paris or Budapest or Lhasa or San Francisco or the Patagonian hinterland." This is not to say that if someone had offered to pay his fare he would not have relished a talk with a lama of Tibet, or a geisha of Japan, or a vendor of spices in the bazaars of the East. He would; and he would have gained great profit therefrom. But as these were inaccessible he did the best he could with the Jesuits of Milltown, and the girls of the canal banks, and the vendors of newspapers in the streets of Dublin; and from these he learned a good deal. But he learned most from the inhabitants of his own back lane off Stoneybatter.

One morning the Philosopher opened his newspaper and read the following passage:

GOSHAWK BUYS BIRDS

WHEAT KING'S LATEST ENTERPRISE

A New York message just received states that King Goshawk has completed negotiations for the purchase of all the blackbirds, robins, larks, and nightingales in the world. The vast bulk of these will be removed at an early date to the great park of Goshawk Palace, but a few will be kept in aviaries near the principal cities for the delectation of their inhabitants.

On King Goshawk's well-known principle that "Anything free is not valued," it is understood that there will be a small charge for admission to these avians.

King Goshawk deserves the gratitude of the public for having thus taken one more step in harnessing Nature to the service of mankind.

After reading this the Philosopher passed his hand three or four times through his hair. Then he went to the window, opened it, and looked down the street. There was a dead wall not far away, on which two flamboyant election posters had been fixed the day before. The Philosopher could read them from where he was. The first ran thus:

VOTE FOR O'CODD
The Yallogreen Party stands for
MAJORITY RULE
If you want PEACE
UNITY
FREEDOM
VOTE FOR O'CODD

The other said:

VOTE FOR CODDO
The Greenyallo Party is out for

DEMOCRATIC GOVERNMENT
If you want TRANQUILLITY
HOMOGENEITY
LIBERTY
VOTE FOR CODDO

The Philosopher smiled. Then he noticed that two mean little hand-bills had been stuck up underneath the flamboyant posters, and he went down into the street to read them. The one under O'Codd's poster said:

O'CODD DRINKS
Would you entrust the
Destinies of Ireland
to such a man?

and the one under Coddo's poster said:

CODDO KEEPS A MISTRESS
Is such a man fit
to legislate for the
Island of Saints?

And lastly he noticed that underneath each mean little hand-bill some franker spirit had chalked the same accusation in blunter language than I care to record.

As long as the Philosopher could remember, the Yallogreens and the Greenyallos had been thus abusing one another: nor had they always confined themselves to flamboyant posters, mean little hand-bills, and dirty language. The Philosopher sadly recalled to mind the great civil war that had been waged between them over the question of rejoining the British Empire, from which the Irish people had seceded some years earlier. The reunion was proposed in the Dáil by Seumas Vanderbags, leader of the Yallogreen party, and supported with fiery speeches by Madame Przemysl and Miss O'Grady. The Philosopher had listened to that acrimonious debate from the Strangers' Gallery; had watched the members file into the Division lobbies; and had heard the ringing cheers that greeted the announcement that the motion was lost by seven votes. He could still see in imagination the pale thin face of Vanderbags as he rose to his feet to announce that he would not abide by the verdict, and to utter his famous pronouncement that the people had no right to do wrong. Never could the Philosopher forget the horrors of the subsequent fighting. The Government had been unprepared; the rebels had been silently perfecting their plans for years. Liquid fire, poison gas, infernal machines of every description were brought into play. Half the city of Dublin was laid in ashes, and most of the country devastated. The army of the Republic was annihilated in less than a month; it only remained to dragoon the civil population into submission, and send a formal demand to London for incorporation in the Empire. The Philosopher felt again the shame of that disgraceful day, and at the memory of what followed his whole body blushed: for the English Government curtly rejected the application, and one by one the Dominions endorsed their decision. But the Yallogreens were not to be daunted by such a repulse. Vanderbags declared that the right of Ireland to belong to the British Empire was inalienable and indefeasible; and Miss O'Grady said that the Irish People were citizens of the British Empire whether they or the British liked it or not: such was their love for the Empire that they would lay all its cities in ashes and slaughter every man, woman, and child within its borders sooner than be thrust out of their inalienable inheritance. The sequel of all this was burnt deep into the Philosopher's recollection: the mad declaration of war against the British Empire; the destruction of the Irish navy; the invasion of Ireland by the British; and the forcible re-establishment of the Republic. Neither could he forget the campaign of flamboyant posters, mean little hand-bills, and dirty language that followed.

Regarding the specimens of statecraft now plastered on the wall before him, the Philosopher began to realise that the song-birds could hope for little succour at the hands of his country-men; but the rest of Europe had no more consolation to offer. Half a century of history now whirled like a nightmare before his vision. In his childhood he had seen the French, who once had been content to be the leaders of the world in art, science, thought, manners, and the cultivation of the vine, suddenly seized with the ambition to be its leaders in covetousness, ruth-lessness, and hypocrisy as well; under which impetus he had seen them trample for long years upon their neighbours the Germans, a good-natured, industrious people, who once had put on impe-rialism like a garment, only to have it torn from their shoulders by others more fitted by nature to wear it. Through those years he had seen France preparing her own doom; had seen her filling her pockets, glutting her hatred and fear, and losing her soul. He had seen her building barracks while the Germans built nurser-ies; drilling armies while the Germans begot children. Then one day the giant nation of eighty millions of people had arisen, and shaken off its tormentors as a man might shake dust out of his coat. Once more German armies were on the soil of France; once more the world was in a ferment. Nation after nation was drawn by its fears or its interests into the fray. The war was waged with the utmost ferocity of which human nature is capable, aided by the destructive efficiency attained by generations of scientific progress. Forty million fighting men fell on the fields of battle; a hundred million women and children perished of famine and disease. One-third of the cities and three-fifths of the shipping of the world were destroyed. Two hundred thousand square miles of land was rendered useless. Europe and half America were stripped bare of forests. The world's supply of copper and tin was exhausted. There was no formal peace: the nations simply stopped fighting because they were unable to go on.

These were sad memories for the Philosopher who stood ankle-deep in dust and rubbish contemplating the flamboyant posters and the mean little hand-bills and the dirty language scrawled on the dead wall in the back lane off Stoneybatter; for to one to whom things external to himself are a matter of serious import, there is cause for sorrow and apprehension in the discovery that whereas a man in fifty years may grow from helplessness and innocence to strength and wisdom, mankind in a hundred does not change at all. But no sooner had this reflection entered the Philosopher's mind than he began to examine it, to question it, and to doubt it, as was his nature.

"Hold," he said. "This may be a misjudgement: for it is many years since I have given any thought to public affairs. I will go down and speak to the people and see whether I am wrong."

He went down accordingly, and came upon a public meeting among the ruins of College Green, where an orator, standing upon the pile of wrecked masonry that had once been Trinity College, was urging the claims of Coddo upon the suffrage of the multitude. With the birds of Eirinn in jeopardy, the Philosopher could not long endure such folly. Mounting therefore upon the pedestal that had once borne Grattan's statue, he began to harangue the people near him. "Citizens," he said, "I am a foolish and ignorant man."

"Indeed y'are," replied some of them.

"I am," said the Philosopher, "and I know it. You also are foolish and ignorant."

"What!!!" yelled the citizens.

"But you do not know it," said the Philsopher.

"Ye're right there," said the citizens.

"Do not vote for O'Codd," said the Philosopher.

"Hear, hear," said the supporters of Coddo. "Don't vote for Coddo either," said the Philosopher.

"Hear, hear," cried the supporters of O'Codd.

"What does it matter to you," said the Philosopher, "which of these fools misrepresents you in Parliament?"

Here the Philosopher's speech was cut short by an egg, which came sailing through the air and smashed in his mouth. Next minute he was plucked from Grattan's pedestal and fell among a roaring, raging mob, who began beating him and kicking him and tearing him and trampling on him, and even fighting with one another in their efforts to get a blow at him. Some spat in his face; others threw dirt at him; one died of rage because he could not reach him. Nor were the women backward in the fray. Some stabbed him with hatpins; others clawed his face; more, who could not get near him, went into paroxysms of fury, foaming at the mouth and yelling "Kill him! Tear his eyes out!" and similar objurgations. Several fainted with fury; others in their transports went black in the face, and with hideous grimaces and frantic bodily contortions flung themselves on the ground, kicking up their legs and screeching like demoniacs. In the end some stout young fellows picked up what was left of the Philosopher and flung him in the river; whence he was with much difficulty and some danger rescued by a man who was later prosecuted under the Blasphemy and Indecency laws and the Treason-felony laws for the utterance of a blasphemous, indecent, treasonable, and felonious sentiment, to wit: "Politics in this country are a damned cod"; and being duly convicted was sentenced to penal servitude for life.

CHAPTER III

How the Philosopher, without Mechanical Aid, was translated to the Twentieth Heaven, and held Converse with one who has not spoken by the Ouija Board

THE PHILOSOPHER, IN SPITE of his years, was of a sound constitution, having at no time eaten when he was not hungry, or drunk when he was not thirsty, as does your ordinary sensible person to the detriment of his liver and the enlargement of his belly. He was not long, therefore, in recovering from the hurts he had suffered at the hands of the citizenry; in whose blows indeed there was more malice than strength, more will than power to do injury. As soon as his mind had regained its vigour and clarity, he said to himself: "So I was right after all." And when he was fully healed and able to regard the matter with complete impersonality he confirmed that judgement. "And alas," he said, "it is beyond my power to remedy this evil, for if I speak to the people again they will only treat me as before, to the undoing of their souls." He began, therefore, to ponder how man might be redeemed from the course of wickedness and folly by which he was travelling to destruction; and to that inquiry he devoted the full labour of his mind for a period of thirty days; at the end of which time he came to the conclusion that the task was beyond the power of mortal man, and could be accomplished only by one returned from the life beyond.

Then the Philosopher set himself to recall to memory the words and works of the great men of the past, in order to discover which of them would be the most fitting to invoke for the purpose: whether Zoroaster or Confucius or Socrates or Plato or Aristotle or Aquinas or Descartes or Hegel or Ibsen or Mill. After prolonged cogitation and a most scrupulous weighing and comparison of the faculties, dispositions, and accidental circumstances of each (and indeed of many others whom he also considered), his choice fell upon Socrates as being the most distinguished of all the wise men for charity and equanimity; as was shown by the answer he gave Xanthippe one day, when, after rating him soundly for his gadabout habits, the low company he kept, and the talk he excited among the neighbours, she was so irritated by his refusal to answer back that she threw a bowl of soup over him: whereat, "After the storm," said he, "we may expect some rain." The Philosopher felt that only by such a spirit as this could reason be restored to the counsels of mankind, and he made his decision accordingly. As to a way of carrying it into effect, that did not seem to him a matter of overwhelming difficulty; neither did he spend any time devising such methods as those by which Odysseus and Aeneas penetrated to the infernal regions, nor those by which Cyrano de Bergerac, Mr. Cavor, and the members of the Gun Club travelled to the moon; for he well knew that the mind of man can conceive more devices than the powers of his body can execute; on which account he was resolved to set his mind upon the quest alone, and to leave his body behind if need were. Locking himself, therefore, in his room, that he might not be disturbed, he gave his thoughts wholly to Socrates for the space of three days and three nights, during which time also he neither ate nor drank; whereby, as he became purged of earthy matter and gross desires, his mind was set free to journey among the stars, until at length it found the spirit of Socrates wandering in a valley of austere beauty lit alternately by twin suns, red and blue, that whirl in the outer regions of space.

Said the spirit of Socrates: "Who are you?"

"One," said the mind of the Philosopher, "who is looking

for Truth."

"So am I," said the spirit of Socrates.

"What?" said the mind of the Philosopher. "Is the Truth not to be found in heaven?"

"Only this truth," said the spirit of Socrates: "that it is not to be found. And this we learn when we come to the twentieth heaven, which is here. For in seeking there is life; but in finding there is stagnation, and stagnation is death."

"That," said the mind of the Philosopher, "does not seem to me to be just or reasonable."

"It is plain, then," said the spirit of Socrates, "that you have come here direct from some corporeal world, and not from one of the lower heavens. Know then that the justice of heaven is this: that we obtain our desires. Now the desire of the many is for peace; and there is no peace but in death. But the desire of the few is for knowledge; and knowledge is infinite; so that its pursuit is life everlasting. But tell me—for I must not reveal the secrets of paradise—what is your errand?"

"Man," said the Philosopher, "is full of wickedness and folly."

"He always was," said the spirit of Socrates. "Nay, but," said the Philosopher, "he had not always the powers of which he is now the master; which indeed are so great that a wise and just people could not safely be entrusted with them, and in his hands are likely to bring him to utter destruction."

Said the spirit of Socrates, pausing in the middle of the valley of austere beauty, bathed in the purple twilight of the rising and setting suns: "If so, so good; for there is no more use for him."

"Nevertheless," said the mind of the Philosopher, "I wish to save him. For we are of one blood, and I cannot but love him."

"Save him, then," said the spirit of Socrates, "but do not interrupt my contemplations with any further talk of his follies."

"I cannot save him," said the mind of the Philosopher, "because he will not hear me. Therefore, I came here to ask you to speak to him instead, for he would listen to one from beyond the grave."

"I have greater work than that before me," said the spirit of Socrates.

"It is your own kin," said the mind of the Philosopher, "— maybe your own descendants—that I want you to save."

"I am beyond love and hate," said the spirit of Socrates.

Said the mind of the Philosopher:

"There was a rich man once who owned mines and factories and lands without number; and he had twenty palaces and thirty motorcars. His fingers, which were as fat and flabby as white puddings, were covered with diamond rings; a most impious practice, for precious stones were made for the adornment of beauty, not for the extenuation of ugliness. He had five chins, and his belly was of obscene proportions and very foul within. For this man was a most insatiable eater and drinker. His meals followed so hard upon one another that he had never in all his life known what it was to feel hungry; and it is even reported that in the night hours his attendants administered nutriment to him while he slept, but whether by injection or inunction I cannot tell. Neither was he ever known to take any exercise, but in the most trivial and intimate actions was assisted and forestalled by the attendants aforesaid. Can you picture him so? Pah! What a parcel of tripes was this, to be so carefully handled and so honourably observed by decent men.

"There was also living at this time a poor widow, who had nothing at all but one only son, whom she supported by working in one of the rich man's factories; for which work he paid her as little as he could, charging her mightily for the kennel he assigned her for a habitation, and for the clothes and food she bought in his shops. Those who have little want less than those who have abundance; and this woman wanted nothing but the happiness of her son, whom she loved with every fibre of her body and every power of her soul. When she looked at him sometimes sleeping in his bed her heart would stand still for very love, and she yearned to take him back to her and enfold him again in the warmth of her being. 'God bless him: God bless him!' she would say, and then go and darn his socks or patch his breeches with fingers weary with toil.

"The youngster loved her too, but easily, as is the way of boys. Under her care he grew up strong, handsome, and intelligent. For his sake she denied herself every comfort, and by diligent saving she was able to keep him on at school beyond the age at which the poor are usually taken away from it for the better preservation of their inferiority. Then when she saw with what zeal he applied himself to learning, and when she looked with eyes of loving pride at the growing, shelf-ful of prizes he brought home to her, a new pleasure came into her life: that of dreaming golden dreams of her dear boy's future.

"One day the rich man, wishing to add a few more millions to his wealth, bought up all the sugar in the world and doubled the price.

"The shopkeepers promptly quadrupled it, and forthwith there arose such an outcry of indignation that the Government was forced to appoint a Commission to inquire into the matter. The rich man bought the souls of the Commissioners, and then, to divert public attention from the question, he purchased an oil-field in a distant part of the world where the frontiers were not very clearly defined, and by maneuvers which I shall not particularise, as I had not the wit to understand them, presently succeeded in involving the two governments concerned in a war which soon spread over the whole world.

"After two years of warfare the rich man's country was in terrible straits for men and money; and the Government, knowing that the poor were already taxed to the last penny that could be got from them without violence, decided to levy a special tax on the rich. And they took from the rich man of whom I am telling you nearly six million pounds that year, leaving him barely two millions for himself, less than a quarter of what he was used to;

and they also took ten of his motor-cars to carry the wounded from the battle-fields, and one of his palaces to house them; at which the rich man grumbled exceedingly.

"'O misery!' said he. 'O my cars and palace! O my two paltry little millions!' and he began to cry, shedding great lardy tears as big as new potatoes into a golden cup proffered by the attendants. This outburst of grief was followed by one of anger. 'I am robbed,' said he. 'Plundered and oppressed by a tyrannical Government. What is the meaning of this differentiation against one class when all should be united in the national emergency? Why do they not tax tea and sugar, that the common burden may fall on the common shoulders?' By which meditations he worked himself at last into such a frenzy of indignation that his bile broke all the dams of his liver and flooded his guts, so that he would have burst then and there had not the two doctors, who were always in attendance on him, made a lightning diagnosis, and by operating on him forthwith, saved his precious life. So the rich man lived, and continued his grumblings.

"But being also short of man-power they called up all the lads who were old enough to die: namely, those who were seventeen years and over. And they took the widow's only son, and drilled him, and taught him how to shoot, and sent him out to the war, where, after he had slain several other women's sons, he was killed in his turn. Then the light went out of his mother's life; yet though she had nothing left to live for, she lived on. But they compensated the rich man for the motor in which the boy was carried from the field, and for the palace in which he died."

Said the spirit of Socrates: "I am also beyond anger and pity."

"Nevertheless . . ." began the Philosopher.

"What?" said the spirit of Socrates. "Do you ask me to leave the pursuit of truth and the contemplation of God to endure again the wickedness, ignorance, and folly which I so thankfully left behind me?"

"I have not finished yet," said the Philosopher. "This pestilent, gross, lardacious fellow, who already owns all the wheat in the world, and all the sugar, as I have told you, has even now, out of the plenitude of his coffers, bought up all the song-birds, a nd proposes to cage them, and charge a fee to those who would hear them sing."

At these words perturbation ruffled for the first time the celestial serenity of the spirit of Socrates; and the anger that shook him rolled forth in thunder that rocked the stars in their courses; for, as the poet says:

A robin redbreast in a cage
Puts all heaven in a rage.

But presently, being calmer, he spoke, saying:

"You should not have come to a philosopher on this errand, nor to any of those who inhabit the higher heavens. A hero would better have served your turn. Follow me."

Then he led the mind of the Philosopher forth from the valley of austere beauty to the rim of the encircling hills, and he showed him the sky suffused with a twilight of purple splendour, with a few great stars shining like sapphires, and a thousand pale nebulae glimmering feebly like phosphorescence on the seas of earth. And he said: "These stars are the heavens; and those nebulae are the material universes. See that dim one yonder of the size and shape of a man's thumb: that is the universe from which you have come. Lost in its texture are Sirius and Aldebaran and the Pleiades and the Hyades and the inconsiderable sun whose dust is the planets of which your earth is one.

"Now see yonder star of golden hue, lying low on the horizon. Two planets have it for sun, of which the inner is the third heaven, which is Tir na nOg. There you may find one to help you. . . . No, do not stay to thank me, but take yourself out of my contemplations with what speed you can."

The blue sun set, and the red sun rose in a blaze of glory;

but to the mind of the Philosopher they were already fused to one purple star as he sped through the black resistless ether of the infinite void. Other stars opened up before him into double, triple, quintuple, or sevenfold suns of divers colours, and closed again at his passing. Right across the vault of the heavens he rushed, through black cold eons of space, throbbing with the heavy music of the spheres, till he came within the zone of the golden sun that lighted the plains of Tir na nOg.

CHAPTER IV

How a Champion took up the Gage of King Goshawk

THE PHILOSOPHER CAME UPON the spirits of the heroes walking in the meadows of asphodel in Tir na nOg. They were not like the spirit of Socrates, which resembled a still flame; but they had the forms of men, glorious and ethereal. A hero is a person of superabundant vitality and predominant will, with no sense of responsibility or humour, which makes him a nuisance on earth; but he is in his element in the third heaven. There the heroes take themselves and one another at their own valuation, regarding their weaknesses as strength, their defects as merits. Their life is in their fame: every time an earthly orator recites their names they experience thrills of pleasure; if they are forgotten they die.

The Philosopher recognised many of the heroes as they walked in golden sunlight over the meadows of asphodel: Hector and Achilles arm in arm; Horatius in friendly colloquy with the Tusculan Mamilius; Henry V of England; Patrick Sarsfield and Shane O'Neill; Bertrand du Guesclin; Garibaldi; and there were many more whom he did not know, mighty men of every race and nation that has shed blood on the green fields of earth. To none of these did the Philosopher address himself, but ever kept a watch for the one that seemed to him best suited for his purpose: namely, Cuchulain of Muirthemne, son of Dechtire and of Lugh of the Long Hand, of whom it was said in his time that there was none to compare with him for valour and truth, for magnanimity and courtesy, for strength and comeliness among the heroes of the world. In the crowd that went by there was none that resembled him. The Philosopher therefore passed on, and crossing another field he came to a glade, and saw before him a bush spangled with blossoms of ever-changing colours, that played sweet music in the breath of the wind. In the shadow of the bush reposed a youth of exceeding beauty. Three colours were in his hair: brown at the skin, blood-red in the middle, golden at the ends. Snow-white was his skin; as seven jewels was the brightness of his kingly eyes. Seven fingers had he on each hand; seven toes on each foot; and if you doubt it, go straightway and poke your misbelieving nose into the pages of the Book of Leinster or the Book of the Dun Cow or the Yellow Book of Leccan, where all these things are faithfully recorded, with a good deal more that I spare you. Certain it is that it was by these marks that the Philosopher knew that the youth in front of him was Cuchulain.

By the hero's side lay a woman, with her head resting amorously on his shoulder. Very fair she was, with two plaits of hair of the rich hue of marigolds, eyes as blue as the wood anemone, and her naked body as white as the foam of the sea. The Philosopher took her at first to be Erner; but presently in their love talk, which held him entranced as by celestial music, he heard Cuchulain call her Fand; at which the Philosopher was moved to indignant speech. Said he:

"I thought that affair was over since Manannan Mac Lir shook his cloak of forgetfulness between you. And surely it were only just to render to Erner in heaven that faithfulness you denied to her on earth."

"You forget," said Cuchulain, "that in heaven there is no marrying nor giving in marriage. As for this"—looking down at the woman—"I am tired of it," whereupon he cast her from him, and she vanished. "She was but the figment of my imagination," said he, "made with a wish; unmade with another: for heaven is but the fulfilment of the heart's desire."

"I do not care for this heaven," said the Philosopher.

"Your desire is nobler," said Cuchulain.

"You should seek a higher heaven."

"I am not a spirit," said the Philosopher. "I am the mind of a man, and I have come all the way from Earth to find you."

"What is your errand?" asked Cuchulain. "Man," said the Philosopher, "is full of wickedness and folly."

"True," said Cuchulain. "Tell me what wickedness and folly he has done since I left the earth."

"In the first place," said the Philosopher, "he is never done fighting and killing."

"That," said Cuchulain, "is foolish, but it is not wicked. I fought and killed many in my time on earth. I am since convinced of folly, but I am clear of guilt."

"In those days," said the mind of the Philosopher, "men fought with men in hot blood, hand to hand, strength against strength, feat against feat, and knowing well what it was they were fighting for. But for many centuries they have been possessed of a devilish powder which enables them to kill at a distance; and by labouring hard at its improvement they have learnt how to kill without seeing one another at all. So that now when countries are at war they do not send forth armies, but each hurls millions of missiles over mountains and seas at the other, destroying lands and cities, men, women, and children, until one or other is utterly overwhelmed. Some of these missiles are so cunningly devised that when they hit they divide up into thousands of particles which riddle and macerate the body; others contain deadly poisons; others scatter the contagion of leprosy and such foul diseases through the air; others on bursting are converted into a fine dust which is borne on the wind and blinds every eye in which it finds lodgement. They inflict on each other besides a thousand more abominations of which I cannot tell you, for already I grow weaker and must soon yield to the earthward pull of my body. But you must know this also, that nobody ever knows the real cause or meaning of these wars, and that if any one asks he is immediately put to silence."

Said the spirit of Cuchulain: "This is indeed a most iniquitous way of fighting. But is the tale of man's wickedness and folly complete?"

"No," said the Philosopher. "That is only the beginning. While the many are thus fighting, the few are contriving against their liberties, and robbing them of their bread and their homes, so that all the wealth of the world has now passed into the hands of usurers. And at last, infamy of infamies, these have begun to covet the beauty of the world as well." Then he told Cuchulain of the bird-purchase of King Goshawk; and at that the hero was thrown into a rage surpassing even that of Socrates.

"Enough!" said he. "I will rest here no longer. Let us to earth at once."

CHAPTER V

How the Philosopher borrowed a Body for Cuchulain

O THE PHILOSOPHER'S MIND returned to him in the little room
in the back lane off Stoneybatter; and having rubbed his natural
eyes he saw the spirit of Cuchulain standing before him, glorious
and resplendent as a flame in a dark place, as a fountain among
stagnant waters.

"Welcome to Earth and to my humble abode," said the
Philosopher. "And pray pardon me if I leave you for a moment:
for I must find you a body, in order that you may go inconspic-
uously among men, and see for yourself the folly and wickedness
from which you would redeem them." And at that he took himself off, leaving the hero gazing in bewilderment at the strange
habitation of the heir of the ages.

Now there was a man dwelling on the same Boor as the
Philosopher who thought life was not worth living; for he had
to spend most of it making up pounds and half-pounds of tea,
sugar, flour, butter, cheese, bacon, sausages, and the like into
parcels, and being polite to the fools that bought them; and he
had to subsist himself on the same commodities, which he hated
with the same intensity and for the same reason as the slaves who
built the Pyramids must have hated the architecture of Ancient
Egypt. He felt that it was no life for a man to rise in the morning
before the sun had taken the chill from the air, to be at every
one's beck and call during the best hours of the day, and not to
be free till its tag end when there was nothing to do but sit in
a stuffy picture house puffing fags. Of course there were also

Saturday afternoons and Sundays: but what could you do with a half-day beyond killing time at the pictures or a football match? And most of a Sunday was gone by the time you had heard Mass and finished dinner, and the picture-houses didn't open till eight o'clock. Oh, it was a hard life and a dull life to be doomed to, very different from the life of his dreams. He would have liked to be rich, to be exquisitely dressed, to live in a gorgeous house, to have abundance of leisure, to have silent, smoothly gliding servants and automobiles always at his command, to be loved and won by glorious shining women—in short, to live like the heroes of his favourite film dramas. Instead of that he had to work, to obey orders, to loiter aimlessly between whiles, to wear cheap readymade suits, to dodge other people's motors and serve their servants with sugar and sausages, and every hour of the day to be tempted by the sight of women customers and passers-by with pretty ankles and swelling hips and bosoms, that would stir up hot tormenting passions which he could only satisfy by risking damnation to eternal brimstone, or else by getting married—which he couldn't afford, and besides the girl he was walking out with was no great marvel, with her pale lips and her flat chest and her thin legs that didn't properly fill her stockings. Oh, a very dull life, thought Mr. Robert Emmett Aloysius O'Kennedy.

It was to this man that the Philosopher came seeking the loan of a body. He was standing before his mirror wondering whether he ought to wash his neck that morning when he heard the Philosopher's knock.

"Come in and sit down," he said hospitably, for he liked the Philosopher, thinking him an amusing old ass. "You don't mind if I go on washing?" he added. "Because I'll be late if I don't," and, having decided to spare his neck for yet another day, he began vigor ously to sponge his face.

"You told me the other day," said the Philosopher, "that you didn't consider life worth living."

"I did," said Mr. O'Kennedy.

"Do you still think the same?" asked the Philosopher.

"I do," said Mr. O'Kennedy, and began to dry his face in an exceedingly dirty towel.

"Would you like to quit it for a time?" asked the Philosopher.

"I'd like to quit it for good," said Mr. O'Kennedy emphatically.

"For ever is a long time," said the Philosopher. "But I think we could manage a month."

Mr. O'Kennedy would have winked here if there had been anybody to wink at. The old boy was certainly more cracked than usual this morning.

"What is your body worth?" asked the Philosopher.

"Couldn't be sure," said Mr. O'Kennedy. "The boss pays me three quid a week for the buse of it . . . but I think he includes my soul in the bargain."

"Your body is all I want," said the Philosopher. "What do you say to two pounds ten? And while I'm using it your soul can go off to heaven for a rest."

"Done," said Mr. O'Kennedy, who thought he had a yarn that would keep his friends in stitches for a week.

Then the Philosopher put Mr. O'Kennedy sitting in a chair; and he made three passes with his hands; at which the body of the young man became fixed and immovable, and his soul was filled with fear.

"Stop!" he cried. "You are killing me."

"You said that was what you wanted," said the Philosopher.

"I didn't mean it," said Mr. O'Kennedy.

Then the Philosopher made three more passes; and the soul of the young man departed from him, and went wandering into space. But the Philosopher took his body, and stripped it, and washed it thoroughly, and brought it to his own room, where he set it down before Cuchulain, saying:

"Come, now. Here is a body: a poor thing; a pitiful thing; not too well made, and somewhat marred in use; but still a semblable human body. Put it on."

Cuchulain looked at the body and did not like it at all; for it was meanly shaped, without sign of beauty or strength. The muscles were small and flabby; the spine curved; the feet distorted fantastically by ill-fitting boots: a body unsuited to a hero. Cuchulain picked it up distastefully, as one might handle another's soiled combinations. Then he gave it a shake and clasped it to him; the spirit seemed to melt and blend with the body; and presently the heart of Robert Emmett Aloysius O'Kennedy began to beat, his lungs to breathe, his eyes to open, and his limbs to stretch themselves, as if the soul within were testing its new tenement. For some minutes after the figure stood motionless, with introspective eyes, like one in contemplation. Then came a lightning change: convulsions seized upon the body of Mr. O'Kennedy, and in an instant Cuchulain had cast it from him with a cry of horror.

"O pitiful brain of man," he said. "What fears, what habits, what ordinances, what prohibitions have stamped you slave. I thought just now that I was in a very sweat of terror of some dreadful being named the Boss, who held over me mysterious powers, and from whom I anticipated chastisement if I were late in his service to-day, as I most assuredly expected to be. At the same time I felt a certain small satisfaction in remembering that yesterday I had done him some underhand injury which he would be unable to trace to my account. It was but a small weed of joy in a forest of fears. I had a fear that a man I knew might have heard that I had spoken ill of him that day; and another fear that a man I had lied to might find me out. I had also a fear that my clothes were not quite the same as were worn by everyone else, and a fear of what all the people I knew might be saying or thinking of me at the moment. Then there was in me a fear that had been inspired some time ago by a play I had seen, which made me seem to myself a mean, stupid, and malicious creature; and of that fear there was born in me a hatred of the play and of the man who wrote it. I hated him for using the theatre, where I went to enjoy myself, as a means of making me hate myself. And that recalled to my memory the worst fear of all those that beset me. For in the same theatre a few days before I had watched some women dancing, and my eyes had feasted on the roundness of their limbs, and my body had been bathed in warm desires. For that sin I was damned eternally to a pit of flame unless I should repent and confess. I was afraid to confess, for fear of what the druid should think of me: and I was afraid not to confess for fear of the pit of flame. Then I began to make excuses for myself, saying that I had not looked very long and that after all there had not been much to see, so that I had not sinned mortally, and had earned only some temporary fire. But I could not make myself feel quite sure of that; nor could I decide whether I was more afraid of the confession or the pit of fire. Then I began to wonder whether there was really a God or a pit of fire at all. But I dared not let myself think of that, lest I should be struck dead and buried in the pit of fire forthwith: whereupon I—even I, Cuchulain—was seized with a loathsome terror, to escape which I cast the foul body from me. And let you, O Philosopher, remove it now; for I swear by the sunlight of Tir na nOg that I will not take to me such a horror again."

"That is not spoken like Cuchulain," replied the Philosopher, "who in the olden times, when he was a man and a hero, was never known to look back from a task that he had once undertaken. It is clear, however, that the spirit is affected by the condition of the somatic substrate on which it depends for expression, so I will clean it up and let you try it on again."

So saying the Philosopher took scalpel and forceps, and, having opened the skull of Robert Emmett Aloysius O'Kennedy, and carefully reflected the membranes, he exposed the brain to the full glare of the morning sun. Then in a bottle he compounded a lotion of carbolic acid, cold horse sense, and common soap, with which he thoroughly scoured and irrigated both the psychical centres of the cerebral cortex and the association fibres connecting them with each other and with the sensory centres: for, as Halliburton or another hath it, *Nihil est in intellectu quad non prius in sensu fuerit*. After this operation, Cuchulain entered again into the body, which straightway began to glow with a divine beauty. The skin glistened like white satin; great muscles swelled and rippled beneath it; the chest expanded to a third as much again as it was; the back straightened like a spring released; the eyes flashed fire; and the sheepish countenance of Robert Emmett Aloysius O'Kennedy shone like that of a hero in his feats. Again Cuchulain began to test the strength of his borrowed frame, stretching the arms above his head, expanding the chest, stamping the feet on the ground: until at last the Philosopher cried:

"Hold now! Enough! Do you not remember all the war-chariots and the swords and spears you broke in the testing the day you first took arms and went foraying against the Dun of Nechtan's sons? This bag of bones is too frail for such experimenting, and if you wreck it I cannot get you another. Besides it is only hired by the week."

Then sounded the voice of Cuchulain from the vocal chords of Robert Emmett Aloysius O'Kennedy like a symphony of Beethoven from the brass trumpet of a cheap gramophone, saying: "Excellent advice, O Sage, and none too soon, for already I feel my shoulders crack. I will forbear in other respects, but the ghosts of my seven toes are most uncomfortably crammed into the warped and etiolated extremities of this starveling here, so that I seem to tread on dried peas: therefore stretch them I must." So he sat down, and began bunching his toes as one might do to expand a shrunken stocking; and with the effort the metatarsal bones straightened out, the phalanges uncurled, a shower of corns and bunions fell on the floor, and the two feet, which had hitherto looked more like the bleached rhizomes of some un known plant than any part of an intelligent animal,

assumed a healthy shape and hue, and heroic proportions. Even
so Cuchulain was not yet comfortable in his corporeal tenement,
but presently said to the Philosopher, very wry in the face: "I
fear I can never wed myself peaceably to this flesh. Lo, I have
here"—pointing to his belly—"a most woeful and disturbing
sensation, as of a griping emptiness, and unless it is soon relieved
I will abandon this carnal vesture yet again and return to Tir
na nOg."

"That is most unfortunate," said the Philosopher. "I had
hoped you would be free of the human frailties and the physical needs which hamper us. This pain you feel is called hunger,
and it is the prick of the goad with which King Flesh reminds
us that we are his slaves, forcing us to cram ourselves with bread
and meat, which we metabolise into energy, which we must use
to procure more bread and meat, thus remaining in a vicious
circle of uselessness, eating to live and living to eat, instead of
turning our minds to the pursuit of wisdom. And now that I
come to think of it, I am hungry myself, and no wonder, for I
have forgotten how long it is since my last meal. Have patience
now, and in a moment both our pangs shall be assuaged."

The Philosopher then went out, and in a shop at the corner
of the street he bought a loaf of bread, a piece of cheese, and
a quart of milk; on which provender he and Cuchulain fared
right joyously, charging their batteries with peptone and the
other approved albuminoids, not forgetting a due proportion of
vitamines as prescribed by the medical columns of the Sunday
papers. Believe me, bread and cheese and milk is the best food
in the world for hungry men, when you can trust your dairy-
man and beer is under a ban: the proof of which is that when
Cuchulain had finished he rose from his chair, and, stretching
himself, put a foot through the floor and both hands through
the ceiling.

"Steady!" said the Philosopher. "This is not Bricriu's Palace.
It is time your limbs were fettered with the garments of civilised

society." So saying, he took out some spare ones of his own and showed Cuchulain how to put them on. Be sure that Cuchulain in donning the trousers and tucking in the shirt showed no more grace or dignity than your mortal man-poet, priest, politician, soldier, average fool, or father of ten. I wish, indeed, that all men who hold position or notoriety could be compelled to put on their trousers publicly at least once a year: by which means we should rid ourselves of a vast quantity of that humbug and hero-worship which make the world intolerable for honest and self-reliant men. For, as the proverb says, no man is a hero to his valet: the reason being that the valet sees the hero getting into his trousers.

CHAPTER VI

Cuchulain takes a Walk

THUS CLOTHED AND FED, Cuchulain set forth with the Philosopher to explore the city. What a sight was here for eyes accustomed to the splendours of Tir na nOg. Come, O Muse, whoever you be, that stood by the elbow of immortal Zola, take this pen of mine and pump it full of such foul and fetid ink as shall describe it worthily. To what shall I compare it? A festering corpse, maggot-crawling, under a carrion kissing sun? A loathly figure, yet insufficient: for your maggot thrives on corruption, and grows sleeker with the progression of putridity (O happy maggot, whom the dross of the world trammels not, had you but an immortal soul how surely would it aspire heavenward!). But your lord of creation rots with his environment; so the true symbol of our city is a carrion so pestilent that it corrupts its own maggots.

What ruin and decay were here: what filth and litter: what nauseating stenches. The houses were so crazy with age and so shaken with bombardments that there was scarce one that could stand without assistance: therefore they were held together by plates and rivets, or held apart by cross-beams, or braced up by scaffoldings, so that the street had the appearance of a dead forest. (Was it not a strange perversity that slew the living tree to lengthen the days of these tottering skeletons?) Many of the houses were roofless; others were inhabited only in their lower storeys; some had collapsed altogether, and squatters had built the huts of wood or mud or patchwork on the hard-pounded rubble. The streets were ankle-deep in dung and mire; craters yawned in their midst; piles of wrecked masonry obstructed them. Rivulets ran where the gutters had been. Foul sewer smells issued from holes and cracks.

Fit lairage was this for the tragomaschaloid mob that jostled the celestial visitor to the realms of earth. What stink of breath and body assailed his nostrils; what debased accents, raucous voices, and evil language offended his hearing; what grime, what running sores, what raw-rimmed eye-sockets, what gum-suppuration and tooth-rot, what cavernous cheeks, what leering lips and hopeless eyes, what pain-twisted faces, what sagging spines, what streeling steps, what filthy ragged raiment covering what ghastly-imagined hide ousness of body sickened his beauty-nurtured sight.

Yet with all this putridity and squalor there were not wanting, even in those bygone days, many signs of progress and private enterprise. At every street corner there were loud-speakers which yelled forth news and advertisements. Airplanes circled like great dragon-flies in the sky, squirting out smoke-signals such as: "Read Cumbersome's Papers", "Why have a Bad Leg? Try Popham's Pills", "Trust the Trusts that Feed You", "Vote for Coddo", "*To him that hath shall be given.* Scripture backs the Trusts", "Are you Languid? Try Peppo". But these were but superficial signs of civilisation. If the hero had taken the pains to inquire, he would have learnt that every foot of land in the neighbourhood was worth fabulous sums of money; and that by a miracle of organisation every square inch of rag on the backs of the people, and every crust fermenting in their bellies had helped to make millions for somebody. Cuchulain, however, was too preoccupied with the uglier side of things to make any such inquiries. Was he not a morbid ghoul and gloomy pessimist thus to nose and grope in the dark for hidden horrors, with the best of life dancing before him in the warm sunshine?

In the pother and hurly-burly I have described, owing to

the celestial vigour of Cuchulain, which was chafed rather than impaired by his catatheosis, and to the enfeeblement of the Philosopher, in whom the milk and cheese had not yet replenished the loss of tissue occasioned by his fast, the two became separated, Cuchulain pursing his way alone, and the Philosopher, after a vain attempt to overtake him, returning to his lodging. Cuchulain, however, not perceiving the loss of his companion, strode onward with more than earthly vigour, to the grave detriment of his borrowed body, which was thereby shaken up, loosened, and derivetted, like a cheap car fitted with a too powerful engine, so that soon the stomach of Robert Emmett Aloysius O'Kennedy began to clamour for more nutriment.

Just as this clamour was beginning to be unbearable, Cuchulain espied a shop window most alluringly arrayed, with a cargo more varied and of more diverse origins than ever was carried by Venetian argosy or Corinthian trireme or galley of Tyre or ancient Sidon. There were oranges there from Jaffa and Seville, and little golden tangerines from Africa nestling in silver tinfoil. There were lemons from Italy and Spain; olives and currants from the land of Hellas; raisins from the Levant, and sultanas and muscatels. Figs were there from Smyrna, and dates from Morocco, Tripoli, and Cyrenaica; bananas, the long straight kind, from Jamaica, and short curved ones from the Canaries; and pineapples and cocoanuts from the islands whose palm-trees fan the Pacific. Then there were cheeses of a hundred species: great Stiltons like mouldy casks from a tangle of jetsam; Gorgonzola streaked like marble; rich yellow English Gloucester; Dutch cheeses like bloated beetroots; hygienic cheeses done up in jars to keep in the vitamins; evanescent-flavoured Gruyere and sharp-fanged Roquefort; simple chaste Cheddar, and sensuous Camembert. There were teas also from China, India, and Ceylon, coffee from the East Indies, cocoa from Brazil and Ecuador, and sugar from five continents and a hundred isles. Rice was there from many lands—China and Japan, Persia and

Siam; and with it were pearly sago and slippery tapioca. There were tinned sardines there from France and Scotland; tinned salmon and potted meat from America. From Canada there was shredded wheat and macaroni; and macaroni also from Italy. Great pyramids of apples there were, from England and from the home orchards: some red as the blush of a country maiden, some yellow like shining taffety; with pale Newtown pippins and quiet green baking apples. Over all hung fine well-smoked hams and bacon from Denmark (with a few from Limerick), and American bacon like greasy tallow. And there were biscuits and chocolates and candied fruits and nuts and odds and ends from the Lord knows where. All these things came as tribute to the men of Eirinn: they made nothing for themselves.

Here, therefore, Cuchulain turned in that he might find the wherewithal to appease the revolt of the baser nature he had put on; but he had scarce set foot in the shop before he was accosted by a large and ferocious person with stand-up hair and waxed moustaches, who, hauling him forward by the lapel of his coat, bawled into his face: "What's the meaning of this, you blasted young slacker? An hour late! You can leave this day week; and go behind the counter this minute and make up the orders or I'll smash your face in."

"Sir," said Cuchulain, "I know not what your rank is, nor what you take me for. Howbeit, I am not used to being handled thus, or being spoken to in such fashion as you have assailed me withal. Loose me, therefore, lest the grossness of this body which I am wrapped in should foul my spirit with thoughts of anger."

The Manager, however, had not in all his life been conscious of the image of God in any shop boy: neither were his eyes opened now. Therefore, taking a stronger hold of Cuchulain, he would have thrust him ignominiously before him, had not the hero, by a sudden exertion of his muscles, maintained himself as if rooted to the floor.

"Come on, now, you obstinate young devil!" cried the

Manager, giving him a flip on the ear with his great fat hand. Anger came on Cuchulain at that, and a terrible appearance came over him. Each hair of his head stood on end, with a drop of blood at its tip. One of his eyes started forth a hand's-breadth out of its socket, and the other was sucked down into the depths of his breast. His whole body was contorted. His ribs parted asunder, so that there was room for a man's foot between them; his calves and his buttocks came round to the front of his body. At the same time the hero-light shone around his head, and the Bocanachs and Bananachs and the Witches of the Valley raised a shout around him. For such was his appearance when his anger was upon him; as testify the Yellow Book of Leccan and the other chronicles; which, if any man doubt, let him search his conscience whether he have not believed even stranger things printed in newspapers. For myself, I think the chroniclers are the more trustworthy, as they are certainly the more entertaining; for, if they lie, they lie for the fun of it, whereas the journalists lie for pay, or through sheer inability to observe or report correctly.

Now when the Manager of MacWhatsisname's grocery saw Cuchulain facing him in the same dreadful guise wherein he overcame Ferdiad at the ford and drove Fergus before him from the field of Gairech, the strength went out of his limbs, and the corpuscles of his blood fled in disgraceful rout to seek refuge in the inmost marrow of his bones. Dreadful were the scenes that were then enacted in the arched and slippery dark purple passages of his venous system. Smitten with a common panic, Red Cells, Lymphocytes, and Phagocytes rushed in headlong confusion down the peripheral veins, which soon became choked with swarming struggling masses of fugitives. Millions of smaller Lymphocytes and Mast Cells perished in the crush, but the immense mobs poured on towards the larger vessels. Yet even here there was no relief: for as each tributary stream ingurgitated its protoplasmic horde, these too became stuffed to suffocation; so that, though every corpuscle strove onward with all his strength, the jammed and stifled cell mass could scarce be seen to move. Here and there bands of armed Phagocytes, impatient of delay, tried to cut themselves a passage through the helpless huddled mass of Lymphocytes and Platelets: but they succeeded only in walling themselves up with impenetrable mounds of slaughtered carcasses. Still more frightful scenes occurred when two mobs, travelling by anastomosing vessels, met each other head to head: for while those in front fought in grim despair for possession of the road until it was totally blocked and thrombosed with their bodies, the cells behind, still harried by fear, pressed onward as vigorously as ever, to the great discomfiture of the dense crowds packed between, who, thus driven by an irresistible force against an impenetrable obstacle, perished in millions.

Thus was the Manager's blood very literally curdled. And straightaway Cuchulain made his salmon-leap and fisted him a smasher under the third waistcoat button, breaking four of his ribs, and hurling him backwards against the counter with enough force to crack the front of it; yet he was so well covered behind that he took no further hurt, though by his screams you would have thought he had been dumped upon the hob of hell. Then, having wrecked the shop and all it contained, Cuchulain went forth into the street, breaking a thigh or a collar-bone for any that attempted to stop him: for all which he was most soundly rated by the Philosopher when he returned to him at the close of the day.

"What have I done?" said the Philosopher. "Old footling dunderhead that I am. What have I fetched out of heaven to show mankind his wickedness and folly? Have you no respect for our civilisation that you must sally forth, as fiery-wild as upon that first foray of yours in the barbarous youth of the world, and the first grocer's shop you come to, must leave your sign of hand upon it as though it had been the Dun of Nechtan's sons. This will never do. If two thousand years of heaven have not tamed your soul, you must tame it now; or if it is the body of Mr. O'Kennedy that is at fault, then you must bring it into subjection right rapidly: for this sort of thing cannot be done in these days."

"What," said Cuchulain, "have you no such pests now as these sons of Nechtan? whose Dun lay athwart the road out of Ulster into Meath, and they took toll of blood and treasure of all that came by. A right strong place it was, not to be easily taken; and the sons of Nechtan were protected by magic also, so that Foill, the eldest, could not be killed with edge of sword or point of lance; and Tuachel, the second, if he were not killed by the first thrust or the first cut, could not be killed at all; and the youngest, Fandall, was swifter in the water than a swallow in the air: yet I slew them all, and gave their Dun to the winds to howl in, and to the wild beasts of Sliabh Fuaith for a lairage. Have you no such pests now?"

"A many!" said the Philosopher. "Their duns lie across all the ways of the men of Ireland, and none may eat or drink or walk abroad without paying them toll. But they cannot be brought low by such tactics as these: for they are more cunningly fenced in, and protected by more potent magic, than ever were the sons of Nechtan. This Goshawk that I told you of is one of them: and I wish you would learn to control yourself, lest you find yourself in a gaol before you can cross swords with him. But, come now. When you had vindicated your honour by thrashing the grocer, what was your next exploit? Tell me all."

"When I had left the grocer," said Cuchulain, "I walked farther up the street until I came to an eating-house, which I entered very gladly, as I was feeling the pangs of my adopted stomach more keenly than ever. Here I was received at first more courteously than in any other place in this earth of yours. The master of the house bowed low to me, gave me a chair by a table clothed with fine linen, and summoned a servant to attend to my wants. Right generous and goodly fare was then put before me, and I fed full, to the manifest enjoyment of this voracious body. Afterwards, when I had rested me a while, I sought out the master of the house that I might thank him for his hospitality: but in the midst of my speech I was interrupted by the aforesaid servitor, who thrust a piece of paper into my hand, saying, 'Your bill, sir,' whereat the master of the house said, 'Good morning, sir; much obliged; pay at the desk.' Then there came upon me a most noble rage, not this time out of the spleen of O'Kennedy, but out of my own soul; and I said: 'Pay! Thou kindless, impious, inhospitable boor! What shall I pay?' for I had thought the place to be a hostelry for the free entertainment of strangers, such as they have in all the planets I have ever visited, and as they had in Eirinn in the olden time. Then said my host: 'I don't know what part of the world you come from, stranger: but in this benighted country you don't get nothing for nothing.' 'Very well, then,' I said, 'I will pay. But not now, since I have not the wherewithal. Good day to you, therefore. I will return anon.' So saying, I would have departed in peace, but the fellow laid hand on my shoulder, saying that he would not suffer me to go until I had paid what I owed. By my hand of valour, my word never was doubted before. Therefore I smote him, yet not very hard: only so as to lay him senseless at my feet, but with the life still in him." (Here the Philosopher groaned.) "After that," said Cuchulain, "two warriors, twins, clad both alike in blue, and their helmets embossed with shining steel, came to his assistance. To these I would willingly have explained the justice of the case, but before I could speak they seized upon me, so that I was compelled to defend myself. Yet, pitying their ignorance, I did them no injury, only binding them back to back with their own harness."

The Philosopher groaned again, and said: "How many people altogether have you maimed and killed? Speak out. Let me know the worst at once."

"Venerable sir," said Cuchulain, "I maimed no more; neither did I kill any. After that I went to a picture-house, but seeing that there was a charge for admission, I did not enter. And by my hand of valour, there is no other planet in the universe—not even among the savage seventy that revolve around the Dog Star—that acts so scurvily: for pictures were meant to elevate the soul, and therefore cannot be priced."

"What a pity you had no money," said the Philosopher.

"After that," said Cuchulain, "I entered a car driven by electricity. What do you call them?" "Trams." "Trams. I thank you. Your trams are tolerable. Nay, I have seen worse, but I have forgotten where. In this tram there were seventeen people, whom I observed with great interest. Nine of them wore discs of glass before their eyes, held in place by a band of metal fixed to the nose. Why did they do that?"

"To enable them to see," said the Philosopher. "Their eyes were bad."

"Why?" asked Cuchulain.

"Civilisation," said the Philosopher.

"Twelve of them," said Cuchulain, "had strange looking teeth of a most unnatural aspect."

"They were false teeth," said the Philosopher.

"What became of their own?" asked Cuchulain.

"Rotted," said the Philosopher.

"Why?" asked Cuchulain.

"Civilisation," said the Philosopher.

"Ten of them," said Cuchulain, "had complexions of a pale green colour, with dull eyes and drooping lips. What was the meaning of this?"

"They were poisoned," said the Philosopher, "by eating too much preserved food."

"Why did they do that?" asked Cuchulain.

"They could afford no better."

"Why?" asked Cuchulain.

"Civilisation," said the Philosopher.

"Eight of them," said Cuchulain, "had sores on their faces; and there were two that could not sit straight, but balanced themselves tenderly on half a rump. What was wrong with them, venerable sir?"

The Philosopher, with all commendable delicacy, gave explanation of the phenomenon.

Said Cuchulain: "The bottom of your civilisation is in no better case. Never have I seen so many and such strange diseases as upon this little planet. Yet you have learned and charitable physicians to cure these ills, whose advice was written plain upon the windows of the tram; as, for instance: *Are you jaded, weary, dispirited? Have you that tired feeling? Then try Peppo; and, Is your Liver bad? Mixo will set you right; and again, You feel well to-day. But who knows what loathsome diseases the Future may bring in its train? If you want to KEEP well, dose yourself daily with Absoluto.* How is it, then, that these diseases persist?"

"These were no physicians' prescriptions," said the Philosopher. "They were but the advertisements of the Patent Medicine Trust. All these sick people you saw were sick because they were poor, and so had to stint themselves in food. To pay for these pills and bottles they must stint their food again, and so again become ill."

"I begin to understand your world," said Cuchulain. "While I was making these observations the Guardian of the tram came to me and held out his hand in a manner that I had at last come to know the meaning of. Can you get nothing in this world without money, my friend?"

"No," said the Philosopher.

"Therefore," said Cuchulain, "I got up to leave the tram quietly, whereupon the Guardian laid hand on me as though to detain me. Nevertheless I smote him not, but, stopping, held his arm a moment, so that he paled and offered no further hindrance. Having dismounted from the tram, I accosted one who passed, asking him to direct me to Stoneybatter. Very quickly he gave me a description that I could not understand, and would have hurried away had I not detained him by the shoulder, saying: 'What, churl! Is this your courtesy to a stranger? I have a mind to slay thee, but lead me on straight to Stoneybatter, and perhaps I may pardon thee.' Said the man of Dublin: 'What sort of a joker are you? Do you know who I am?' I said I did not.

"'I am Solomon Beetlebrow,' quoth he, 'Minister of the Interior.' 'Your humble servant,' said I, bowing. 'But time presses, therefore lead on.' At that I took him by the ear, and in this wise he led me to Stoneybatter, but not without exciting some admiration in our course."

CHAPTER VII

How Cuchulain treated a Minion of King Goshawk

AFTER SUCH ADVENTURES THE Philosopher dared not let Cuchulain give him the slip again. On the next day, therefore, they went linked arm-in-arm throughout the whole of their explorations; by which, as they were both far and wide, and as the slowest pace to which Cuchulain could restrict himself was nearly twice as fast as the Philosopher could tolerate, he was so much exhausted that on the third day he readily agreed that the hero should go forth alone, but laid on him this geasa: that for no cause whatsoever, and under no provocation whatsoever, should he strike or otherwise mishandle any human being, or any property of any human being whatsoever.

Thus bound, Cuchulain walked rapidly through the city till he came to the open country about Lucan. Presently he met with a man in the scarlet uniform of King Goshawk, bearing on one arm a wicker cage, and under the other a strange-looking apparatus somewhat resembling a set of war-pipes, the bag of which he squeezed with his elbow, forcing from the nozzle a stream of violet-coloured gas wherewith he sprayed the hedges and the trees that lined the road. Under the discharge of this noxious vapour there fell at his feet great numbers of asphyxiated birds, from which he selected the robins, thrushes, and blackbirds to put in his cage, and then walked on, whistling a merry note, trampling through the fallen wrens, finches, sparrows, and other such common truck as if they had been drifted leaves in autumn.

"Fellow," said Cuchulain, "what are you doing?"

The bird-catcher cocked an impertinent eye, and, tapping the breast of his tunic, said: "See my livery? Then hold your lip." Cuchulain, mindful of his geasa, put constraint upon his wrath. Then, laying a hand upon the bird-catcher's shoulder, he said: "Friend, I have asked you a civil question: I want a civil answer," fixing him with a look so persuasive that the bird-catcher made haste to propitiate him, saying: "No offence, boss. I'm gathering birds for King Goshawk."

"Why?" asked Cuchulain.

"They're his birds, boss. The robins, thrushes, and blackbirds, that is. I take no others, as you see."

"How are they his?" asked Cuchulain. "He's bought 'em," said the bird-catcher. "Is that any reason why you should gather them for him?" asked Cuchulain.

"I do what I'm paid for," said the birdcatcher.

"Vile slave," said Cuchulain, "why do you not do what you will to do, and get paid for that?"

"Now, God help you, sir, for a poor innocent," said the bird-catcher. "Wouldn't we all do that if we could? But we can't. Personally I'd like to carve wooden toys for children—I carve 'em for my own kids in my spare time: cows and donkeys and crocodiles and things, you know, all done with a penknife— amatoorish, of course, but the kids like 'em. But bless you, how could my penknife compete with the Toy Trust?—I mean if it came to business. And if I went into one of the Trust's factories, I'd just have to stand seven hours a day feeding lumps of beech-wood into a damned machine. No thank you. Not for me. The open road for this child. Now just stand aside, sir, if you please, for this job is piece-work."

"O thou pitiable slave," said Cuchulain. "Give me that cage and gas-battery: for, by my hand of valour, you shall spray no more."

At this speech the bird-catcher began to feel some alarm, for to his ears it seemed to smack of lunacy: so he set to coaxing and reasoning with Cuchulain, saying: "Easy, boss, easy. Where's your Majesty's oil-field?" for it was a common infirmity of the mind in those days to imagine oneself possessed of boundless wealth, and Cuchulain spoke with the haughtiness characteristic of one so afflicted. "A truce to this jesting, slave," said Cuchulain, his anger kindling. "Give me that cage and gas-battery, or must I take them by force?"

"Please, your Majesty," said the bird catcher, "I am but a poor man, and these are the property of his Majesty King; Goshawk, whose subject I am. Will your Majesty deign to walk down the road some fifteen perches, and at the third turning to the left you will find your Majesty's oil-field."

Still mindful of his geasa, Cuchulain enforced himself to a meek behaviour, taking the bird-catcher very gently around the neck with one hand, while with the other he caught the wrist that held the cage. The birdcatcher tried to struggle, but Cuchulain mildly repressed him, and having quietly relieved him of cage and gas-battery, laid him tenderly on his back upon the road. If you will believe me, the neck and wrist of the thrall took not more than a week or so to regain their normal flexibility: yet for this moderation Cuchulain got small thanks from the Philosopher, who laid sterner geasa than ever upon him, declaring that if he had thought the songbirds could be saved by such simple methods, he would not have gone beyond the skies for a liberator.

CHAPTER VIII

How Cuchulain courted a Girl of Drumcondra

THE NEW GEASA THAT were laid upon Cuchulain were that he should not again go forth alone until, by the Philosopher's instruction, he should have become thoroughly acquainted with the manners and customs of the people. So for the next two days the hero applied himself diligently to this course of study. But when the third day dawned, because of a prick and urge of the flesh, together with a dancing of the blood and a singing of the spirit, that could no longer brook such inaction, with the temerity that had once brought dark disaster and woe upon Conaire Mor, he broke his geasa and sallied forth by himself till he came to the district of Drumcondra.

There he beheld a young girl leaning over the garden gate of her father's house, watching the people go by in the sunshine. When she saw the young man looking at her, she blushed and smiled; for the spirit of Cuchulain had imparted to the smug features of Robert Emmett Aloysius O'Kennedy a moiety of the beauty and the fire that in the olden times had won the love of Aoife, and Erner, and Fand, and Blanadh, and Niamh, and of three times fifty queens that came to Emain Macha from the four quarters of the earth to look upon the Hound of Ulster. Cuchulain, turning to the maiden, saw that she was fair: for though she was pasty-faced and lanky of figure, yet was she pleasing to the eyes of Robert Emmett Aloysius O'Kennedy, through which he looked upon the world. O'Kennedy's body was thus smitten with a yearning for the damsel which infected even the soul of Cuchulain, so that he stopped and spoke to her, saying:

"Fair maiden, you are beautiful as a morn of spring when the cherries are in bloom."

"Galong out o' that," answered the girl, smirking.

"Nay," said Cuchulain, "send me not away from your gracious presence, for truly your voice is like the love-song of birds on a musky evening, and the Twin Stars shed not sweeter light than your wondrous eyes."

The girl blushed fiery red, and kicked the gate nervously with her shabby toe; but she made no answer. Then Cuchulain said:

"Bid me again to go, and like the lightning I will be gone: for no woman yet asked me a boon that I refused her. Nevertheless, bid me not; for bitter is the air that is not sweetened by your breath. Speak, therefore: shall I go or stay?"

"Sure, why would you go?" said the girl. "I was only joking."

Then Cuchulain kissed with his ambrosial lip the grubby finger-tips of the maiden; and he said:

"In the gardens of Paradise the winds play a melody as of silver flutes over the golden heads of the swaying asphodels. But now my desire is for a cool spot by a woodland stream, amid odours of fern and damp earth, with wild hyacinths, maybe, in the long grass, or wood anemones, and yourself stretched beside me, plashing your white feet in the water."

The girl, playing with a faded ribbon on her blouse, thrust it between her teeth and giggled. Cuchulain, watching her, said:

"My thirst is for the honey that is gathered from a bed of scarlet flowers."

"I don't care for the kind you get in them combs," said the girl. "I prefer the bottled stuff. But I like jam best."

Silence fell between them at that; but presently the girl, thinking he would have invited her for a walk or to the pictures but had been prevented by shyness, said: "What was it you wanted to ask me about?"

Cuchulain answered: "My desire is for two snowy mountains, rose-crowned, that are fenced about with thorns and barriers of ice. What shall I do to melt the ice and turn aside the menace of the thorns?"

"What do you mean?" asked the maiden.

Then said Cuchulain: "It is your fair bosom that is the fruit of my desiring, and your red lips ripe for kissing, and your warm white body to be pressed to mine in the clasp of love."

"O you dirty fellow!" cried the girl, and turning, she fled into her house.

Cuchulain would have pursued her, but a tap on the shoulder made him turn round, and he found himself confronted by two men of singular aspect. Their clothing was all white, though somewhat soiled, with buttons of ivory and facings of swansdown. On their heads they wore helmets in the likeness of a sitting dove; and they carried batons of some white metal wrought in the shape of a lily. On their collars were these words in letters of ivory: CENSOR MORUM.

The official who had tapped him addressed Cuchulain, saying: "What were you wanting with that girl?"

Cuchulain, mindful of his geasa, restraining his desire to smite him, answered: "That, sir, is a matter between her and me."

"Now, then," said the Censor, "none of your lip. I've reason to suspect that you were asking her more than the time of day; and I've power to put you under arrest unless you can give me a satisfactory explanation."

"I can tell you nothing of what passed between us," said Cuchulain, "without the consent of the lady."

"Tush, sir," said the Censor. "You must be one of these foreigners if you think we would so outrage the modesty of our Womanhood by questioning them on such a subject. Come, now. What is your explanation?"

More difficult was Cuchulain's task to bridle his wrath at that moment than once had been the feat of bridling the Grey of Macha by the dark lake near Sliabh Fuaith. The veins of his forehead stood out like black and knotted cords; his collar at his neck was scorched deep brown; his heart missed seven beats; but calling to mind the calm visage of the Philosopher, he put constraint on his voice and said: "I was making love."

"With matrimonial intent?" asked the Censor, entering the reply in his lambskin covered notebook.

"I do not understand you," said Cuchulain.

"Do you want to marry the girl?" explained the other Censor.

"Indeed, no," said Cuchulain. "There are no marriages in heaven."

"Then you must come with us," said the Censors, laying hands on him.

"Whither?" asked Cuchulain.

"To the Lothario Asylum," said the Censors, and began to haul him away between them.

"Dogs!" cried Cuchulain. "Let me be"; and he put forth his strength so that his feet dug deep holes in the stone pathway, and the Censors could not move him. Thereupon these raised their lily-shaped truncheons to beat purity into the son of Lugh: but he, taking them up one in each hand, entwined the right leg of the one with the left leg of the other in a truelove knot, and left them there on the pavement for the gathering throngs to admire.

CHAPTER IX

Why the Censors were so Zealous

YOU MUST UNDERSTAND THAT in those days every action, word, and thought of which man is capable was most thoroughly regulated by law. Like every other product of human endeavour, the process of legislation had been so perfected and accelerated by the marvelous progress of science during the previous quarter of a century, that the output of laws at this period baffles computation. Indeed, there were so many that it had been found necessary to double the number of judges; yet even so it would have been impossible to administer all the new statutes and punish all the new crimes without rather neglecting the old ones. (It was for this reason that Cuchulain was able to get away with an assault or two, so long as he kept his hands off millionaires.) The penalties for breach of any law were necessarily very severe, for the complexity of the system made the smallest infringement a matter of such consequence that only the most powerful deterrents could save the courts from being glutted with cases. So great, however, was the legislative zeal of the age that although, as a contemporary wit observed, there were already so many laws that it was almost impossible to obey one without breaking another, nevertheless the promulgation of new ones continued unabated, so that it had become a matter of vital necessity for every citizen to read his newspaper in the morning with the closest attention, lest inadvertently he should commit an act which had been made criminal while he was in bed; as happened once to some forty thousand people of Dublin, who on a morning in March found themselves lodged in gaol for blowing their noses in public, being unaware that this action had just been incorporated as Schedule 678 of the Public Modesty Act. However, there was as yet no law to protect the wise from the malice of the ignorant; though there were many to protect the ignorant from the assistance of the wise. Hence the fate that befell the Philosopher in our first chapter.

You must further understand that these were the days of paternal government. All over the world the governments had decided to abolish temptation, it being generally conceded, by philanthropists, social reformers, and statisticians, that man's character was now so weak that at the mere appearance of temptation he must instantly succumb. The manufacture of wine, beer, spirits, and tobacco had long since been entirely suppressed. The vine and the tobacco plant were actually extinct, and in France there was a law ordaining that anyone who should see a wild seedling of either must, under severe penalties, report it at once to the authorities for destruction. Substitutes for the banned commodities were, however, illicitly manufactured in great abundance. The Germans invented an imitation beer, made by soaking scrap iron in a mixture of vinegar and water; there was an insuppressible trade in Ireland in a kind of whisky of immense strength and unknown origin; and the in genuity of the French had succeeded in extracting a very potent liquor from the common blackberry. For tobacco-substitute, every con ceivable plant had been put under contribution, the chopped and dried leaves being usually smoked in pipes of plain deal, which, in the event of a raid by the Inspectors of Morals, would be readily consumed if thrust into a fire. Some of the more venturesome would even smoke cigars of brown paper in the street, and if they saw an Inspector approach, would extinguish and unroll it and wrap it like parcelling round a cake of soap or some such trifle kept for the purpose.

Even more thorough were the methods employed to save

the citizens from the temptations of the flesh. The costumes of women, both as to cut and material, were all regulated by statute, the length of the skirt and the thickness of the stockings being the subjects of most stringent legislation; for the enforcement of which the Inspectors were furnished with tape-measures and calipers, with instructions to test any garment that might excite their suspicions.

Needless to say, the arts had received a full share of the attention of these paternal governments. The nude was a forbidden subject; and there had been a great holocaust of existing works in this genre many years ago. Fully two-fifths of the world's literature had suffered the same fate, and another fifth had been so mutilated by the expurgators as to have been rendered unrecognisable to its authors. The Old Testament had been reduced to a collection of scraps, somewhat resembling the Greek Anthology; and even the New Testament had been purged of the plainer-spoken words of Christ which were offensive to modern taste. All new works had to undergo a prolonged inspection by a board of Censors, whose jurisdiction, however, did not extend to musical comedies or Sunday papers.

But the efforts of the governments to abolish the occasions of sin did not end here. It was ordained that if a person were to behave in such a way as to tempt any one to murder him, he could be arrested and imprisoned at the President's pleasure; to abolish the temptation to bear false witness, the practice of calling witnesses in legal proceedings was being gradually discontinued; and anybody whose poverty might render him liable to steal could be put under restraint until such time as his circumstances should improve. The Party of Civil Liberty, however, had by tremendous exertions succeeded in preventing the passing of a law forbidding the rich to flaunt their wealth in the faces of the poor. It was but a trifling omission from such an exhaustive code. Such indeed was the zeal of the authorities in their war against temptation that it was a frequent occurrence for the police on duty in the law courts to arrest all the members of the public present, the jury, the lawyers, and even the judge himself, to save them from hearing some unsavoury detail of a case.

Yet in spite of all these laws and regulations the general behaviour of the human race was in no wise improved; a thing which the purveyors of morals were hard set to explain. Wars and individual murders were more frequent than ever before; thoroughfares in the great cities were often rendered impassable on Saturdays and Sundays by the prostrate forms of men and women drunk with poteen or blackberry wine; and the white slave traffic was paying dividends of sixty-two per cent on its ordinary shares, which were openly purchased by respectable citizens. Governments and peoples still preserved an attitude of mistrust and feelings of hatred in their relations with one another; and internal politics were largely a matter of flamboyant posters, mean little hand-bills, and dirty language.

So much for the measures taken for the elimination of moral temptations from the ways of the world. Political and social stability were preserved by the same means; there being in every country a law forbidding the speaking or writing of any word declaring, implying, or insinuating that the legislative, executive, or judicial system of that country was not the best conceivable for that country. Thus in one country it would be forbidden *to* criticise plutocracy disguised as monarchy; in another to criticise plutocracy disguised as republicanism; and in Ireland it was high treason to condemn the system of flamboyant posters, mean little hand-bills, and dirty language. It was customary also for states entering into an alliance to make a mutual compact by which each state was to suppress criticism of the government of the other. Hence the Spaniards and Portuguese could criticise neither monarchy nor republicanism; and the Irish and Russians were debarred from comparing capitalism with communism; as for the English, so multifarious were their alliances and understandings that they could criticise nothing at all: which suited their temperament to perfection.

CHAPTER X

Why the Devil is not to be debited with all our Sins

FOR MYSELF, I CANNOT tell whether this love impulse of Cuchulain's came from God or from the Devil; and you who are cocksure of the origin of all such irregular perturbations, pray tell me, was it by infernal promptings that Robert, Duke of Normandy, fell in love with Arletta, the tanner's daughter: for, if so, you say that the Devil founded the British Empire, which is a wicked, unnatural, and traitorous opinion, and absurd withal, seeing that it cannot be abbreviated, nor thwarted in its policies, without infringement of the laws of God. On the same theme here's a tale that I found in an ancient book of Eastern legends which I picked up for a song on a cart by the Liffey side.

You know that King David, loitering in Jerusalem while his armies were besieging the city of Rabbah, one day, when walking on the palace roof, saw Bathsheba, the wife of Uriah, washing herself in an upper room of her husband's house, and straightway fell into an amorous desire of her. Now the Devil, so far from playing pandar to the twain, well knowing what injury was to accrue to his kingdom from their union, made haste to forestall it, and, perching himself upon the King's shoulder, spoke in his ear as follows:

"David, David, what abasement and degradation is this? What will the princes and the captains say when they learn that their King is enslaved by a woman of the people by the wife of an Hittite?"

"I care not what they say," replied David, thinking that it was the voice of Conscience, or Common Sense, or some such monitor that was addressing him.

"Royally answered," said the Devil. "But what aileth David's eye that it so gravely misleads the King's affections? Is not that left leg bowed somewhat? And is not that a hairy mole I see upon her chin?" So saying he offered David a pair of magic binoculars with distortionary powers; but Love, which conquers all things, wrought upon those lenses in Bathsheba's behalf, so that she appeared ten times more beautiful even than she was, and David's passion blazed up afresh. Then said the Devil:

"Bethink thee, David, that by this sin thou dost contemplate thou kill'st thy soul as surely as thou would'st kill thy body by transfixing it with a sword."

"Nay!" quoth David. "I am a fighting man, I, and have been transfixed by many swords in my time: yet here I am, alive, and fresh in love."

"True," said the Devil. "But by each successive yielding to carnal pleasure the soul is drugged and stupefied, weakened in its powers, and deflected from that heavenly aspiration by which alone it can rise to the after life when the body is sloughed in death."

"And yet," said David, "methinks now that I would count the after life well lost if I could but hold her once in my arms."

Thus baffled, the Devil recoiled for a better leap.

"Take the wanton," said he. "But first weigh well the cost. Did you ever hold your finger for one instant in the flame of a candle? Could you bear to hold it so for five minutes? for an hour? for a day? for a year? for ever? Yet a candle flame is like the cool spray of fountains compared with the brimstone lake of Hell, in which your sin will plunge you, body and soul. You shall be salted with fire. Every sense shall be unceasingly tormented: your eyes with the perpetual sight of the devils and the damned leaping in agony amid the flames; your ears by the clamour of infernal voices, by yells and screeches, and by a jarring cacophony as of steel-sawing, stone-grinding, and slate-scraping; your nose and taste by the odious and mephitic slime in which you will be engulfed. O the tortures and the horrors of the damned! Words fail me when I endeavour to depict them. Amend thy ways therefore, O King, amend thy ways, and turn thy desires away from this woman."

"What a figure she has," said King David, "and with what grace she plies the towel."

"Wretched man!" cried the Devil. "Consider yet further. All these pains and terrors might be in some sense endurable if at some time, however remote, they were to have an end. But they are endless. The tiniest inconvenience becomes a torture if long continued; but these horrors I have described will continue unceasing for ever and ever, for ever and ever. Think upon it. Man after man shall be born, live, reproduce himself (if I may speak so plainly), and die. Generation shall succeed generation, century succeed century, and millennium millennium; and still you shall burn. The world shall perish, and the universe, and new worlds and universes have their being; and still you shall burn. For ever and ever; for ever and ever. The inexorable pendulum shall swing like that: for ever and ever; for ever and ever; for ever and ever."

"I shall be sorry for ever and ever," said King David, "if I let slip this chance. Did you ever in all your life see such glorious hips?"

"O insignificant mind of mortal man," said the Devil. "It is plain you have no conception of the immensity of Eternity."

"Doubtless it is very long," said King David, "but not so long as a minute spent waiting for one's beloved."

"Shallow fool," said the Devil. "Listen awhile, and I will endeavour to convey to you some faint intimation of the dread reality." Here the Evil One lowered his voice a tone or two, and spoke in slower measure. "Imagine a vast ball a million times the size of this earth, of a substance a million times harder than burnished steel, hanging in the night of space. Suppose that once in every billion years a butterfly were to flutter past and just graze the ball with the tip of one of its antennae. How many billions of billions of years would it be, think you, before he should make a depression deep enough to hold a dewdrop?"

"He would rub away his antennae first," said the King.

"Do not trifle," said the Devil. "This is a metaphorical butterfly, and its antennae are indestructible."

"I was never a mathematician," said David. "To resume," said the Devil. "How many trillions of trillions of years must elapse before the depression should be enlarged to the size of a man's head?"

"I cannot think," said King David.

"And how many quatrillions of quatrillions of years before it should be as large as this palace."

"Do not ask me," said King David.

"After sextillions of sextillions of centuries," said the Devil, "we will suppose that there shall have been rubbed from the globe a moiety equal in size to this land of Palestine, with all its fields and deserts, mountains and valleys, forests and cities. Do you know what even *one* sextillion is?"

"I do not," said King David.

"It is written thus," said the Devil, and with his finger he wrote in flaming characters upon the air, as follows:

1,000,000,000,000,000,000,000,000,000,000,000,000.

"That is a power of noughts," said King David. "Enough to fright an astronomer. But what comes at the heel of them? Continue, I pray."

"The butterfly shall continue," responded the Devil grimly. "Picture him still at his task, fluttering out of the blackness of space at the end of every billionth year, flicking the ball with his antennae, and vanishing again into space like some infinitesimal comet. Picture him doing it through octillions of octillions of centuries, until at last he shall have obliterated a portion equal in bulk to this mighty earth. Behold, the scar is scarcely noticeable. After all his labours there yet remains a mass nine hundred and ninety-nine thousand nine hundred and ninety-nine times as large to be comminuted in the same fashion."

King David whistled.

"To continue our meditation," said the Devil. "Let us now suppose that after the lapse of inconceivable multiplications of decillions of centuries the whole steel ball, one million times the size of the earth, shall have been thus rubbed away by the antennae of the errant butterfly. Suppose that there is then offered to him another such ball a million times as large; and when by the same process he shall have annihilated that, a third one, two million times as large, a fourth, three million times, and so on. What skilliondillion ramplescallions of billeniums must elapse before he shall have destroyed a million of them. And all this while, mark you, the fire burns with undiminished heat, the stenches stink, the cacophony continues unabated."

"No more! No more!" cried King David, now for the first time taking his eyes off the figure of Bathsheba, and looking full at the Devil; who appeared as an austere and lean-featured person in a black robe, with skimpy black wings at the shoulders.

"Suppose," said the Fiend remorselessly, "that by persevering flicks of his antennae once every billion years the butterfly shall have finally wiped into nothingness a long succession of such balls, to the total number of seven billion trillion quatrillion octillion decillion zillions—"

"Yes," said King David, regaining his composure somewhat.

"At the end of that period," said the Devil in his most impressive manner, "Eternity would be only just about to begin beginning."

"By my soul," said King David, "if the penalty be so vast,

what a very sweet bedfellow must this woman be." And he made her so straightway.

You will find this story, unexpurgated and unabridged, in the seventh book of Apocryphus, cap. ix. Was it not foul slander afterwards to lay the whole responsibility at Satan's door, not only for the seduction, but also for the mean and bloody deeds by which the King sought to hush it up?

CHAPTER XI

How Cuchulain was sick of the World and of all that was in it

BE THAT AS IT may, Cuchulain was conscious of sin, and in the evening he told the Philosopher what had occurred, and asked for an explanation.

"What a hot-headed fellow you are," said the Philosopher, laughing. "A modest maid is not to be wooed after this fashion."

"How are they to be wooed?" asked Cuchulain.

"I will not tell you," said the Philosopher. "I brought you here for work, not for love making."

"It is no matter," said Cuchulain. "I am wearied of this earth of yours. I came here as to a world of war and wickedness, where a hero would find wrongs to right and evildoers to overcome. I find instead a dunghill of meanness and silliness, with a cock on its summit that I may not oust this way, or must not oust that way, or would cause complications by ousting the other way, but must wait and watch for opportunity, and do nothing hasty for fear of shocking the tame capons that pay him tribute for maggots. Go to. Release me from my geasa, that I may cut his throat, or else I will leave immediately."

The Philosopher shook his head, and begged him to wait a little longer.

"No!" said Cuchulain. "I am weary, too, of this mouldy vesture of defilement, this body, with its rumbling digestive procedure, its recurrent exhaustion and demand for sleep. Go to. I'll inhabit it no longer. Whistle me its owner out of what quarter of space you have sent him to, that I may render it back to him. For I am for Tir na nOg this very instant."

"What?" cried the Philosopher. "Will you abandon the song-birds to their cages?"

"Shall I let them out of one cage into another?" asked Cuchulain.

Then the Philosopher went down on his knees and besought the hero not to forsake mankind in its wickedness and folly; to which Cuchulain listened at first without concern, but presently, yielding to the Philosopher's importunity, he stayed his speech, saying: "Very well. I will do this much for you, old man. I will join with some maid in whatsoever fashion your world approves, to engender a child. He shall be as a hero among men. As man he will be able to endure their ways: as hero he will see to it that they shall not continue them."

"Perforce I must be content with that," said the Philosopher.

That Cuchulain might have nice girls to choose from, he persuaded a well-born young man of his acquaintance to put him up for membership of the Bon Ton Suburban Tennis Club.

CHAPTER XII

How Cuchulain was rejected by an Attorney's Daughter

YOU SHOULD HAVE SEEN Cuchulain playing tennis with the gentry and ladies of the Bon Ton suburb. He learnt the whole art and skill of the game in ten minutes, and straightway beat the Champion of all Ireland six-love, six-love, and six-love. Never had such strength and agility been seen before. He could cross the court in one leap; he never served a fault, and none but the Champion ever returned his service; he would take any stroke on the volley; and at the net his smash invariably burst the ball. Thrilled by his prowess and enraptured by his grace and comeliness, the young ladies of the club began to turn from their faithful swains and to inquire about his origin and income.

There was one of these whose form, as it was both ripe and slender, fixed the errant fancy of the Hound of Ulster. The daughter of a struggling attorney, she responded readily to his advances, calculating that no man could attain to such proficiency in tennis who was not tolerably well off. Cuchulain, delighted by her girlish spontaneity, at once informed the Philosopher that this was the woman of his choice.

"Woo her discreetly, then," said the philosopher, "and in way of marriage."

"It shall be done so," said Cuchulain.

The next day, therefore finding himself alone with the girl in the pavilion, the other members of the club being out at play in the sunshine, he took her hand in his, saying: "Fair maiden, I am better instructed than to dally with you, filling your ears with fond and foolish love-talk. Come, therefore. Hie thee with me to some convenient priest, that we may be duly wed; then straight to our nuptial couch and forge us goodly offspring."

At these words the maiden's cheek blushed red as any tulip: you could not have believed the designing minx could have so much blood in her. "Sir," said she, "you are no gentleman," and plucking her hand from his clasp she fled from the pavilion. You may be sure Cuchulain was struck with wonder at such behaviour; yet, fearful of offending her further, he asked no explanation, but went home and told the Philosopher what had happened. "I asked her to marry me," he concluded, "yet she fled just like the other. Now what is the meaning of that?"

"You are too precipitate," said the philosopher smiling. "Why did you not woo her as I told you, discreetly? Heaven help me, it is so long since I courted a girl that I have almost forgotten the manner of it; but you might have gone about it this way. As you were holding her hand, you might have told her it was softer than swansdown and whiter than the lily. Then when she looked up at you to say 'really,' you should have gazed into her eyes as if your one wish was to die then and there."

"But it was not," said Cuchulain.

"No matter," said the Philosopher. "You might have stopped there for the day: it was good progress. Next day you could have taken both her hands and told her she was the most wonderful woman in the world: the more obvious the lie, the better it pleases the girls. Then you should have enfolded her in your arms and said: 'Molly, my darling, I know I am not worthy of you, but I cannot live without you. My one desire in life is to make you happy. Only promise to love me a little, and my love and devotion shall be yours for a lifetime.'"

"In heaven's name," said Cuchulain, "how could I make such a speech? I am well worthy of her: it is she who is unworthy of me. I do not care a whit more for her happiness than for that of any other being. And if she love me for a brief hour it is all that I require of her: nor shall I love her one second longer myself. Pah! If she will not answer to my wooing, a fig for her! I will find one that shall."

"Where?" asked the Philosopher.

"How should I know?" said Cuchulain. "I will go seek her through the world. I will pay court no longer *to* pimply thin-shanked wenches nor to silly giggling young ladies, but will find me a woman of shameless mind, with white shining skin, and a body without flaw."

"Why, then," said the Philosopher, "you must look for a millionairess: and you must catch her young; for they soon go paunchy."

"So be it," said Cuchulain; and, taking leave of the Philosopher, he started on his Journey.

CHAPTER XIII

The Fair Maid of Glengariff

BOODLEGUTS THE TRIPE KING had a daughter, fair and well-formed, and without blemish from the crown of her head to the soles of her feet. You would not believe she could have issued from Bodleguts' loins, so beautiful she was, and fresh, and jocund. A dowry her father had promised with her of a million pounds; but for myself, I would have taken her for her bosom alone, that was white as a bed of sweet alyssum, and for her smile, that was frank and tender, and I make no doubt would have been very sweet when bent on one she loved. Seventeen was her age, and her name Thalia.

For dynastic reasons her father had betrothed her to one Samkin Scallion, son of the Onion King, a podgy and lecherous lout, repugnant to the maiden both to sight and touch. Phew! he was a beastly slug to slaver so fair a rosebud: and piteously she besought her father to spare her so foul a fate. But old King Boodleguts was adamant; nor dared she disobey his behest.

On the eve of her wedding, while they were all busy preparing for the ceremony, she slipped from the company of her attendants, and went walking by herself, sad and apprehensive, through her father's demesne. The summer palace of King Boodleguts was in Glengariff, which had long ago been cleared of the mean dwellings and cabbage-patches of the common folk that had once disfigured it, and been converted into a pleasaunce of sunny lawns and shady groves, with beds of rhododendrons and azaleas and rare exotic blooms that flourish in the balmy air of the Bantry coast. Among these groves and gardens Thalia wandered, savouring the last short hours of freedom and maidenhood, and yet taking no joy of them for fear of what the morrow was to bring.

Presently she came to a little stream that ran sparkling through a green secluded valley. Along its banks fringed with willows she strayed till she came to a pool, deep and crystal clear. There she paused a while in thought; then, slipping her robes, stood gazing at her image in the water, and wept to think that so much beauty should be delivered to the enjoyment of satyr eyes and hands. Thereupon she leaped into the pool, breaking the image into a thousand ripples and splashes, and, after disporting herself a while, stood up, white and glistening, the water tugging at her knees.

And now came a sound of steps on the farther bank; the curtain of willows was parted; and the figure of a young man appeared. He looked at Thalia with gladness lighting up his goodly countenance; whereat she felt neither shame nor fear, for there was neither curiosity nor lust in his eyes. So they stood for a while, he admiring, she joying in his admiration, till suddenly, as if a spell had been broken, she turned and fled, screening herself behind the willows across the stream. The young man followed leisurely, and presently she came back to him, clothed, but with her feet bare, and sat beside him on the bank, trailing her toes in the water.

"Truly," said the young man, "you must be a millionairess."

"Why?" laughed she in silvery notes.

"Am I so fat and proud faced?"

"You are the most beautiful thing," said he, "on this sad earth."

"O my love," said she, holding out her hands to him. "Why, when you come too late, have you come at all?" and fell weeping on his breast.

Cuchulain gave her a loving kiss, and begged her to tell him her cause of woe: which she did most eloquently. "And now," said she, having concluded her tale, "my fate is sadder even than before; for whereas this morning I was engaged to wed unloving, now I must wed loving another."

"That you shall never do," said Cuchulain, "for it is myself you shall wed, and we will away together to Tir na nOg. There we will have fine sport and many kisses, and I will wreathe your hair with asphodels and put a girdle of roses about your waist. There shall the child of our love run wild among the lilies."

"It is a sweet picture," said the girl, "but it can never be. My father is one of the world's great potentates; my betrothed is son of another. They have castles in many lands; their subjects are counted in millions; their interests are everywhere. What can you achieve against them, alone and unfriended? If you carry me off you will be hunted down and killed, or sent to languish for the rest of your days in a dungeon; and as for me, I shall be wedded to this Scallion, with sorrow for your fate added to the misery of such a union. Go, therefore, my lover, while there is yet time, for I see the torches of many searchers flashing in the distance. Kiss me again, and go. Let me but know that you are safe, and the memory of this meeting shall abide with me for ever to sweeten the long bitter days that are to come."

"What?" said Cuchulain. "Do you think I will leave you in the clammy clutch of this vile onion merchant? Or do you think that any slave of Mammon can turn me from what I have a mind to? No, by this hand. With this kiss I make you mine"— here he pressed his lips to hers—"and tomorrow I will take you from their midst, though all the powers of Darkness bar the way."

Looking into his eyes she knew that he would do what he said: and so, when he was gone, she awaited in contentment the coming of the search party. Cuchulain meanwhile went down to the town and wired to the Philosopher in what tenor you may guess.

CHAPTER XIV

How Love and Laughter baffled the Tripe King

NEXT DAY, TO CELEBRATE the wedding, there was a great banquet more gorgeous and delicious than you could possibly conceive; but not more so than the company that presently put themselves outside it. There were three kings among the guests, with huge numbers of and financiers, all good workers behind a knife and fork, and not one among them but was a millionaire or the son or daughter of a millionaire, and a great personality in the financial world. You may be sure they wired in to the feast and packed their breadbaskets thoroughly. What a pity there was no wine served, according to Saint Paul's counsel, for their stomachs' sake. But King Boodleguts, who was of a gouty habit, would abate no jot of the law in this respect: alas! for, for the lack of such emollient, they were all very badly stodged, which was to prove a grave misfortune, as you shall hear.

When they were well gorged, and many of them in a mood to give all their wealth for a thimbleful of Benedictine, or even a pennorth of Aq. Menth. Pip.; just as the Chief Steward was assisting Mr. Garlic, the Best Man, to his feet, and wedging a couple of footstools between the seat of his chair and that of his pants in order that he might make some show of standing to propose the toast of the happy pair; a sudden fierce shout, louder than had ever issued from human throat, rang in the ears of the company. There was not a hair in the room that did not stand erect at this horrific sound, nor a skin that did not break into a cold sweat like the walls of a vault. You would not believe that kings and men of weight and influence could be so dismally affrighted.

It was Cuchulain's voice that had put them into this fluster; who, coming on to the lawn in front of the house, and seeing the door guarded, made a leap at a window of the dining-hall, but fell short almost by the height of a man, to the huge merriment of the guards and other onlookers. At that Cuchulain let his battle-cry out of him, and, taking a longer run, leaped again at the window, reaching this time to the sill, but, like a bird whose power is spent, fell from that perch even as his foot touched it. Then the guards and the onlookers began to laugh and to jeer, and to throw mud and stones at the hero, so that his anger kindled, and, standing back again, he made his salmon-leap and came flying through the window into the hall.

Mr. Garlic had begun to recover his nerve, and was just about to give the toast, holding aloft a tall tumbler overflowing with whipped cream and iced fruit syrup, when Cuchulain landed upon the table with a crash and jingle of glass. Very beautiful and fierce he looked, his eyes flashing fire, a long bright sword in his hand, that had been put there bythe Morrigu herself as he hurtled through the window. "Swine, stay at your troughs," he commanded, as one or two strove feebly to rise. "And you varlets, back"—this to some servitors that had first thought of inter fering but now desisted, fancying from his imperious tone that he must be a financier or monopolist of eccentric habits arrived late for the feast. "I have come for my bride," said Cuchulain, "and will harm no man that offers me no hindrance. Come, Thalia."

So saying he advanced towards the head of the table, over the white damask cloth, through the silver and the glasses; nor could any man rise up to stop him, no more than if the seat of each one's breeches had been caught between the jaws of a crocodile: though there were a few that strove to do so, and flopped off their chairs on to the floor in the effort. Cuchulain offered his hand to Thalia, who, taking it, leaped lightly to the table beside him, leaving a yard of her gown in Scallion's podgy fist. The bosthoon dared no more resistance than that, for the sword of Cuchulain gleamed bright and menacing. But old King Boodleguts at the other end of the board (though he could not rise any more than the rest of the roysterers), being near bursting with choler at the audacity of this intrusion, began bawling for the guards so urgently that these came rushing up from the lower court yard, a score in number, and covered the hero with their guns, awaiting orders. A moment Cuchulain stood facing them with Thalia upon his arm: then he brandished the sword above his head so fast and furious that a shaft of sunlight, striking it suddenly, flashed blinding white in every eye.

When they had recovered their sight, the first thing they perceived was that Cuchulain and Thalia had vanished; and the next was a body that lay wrenched and distorted among the dishes and adornments of the table. It was the disjecta membra of Robert Emmett Aloysius O'Kennedy, now void of the strength and beauty which the spirit of Cuchulain had filled them with; so that none of the company recognised the thing, nor did it occur to them to connect it in any way with the vision that had flashed upon them a moment before. Indeed, the Major Domo had the Chief Steward consigned to the dungeons for allowing such an object to get upon the table, and ordered the guards to throw it upon the refuse heap, where it was presently found by the Philosopher, by whom it was restored to its owner; who had been having rare adventures in far quarters of the universe, of which I will tell you in another book. Meanwhile there was hurry and scurry in Boodleguts' halls and the surrounding demesne, of which there was neither hole nor corner, nook nor cranny, that they did not thoroughly poke into and search. When these efforts proved unavailing, King Scallion spoke winged words to King Boodleguts, and rode away with his son in high dudgeon to have the marriage annulled: there was near being a war between Tripe and Onion on the head of it. After they were gone, a pack of private detectives was called in from London, wily sleuths trained in the school of Sherlock, each with a Watson to heel, who, with high power lens and litmus-paper, scrutinised every inch of the place all over again, afterwards extending their operations over a large part of the surrounding country. Nevertheless they found no clue of any sort except a garter of Thalia's down by the river, which she had forgotten to put on in her hasty dressing. Here was a spicy headline for the newspapers, which a million crafty sub-editors made effective use of. I cannot tell how many variants upon the theme were rung in ribbon and triple column measure by these master musicians; but it is said on good authority that there were forty-three thousand photographs of the garter taken, besides sketches; which were printed in fifteen million papers for the delectation of two thousand million readers. The more reputable of them were content to publish small-scale reproductions on their back pages for the criminological interest of the clue; others, less chary of their reputations, gave it greater prominence, figuring it large upon their front pages, with suggestive descriptions appended; while one very popular sheet, appearing on the Lord's Day, delighted its readers with a full-page picture of the article *in situ* upon a very shapely leg, complete with stocking and knicker-frill. Did not all this call for a far higher degree of enterprise, organisation, acumen, and knowledge of human nature than the mere unravelling of the mystery connected with it? as to which, I do not know what conclusion they came to; nor do I care.

BOOK II

THE COMING OF CUANDUINE

CHAPTER I

The Birth of Cuanduine

THESE TWO, CUCHULAIN AND the fair Thalia, having thus joyously come together, she conceived a child, and bore him the full term; during which she remained always in the warm sunlight, her ears filled with symphonies of sweet music, and before her eyes the golden-spangled meadows of Tir na nOg: which, indeed, are not more beautiful than fields of Earth pricked out with buttercups, only that they are boundless. In due course the child was born, a fine healthy boy, who, instead of crying after the manner of earthlings, broke straightway into a shout of joy, and seizing the breast as if it had been a cup of wine, after a deep draught he stood upon his legs and went running and leaping among the asphodels. He was, indeed, a marvelous fair child, that had learnt more acquirements in the womb than most children in five years of life. He had both his father-tongue and his mother-tongue (that is to say, Irish and English); he could rime and sing; he made him a pipe out of reeds, and played his own melodies upon it. He had the gift of strength and fleetness, the gift of courage and truthfulness, the gift of modesty and courtesy. Being nurtured neither on sterilised powders out of tin cans, nor on new bread and black tea (on which the mothers of Eirinn rear the finest race in the world), but on his mother's milk only; and being naked always in the sunshine, and ever drinking in beauty through his eyes and ears, he waxed daily in strength and comeliness: and as there were none to tell him lies or bid him hold his tongue, he waxed in knowledge and wisdom also. Because of his destiny, and after the manner of his father's naming, they called him Cú an Duine, that is, the Hound of Man.

One day, when he was six months old, the mind of the Philosopher came winging from Earth to see him, and was overjoyed to find him a lad of such promise. But after watching the youngster's gambols for a while, and hearing some of his questions, he began to weep at realising that he could not live to see his work amongst men. At that Cuchulain chid him, saying that it was not fitting that tears should flow in Tir na nOg, and desired him to tell his cause of grief. The mind of the Philosopher having duly complied, Cuchulain said:

"Weep no more. That matter is easily settled. We will consult Aurora."

"Whom?" asked the mind of the Philosopher.

"Aurora. The Dawn Goddess."

"I did not know she existed," said the mind of the Philosopher.

"She lives in thousands of imaginations," said Cuchulain, "more familiarly than many millions whose reality is vouched for in the telephone directory."

"True: true," said the mind of the Philosopher. "Let us seek her. Where is she to be found?"

"In the Ether," said Cuchulain. "In the Nebula of Abstractions."

Swish! went Cuchulain and the mind of the Philosopher through the infinite void, and shot into the radiant realms of Fantasy, where dwell Mr. Pickwick and Don Quixote, Rosalind and Lady Cicely Waynefleet, with the Chimaera and the Hippogriff, the Squirryphant and the Mock Turtle, Puss in Boots and the Whangerdoodle, and the Dong with a Luminous Nose. There the hills are of crystal, and the fields are greener than the pastures of royal Meath. Cloud palaces of alabaster crown the heights, and cascades of pearl tumble into the valleys. There among the amber-dropping forests dance the Nymphs and the Dryads, and scurry the Elves and the Leprechauns. There dwell all the beautiful girls that cloy the senses of novel-readers.

Now darted three spears from the hand of the Dawn Goddess: a grey spear, and a silver spear, and a golden spear; and then Aurora herself came striding in pursuit over the crystal mountains, and overtook and caught them in her hand, shaking them over the valley. A helmet of light was on her head; a vesture of gold covered her rosy flesh.

"Lady," said Cuchulain, "here is the mind of a mortal that seeks extension of life."

Aurora stopped, brandishing her spears.

"Hold," said the mind of the Philosopher. "I would not share the fate of Tithonus by a like remissness of the Goddess. I want a modicum of youth with the extension."

Aurora laughed and said: "What fools you mortals are. Have you not yet discovered the secret of youth?"

"Indeed, madam, we have," said the mind of the Philosopher. "But we have not yet succeeded in making it work rightly. I will tell you briefly the history of the matter."

CHAPTER II

Elixir / Vitae

"You must know," said the Philosopher, "that in the stress of modern life few of those who attain to riches do so at an age when they still have zest to enjoy them. Wealth, too, when injudiciously employed, is a great squanderer of years; and it is a misfortune, that grows harder by geometrical progression, that the more a man can accumulate, the less grows his ability and opportunity to spend it. In brief, the one thing needed to make perfect the happiness of having great possessions is the gift of perpetual, or at least of continuously renewable youth.

"In the early days of the century many crude attempts had been made to discover a scientific substitute for the elixir vitae of fable; and, later on, a handsome prize offered by a Coal King stimulated research in that direction. It was soon discovered that a solution of infants' thymuses in horse serum and chloride of platinum would have the desired effect. Unfortunately, the removal of a child's thymus is a dangerous operation, resulting in premature senility and early death. It was also illegal. It was believed, however, that there must be many thousands of parents in the world who would welcome the opportunity to barter the lives of one or two of their children for a price that would lighten the lot of the remainder: indeed, it was known that there, were many who had cheerfully denied life to a dozen to better the lot of one. A bill was accordingly introduced into Congress to legitimise the operation. It was of course strenuously opposed by the Socialists and others, who characterised it as a deliberate attempt to rob the children of the poor of their youth. To this the supporters of the bill retorted that it had always been a pet argument of the Socialists that the children of the poor had no youth worth speaking of, so where was the robbery? The average poor child, they pointed out, had no real need of a thymus: it was sheer selfishness and class-hatred that objected to its transference to one who had. They denounced also with much heat and zeal this unscrupulous attempt of professional agitators to obstruct a truly progressive measure whose object was the betterment and enrichment of the lower orders. The Bill passed the House of Representatives; but in the Senate a learned statistician demonstrated that if the number of thymuses required were forthcoming (as he had no doubt they would be), it would soon make an end of that floating surplus of labour on which the existence of our civilisation depends. This argument, uttered with such authority, settled the fate of the Bill, the lower house concurring with the Senate in rejecting it.

"The scientists immediately renewed their experiments, hoping to find a substitute for the forbidden gland. Every known animal substance was tested, from the pseudopodium of the amoeba to the prosencephalon of the larger anthropoid apes. At last Professor Pepper, of Harvard, a pioneer in this work, succeeded in darkening the grey hairs of a favourite cat which he had been dosing with a preparation, the recipe of which has been unfortunately lost. Discoveries now came hard and fast on one another's heels. Six months after Pepper's discovery, Brainstorm, of Berlin, caused a dog thirty years old—blind, toothless, and unable to stand—to frisk, yelp, and wag its tail, by injecting it with extract of capercailzie gizzard. Two years later Assenhead obtained a pint of milk daily from a moribund cow which had been sold for cat's meat, by treating her with an ointment compounded of the gelatinised bills of embryo ornithorhyncuses. The very next year brought mankind to the threshold of triumph, when an ancient spavined cab-horse with a tube in, after treatment by Fuhzler with subcaudal fomentations of skunks' bile, won both the Grand National and the Derby in a canter, breaking all records for both races. Subsequently the complete rejuvenation of half-a-dozen nonagenarian paupers by this process proved that it might be safely applied to human beings, and even to millionaires. The latter, indeed, were in the early days the only beneficiaries of the great invention, for the cost of treatment was prohibitive. They came at first cautiously, only the bravest and the most desperate venturing on the experiment; but when these began to show good results there was a rush to follow their example, and soon all the world of wealth and fashion was flocking to Fuhzler's consulting room. Then was the great scientist's letterbox choked with testimonials from his grateful clients. 'I am growing younger at the rate of a year a week,' wrote one delighted Oil King; 'I am already spending nearly a tenth of my income,' wrote a charmed stockbroker; and an exuberant milk monopolist testified: 'Since using your stuff I have trebled my harem.' In course of time the cost of treatment was reduced until it came within the reach of the average middleman; nor were there wanting quacks to reap rich harvest of pennies from the credulous poor. You would have marvelled at the vast concourse of seekers after a few extra years on our unhappy planet. So great it was that the race of skunks was almost extirpated, and a fortune was made by a speculator who cornered the whole available supply. From that time the treatment was obtainable, as at the beginning, by millionaires only; who submitted themselves to the process more enthusiastically than ever, even young women in their thirties throwing themselves back into girlhood by its assistance.

"Fuhzler's triumph, however, was short lived. While he was at the very height of his fame a mysterious epidemic suddenly broke out in the Millionaires' ghetto at San Francisco. A few months later there was an identical outbreak at Chicago. Within a year every ghetto in America was afflicted, and before long the infection reached Europe and spread throughout the world. On its first appearance it had been thought to be Chorea (or St. Vitus' Dance), but this theory was soon found to be fallacious. It transpired eventually that the effect of Fuhzler's Process was to infuse more vitality into a body than it could stand. After a certain period of increased health and vigour, the patient began to lose control of his movements. Desiring to rest, he found himself unable to do so. His artificially acquired energy, left without guidance, was forced to express itself in violent jerks and gyrations, which exhausted the patient without appreciably fatiguing itself. Frantic leaping and dancing, ending in collapse, marked the culmination of this first stage of the malady.

"After a prolonged state of coma, consciouness gradually returned, and the second stage of the disease commenced. While the mind regained its normal condition, the body began rapidly to age. The process was so swift as to be easily perceptible. Limbs that could walk on one day were too weak to stand upon by the next. Teeth and hair fell out in a night. Sight and hearing fled like down upon the wind. Thus, in a typical case, a man who had been fomented, say at forty-five, found himself at forty-eight, with all the faculties and desires of a man in his prime, shackled to the body of a dotard of more than a hundred. As he lay helpless in bed he was tormented by feelings of impatience and disgust for this outworn tenement; which, as they could no longer find a vent in physical action, were the occasion of severe mental pain, leading, in some cases, to mania.

"The reached third stage of the disease was now from this point the ageing of the body proceeded at a slower and a constantly diminishing rate, accompanied by a fall in temperature, while the exhausted mind held but one instinct, an intense longing for death. Death, however, was slow in coming. In the early stages of the malady many had sought to end their misery by suicide; only to find that their superabundant vitality was proof against wounds that would have killed any ordinary mortal. Fuhzler himself, broken by failure and disgrace, was one of the first to seek relief in this way, and lived for many years with a bullet in his brain, a ghastly warning to his fellow-sufferers. In the normal course the inertia of the body required from twenty to forty years, according to the age of the patient, to quench fully the vital flame, and the intervention of death was invariably painless.

"I was once permitted to see in a public hospital some poor men in the grip of this frightful malady. One, a faithful old retainer in a millionaire family, had been fomented, as a mark of esteem and gratitude, at the expense of his employers; another had abused his position as valet to steal some of the drug from his master. (Did he not richly deserve his fate?) These two had attempted suicide not long before. The breath of one rustled through his jagged throat, which was cut from ear to ear. The other looked like one who had been many days in the depths of the sea: and so indeed he had been. There were two others in the same ward who were drifting slowly through the last stage of the malady towards death. They lay quite still in their beds, poor shrunken bags of skin and bone, seemingly asleep. They looked to be of incredible age, though they were neither of them, I was told, above fifty. They were hairless, blind, deaf, senseless. Their dried-up skins crackled and flaked; their bones could be heard to crepitate. The loud reverberant thumping of their labouring hearts told of the stubborn fire that burned within.

"Humanity, you may be sure, was staggered by the realisation of the calamity it had brought upon itself. Fully two million persons, mostly millionaires, had undergone the fatal treatment from first to last, and one after another found himself falling victim to its inevitable consequences. Moreover, in the first panic of the revelation, there had been a disastrous slump in the price of skunk bile, the Fuhzler Trust had gone smash, and the markets were glutted with consignments of the drug going for a song, a dire menace to the public. Governments everywhere at once took action, and legislation was hastily introduced in the various Parliaments, making the manufacture, sale, and application of the drug a penal offence. These measures have had to be reinforced from time to time; for such is the craving for life that has been aroused in human breasts that not all the penalties, legal and physiological, known to be involved can deter some depraved creatures from applying the baneful fomentation to their posteriors. Meanwhile Science, stimulated by liberal benefactions, has been earnestly seeking an antidote which, taken along with the elixir, shall counter its ill effect. Many learned savants have devoted their lives to this research, but hitherto without result."

When the Philosopher had finished his narrative, Aurora said: "This is folly and waste of time. A man can live as long as he wants to."

"I do not understand you," said the Philosopher. "Surely, if any one ever wanted to live, it was those who were willing to endure the pain and shamefulness of fomentation to that end?"

"No," said Aurora. "They only wanted to enjoy themselves. They were like children who long to be grown-up, thinking that manhood means no more than long trousers and freedom to stay up late and eat what one likes. Life is a whole, and enjoyment but a very small part of it: look at it so, and while you want to live you shall not die; but you will not want it long. I will give you this gift besides, which I denied to Tithonus, that, so long as you live by willing, you shall not age."

Dazzled with the effulgence of Aurora's eyes, the mind of the Philosopher fled back to its earthly tenement in Stoneybatter.

CHAPTER III

The Education and Early Life of Cuanduine

MEANWHILE CUANDUINE GREW UP to be a fine sturdy lad, very
bold and ready with tongue and hand. Nor was he by any means
the nasty little leecher and sinkhole that the Professors would
make you believe our earth children are. Indeed he had but three
faults: that he was very disobedient (Adam Complex), that he
was addicted to lying (Ulysses Complex), and that he was in-
fernally curious about women (Gynaecothaumastic Libido); as
to which last, though it seems natural enough to me, no doubt
the Professors would explain it in this way. You may remember
that when his father, Cuchulain, returned to Emain Macha on
the day that he first took arms, all red with battle fury, the men
of Ulster, fearing lest he might run amok and do himself and
them some injury, sent out a band of women to meet him, with
their breasts uncovered; at sight of whom, as he was an innocent
and bashful youth, his wrath left him, and he hid his face in the
cushions of the chariot. Now from that day to the end of his
life he ever regretted his modes y on that occasion, and though
there were many fair bosoms were his for the taking, the desire
for those particular dames, thus thwarted, never left him; but,
being rudely thrust down into the subliminal recesses of his
ego, went on smouldering in his subconsciousness: from which
repression it sprang forth with hundredfold vigour in the ego
of his son. And the moral of this is: Do evil, that your offspring
may escape temptation.

In spite of these faults Cuanduine was, as I have said, a fine
little lad, and he g:rew well and rapidly. When he was seven years

of age he was as big as any other lad of fifteen, and ten times riper in intelligence and character. It was at this time that Cuchulain took him, by way of object-lesson, down to the neighbouring heaven of the Idealists. This was a planet consisting for the most part of vast arid plains, with a few solitary rnountain peaks of naked rock incredibly high. The rays of the golden sun that bathed the meadows of Tir na nOg in living light were here tempered to a dull grey by a veiling of cloud that obscured the sky. Vague formless beings, each with a human head, drifted over the plains and among the jutting crags, driven before the cold currents of the wind: the ghosts of men and women who wrought by principle and conviction; martyrs and makers of martyrs; tyrants and tyrannicides; teachers and preachers and other moulders of minds.

To this heaven go all who know they are in the right, a bloody throng, with more cruelties to their credit than all the childbeaters and murderers in Tartarus. Marcus Brutus was the first the visitors encountered, a gloomy ghoul, muttering to himself as he was blown along: "Hear me for my cause, and be silent that you may hear. Had you rather Caesar were living, and die all slaves, than that Caesar were dead, to live all free men? As he was ambitious, I slew him. I slew him though I loved him: and yet the people around Philippi do stand but in a forced affection. This is beyond reason: I cannot understand it. I tell you I know I did right to slay him. My motives were of the purest. Yet Caesar, who slew more than I, is in the higher heavens. Is that just or reasonable? But here I know that I did right to slay him: therefore I will go no higher."

A very choice collection of opposites was to be found here, all luxuriating in the same conviction of righteousness: Torquemada and Queen Elizabeth; Martin Luther and Ignatius Loyola; Oliver Cromwell and Charles the First; Marat and Charlotte Corday; Trotsky and Tzar Nicholas. All these had but one interest to keep them alive: each was eternally wondering why his opposite, who was clearly in the wrong, was not in Tartarus. Wrapped in contemplation of his own perfection, each went his separate way as the wind listed; but at long intervals they were swept together as by a cyclone, and then they would join as one voice in a proud hymn, worded somewhat after this fashion:

The blood we shed with knife or spear,
The widow's and the orphan's tear:
Of guilt they leave us unconvincible;
For what we did, we did on principle.

Then the gusts would dissipate them again, each on his separate course.

Having seen this much, the hero and his son returned to Tir na nOg. There Cuanduine grew rapidly to manhood, which he reached at the age of ten years. Cuchulain then, having trained him in all the heroic virtues, and having taught him his salmon leap and all other feats meet for one who had such perils before him to encounter, sent him on to the Fourth Heaven, which is the heaven of Realities, where he might gain more wisdom and knowledge than himself could impart. Thence he presently returned well dowered with gifts: namely, the gift of self-distrust, the gift of incredulity, the gift of incertitude, the gift of clear-sightedness, the gift of hardness, the gift of kindness, the gift of unscrupulousness, the gift of shamelessness, the gift of humour.

When he saw the lad thus equipped, Cuchulain considered it was time to send him to Earth: so, summoning him to his knee, he told him of the existence of that planet, and of the manners and customs (so far as he had himself observed them) of its inhabitants, dwelling on those that had seemed to him strangest, in order to whet the youth's curiosity to visit it. Then he told him of King Goshawk and of his encroachments upon the liberty of birds and men; whereupon Cuanduine's eye kindled, and he cried out that it was shame that the stars should witness such villainy.

As he spoke, the mind of the Philosopher came up once more from Earth, laden with bitter tidings. "Woe! Woe!" said he. "Goshawk has put another rivet in our shackles. In return for a rebate of one penny on sugar, they have surrendered to him all the wild flowers of the world; which his henchmen are even now uprooting and transplanting to his gardens. The primrose from its shady bank, the bluebell from the woodland, the loosestrife and mallow from the river's brim, the buttercup and the clover from the pastures, the gorse and the heather from the mountains, the ragged robin from the hedgerow, the foxglove and meadow-sweet, the pimpernel and prunella, even the little pink saxifrage from the crevices of the rocks: they are rending them all from their settings to deck his pleasure-grounds."

"What?" said Cuanduine. "Has no voice nor hand been raised to stay him?"

"But one," said the Philosopher. "My own. I went to the Finance Minister to urge that he should not take the sugar reduction on such terms; who, being friendly disposed towards me, as we had been at school together, heard me out very patiently, though he was not to be moved by my arguments. These, he admitted, were excellent in theory; but, said he, a statesman and. economist must look at the thing from a practical point of view. A scheme which involved an immediate reduction in the cost of an essential commodity, and would give badly needed employment to thousands of workers, counted more with him than fine-spun theories of academic democracy and dilettante aestheticism. Private enterprise was coming into its own, and we could not stop the flowing tide. Besides, if the Government did not adopt the scheme, the Yallogreens would make it a plank in their programme, and would infallibly sweep the country with it.

"After that," the Philosopher continued, "I went out and

denounced the proposal at every street corner, and in letters to all the newspapers: for which I was derided as a crank, scorned as a madman, and roundly abused as one that for a few paltry weeds would tax the sugar of the children of the poor and keep their fathers out of employment; or as a bloodsucking investor in the Sugar Trust, disgruntled by the magnanimous action of King Goshawk. By God, if you do not come soon to our help, young man, he will put the very soil of the Earth in his voracious pockets; nor will our people complain until he orders them into the void that he may take the rock as well."

"I will come straightway," said Cuanduine. "Neither will I rest until the birds and the flowers are freed, and Goshawk chastened in his insolence."

"Spoken like your father's son, my lad," said the Philosopher.

"I must learn to speak better, then," said Cuanduine. "For if a man is no more than his father's son, what is any of us but the great great-grand descendant of a protozoon? Tell me now: when a protozoon first produced bicellular offspring, which do you think should have been proud of the relationship?"

"That is easily answered," said the Philosopher. "But Should is not Would. I'll guarantee that youngster was well snubbed and spanked for his presumption. Nor have we earthlings yet cut our cousinship with the primeval slime."

"We must alter that," said Cuanduine. "Do not think I will rest after the liberation of the birds and the overthrow of Goshawk. I have heard from my father of your other follies: I will teach you the wisdom of Charity."

"Too soon for that," said the Philosopher. "First teach us the folly of killing."

"Too soon for that," said Cuchulain. "First teach them to fight decently."

With that advice Cuchulain bade farewell to his son. Then Cuanduine by his will, and the mind of the Philosopher by the tug of his body, fell swiftly to Earth.

CHAPTER IV

Cuanduine reads a Newspaper

THE PHILOSOPHER'S ATTIC HAD not changed much in the years that had passed, save that it was grown older and the rent higher. The old man had a new suit of clothes waiting for Cuanduine, of a nice pattern of tweed, and fashionably cut, with snow-white shirt and tie of poplin. When he was dressed in these the Philosopher served them a breakfast of milk and bread and cheese, as he had done before when Cuchulain came to Earth; after which he offered the young man a newspaper, and himself opened another.

"What is this?" asked Cuanduine.

"That," said the Philosopher, "is one of the marvels of human civilisation." Cuanduine turned the newspaper over in his hands; looked at it right way up, wrong way up, and sideways; opened it and counted the pages; and finally looked at the Philosopher with an expression of bewilderment on his godlike countenance. "It is called a newspaper" the Philosopher explained. "In it is written down the news of all the things that happened yesterday in the world: and to-morrow I shall get another which will relate all that happened to-day."

"But how," asked Cuanduine, "can the truth be ascertained in so short a time?"

"I did not say that it told the truth," replied the Philosopher. "I only said it told the news."

Then Cuanduine began to read aloud from the newspaper: "Social and Personal. King Goshawk gave a garden party at Tuscaloosa yesterday. . . . The Duke of Dudborough is fifty-one to-day.' Who is the Duke of Dudborough?"

"I don't know," said the Philosopher.

Cuanduine held his peace after that. These are some of the things he read:

Mr. Cyrus Q. Moneybags has had to cancel his European trip owing to an attack of leprosy.

———

Miss Dinkie Filmy has recovered from her fit of the blues, and has consented to resume her part in the great film "Kisses of Fire," the production of which will now proceed.

———

If your breath is bad in the morning, try Punk's Pills. (Advt.)

———

LIMELIGHT CINEMA
All This Week
RODERICK REDLIP and BETTY BRIGHTEYE
in
TAVY'S BROKEN HEART
Adapted from Shaw's touching romance *Man and Superman*.

———

DASHBLANK & Co.'s New List of Masterpieces
Henry Heavynib's Great Novel, *Daisy* . . . . . . .10s.
Amy Slosh's Great Novel, *Girlish Hearts* . . . . 10s.
Lady Dishwater's Great Novel, *Riviera Romps* . . . 10s.

Daisy Deepend's Great Novel, *Fiametta's Frillies*   10s.
Millions of other Great Novels. See our Catalogue.
"All Dashblank's novels are Masterpieces" *(vidt* Press).

DASHBLANK & Co. "Masterpieces Only."

———

A STRAIGHT ISSUE

Once again it becomes our duty to tell the Government in
plain and unmistakable language what the best elements in the
country-and we speak in no undemocratic sense-think of the
way it is handling the present situation. This is a time for plain
speaking; a time to search men's souls, and to apply to every
word and action the acid test of Truth and Jusuce. We do
not count ourselves among those - if there are any such-who
would deny that there is never an occasion when the cause of
true Justice might not be less disadvantageously served by a
not overinflexible adhesion to the strict litera verecundiae than
by a too inopportune application of those solemn precepts
which are the concrete foundation on which morality and true
civilisation subsist. But nevertheless there are occasions such as
the present, when the whole fabric of Society . . .

———

THE WOLFO-LAMBIAN CRISIS

It is a matter of exceeding difficulty to estimate, at the present
stage of the proceedings, the true light in which to regard the
unfortunate misunderstanding that now threatens to involve
the Not-Very-Far-East in chaos and possibly bloodshed. To hold
the balance evenly between causes in which so many questions,
not only of national principle and international morality, but of
widespread interests and deep aspects of policy and diplomacy,

are inextricably intertwined, might possibly at this moment, when even the parties primarily concerned have not yet put their case fully before the public, militate unfavourably against those very principles of reconciling the effectuating of rightful action with the non-impairment of national privileges and financial interests, which it is the first duty of the organs of public opinion to safeguard, secure, and protect.

———

UP AND DOWN

Royal Resource.

When King Henry was driving down the Strand yesterday, a sudden breeze almost blew the royal hat from the royal head. Nothing daunted, his Majesty caught the royal brim with the royal fingers, and by this display of royal resourcefulness saved an awkward situation.

A Prince's Joke.

Prince Reggie, son and heir of the Jute King, is renowned for his sense of humour. The other day his Highness paid a surprise visit to one of his father's slums in Liverpool. As soon as his presence was known, dense crowds came swarming round to feast their eyes on his princely countenance. "They look like sardines in a box," remarked the Prince to an aide-de-camp. Screams of laughter greeted this ready sally.

———

A GREAT SPORTSMAN

Lord Puddlehead, who died last Monday, was almost as distinguished in the field of sport as in that of politics. His greatest kill was on his own estate at Puddlington about five years ago, when he shot 850 brace of pheasants in a day. But his performance in Scotland last year runs it close. On that occasion he shot 3600 head of grouse in five days, an average of 690 per day. Altogether over one million birds and beasts have fallen to his gun during his amazingly active life

---

ATROCIOUS MURDER
Airman done to death in Jungulay

A murder of a peculiarly dastardly character was perpetrated to-day by tribesmen in the neighbourhood of Jhamjhar, Jungulay. The victim was Lieut. Derek Blacktan, an officer in King Goshawk's Air Force stationed at Brahmbuhl Jhelli. Entirely unarmed save for a loaded revolver, he happened to be strolling in the vicinity of Jhamjhar, when he was set upon by three natives and beaten to death. The village had been bombed from the air a few days before, and it is believed that the assassination was an act of vengeance. Reprisals are already in preparation.

THE FAIRLY-NEAR-EASTERN CRISIS
Lambian Reply To The Wolfian Note

WOLFOPOLIS, *Thursday.*

The reply of the Lambian Government to the Wolfian Note demanding reparation for the alleged negligence of a Lambian lighterman in damaging the paint of a Wolfian steamer in Micropolis harbour last week, was delivered here this morning. The Wolfian Note, it will be remembered, embodied the following demands:

1. The Lambian Government to send a grovelling apology to the Wolfian Government.

2. The guilty lighterman, or, if he cannot be discovered, any other Lambian lighterman, to be executed at once without trial,

and the trade of lightermanship to be suppressed in Lambia.

3. The Lambian Bag to be lowered seven times on all public buildings in Micropolis whenever a Wolfian citizen passes by.

4. All citizens of Lambia to prostrate themselves for five minutes at sight of a Wolfian citizen.

5. Lambia to pay an indemnity of £900,000,000,000 in three yearly instalments.

6. The members of the Lambian Cabinet, and the Committee of the Lambian Lightermen's Union, to proceed at once to Wolfopolis and publicly prostrate themselves before Nervolini, the Wolfian Dictator, afterwards accepting his boot in the part prescribed in the Annex.

The Lambian reply is understood to accede to all these demands, with the exception of No. 6. It also asks that the period for the payment of the indemnity be extended to five years.

The Wolfian Fleet has already put to sea in readiness for any eventuality.

LAMBOPOLIS, *Thursday.*

It is reported that the Wolfian Fleet has been sighted off Micronetta.

––––

HOW I DID IT

ACQUITTED MURDERER TELLS HOW HE KILLED HIS WIFE, DAUGHTER, AND SOLICITOR

THE BLANKSTOWN MYSTERY SOLVED AT LAST

WILLIAM BADSTUFF'S OWN STORY

EXCLUSIVE TO THE "ILLUSTRATED SUNDAY SURVEY"
GORY DETAILS   *SENSATIONAL REVELATIONS*

GENUINE NARRATIVE AS ISSUED
FROM THE MURDERER'S REFUGE
IN THE WILDS OF CENTRAL ASIA,
SECURED BY "SUNDAY SURVEY"
AT A COST OF
TWO MILLION POUNDS

MR. BADSTUFF.

First Instalment Next Sunday Tells
HOW BADSTUFF WON THE AFFECTIONS
OF HIS SOLICITOR'S CHIROPODIST

ORDER YOUR COPY AT ONCE

OTHER CONTENTS OF THIS ISSUE
RURITANIA *MUST* PAY – – – – – – By Frantic Blair
IS THERE A HELL? – – – – By Rev. Simon Broadhead
DARNING THE PRINCE'S SOCKS – – By Sylvia Slop

ALL THE LATEST PHOTOS OF SPORT AND SOCIETY
CONCLUSION OF SPLENDID SERIAL, "LAWLESS
LOVE" LONG OR SHORT KNICKERS? MORE VIEWS
FROM OUR READERS ON THIS ABSORBING TOPIC

READ THE
"ILLUSTRATED SUNDAY SURVEY"
SPORTING NEWS
It is understood that the soccer match between Wondrous
Wanderers and Sturdy Stickers has been cancelled owing to the
refusal of the latter team to play for less than £5000 per man.
The Wanderers had contracted for £3500.

A record entry is expected for the Amateur Golf Championship, £1000 having been guaranteed to each competitor. There is a rumour, however, that Mr. Niblick, the present holder, will refuse to play unless guaranteed £20,000, win, lose, or draw.

———

Yesterday's great fight between Bruiser Burke and Slogger Samson for the Middleweight Championship of the World was a magnificent display of fistic talent. Every precaution had been taken to ensure a genuine contest. A sum of one million pounds was to be divided equally between the combatants on condition that the fight should last at least ten rounds, that a full pint of blood should be spilt, and that not less than two eyes should be completely bunged. In addition, the winner was to receive a further quarter of a million, and the loser a further four hundred thousand. The result was highly satisfactory. After six rounds each man had a darkened peeper, and in the eighth the referee announced that the blood measure was full. The next two rounds were uneventful, but as the gong sounded for the eleventh, every nerve in the vast audience was tense with excitement. The two bruisers faced each other for a moment. Then simultaneously each tipped the chin of the other with his left, and, quick as lightning, flung himself backwards on the floor. Burke, being the heavier man, reached it first, and was accordingly declared the loser. Frantic cheering greeted the result. The blood was subsequently auctioned, and was knocked down at £120, which will be divided equally between the pugilists.

———

Bashing Burton has declared himself ready to accept £2,000,000 as a preliminary fee for discussing the conditions under which he might be prepared to fight Kid Coffey for the Heavyweight Championship, without prejudice to his right to refuse to fight him on any conditions.

———

BRITISH LABOUR TROUBLE

A general strike is threatened in British coal mines as a result of the proposed cut of two shillings per week in wages. The Coal Trust have issued a statement that it will be impossible to work the mines at a profit unless the cut is accepted.

———

CENSORS' GOOD WORK
Immodest Women Penalised

In Wolfe Tone Street yesterday two young women wearing immodest dresses, which revealed their throats and ankles, were arrested by Censors, stripped, and taken before the District Court. They were sentenced to a year's hard labour. We hope this will be a lesson to those young persons that the world-wide reputation of Irish womanhood for modesty and chastity is not a thing to be lightly imperilled.

———

BUY THE

SUNDAY MUCKHEAP

THE BEST TUPPENCEWORTH ON THE MARKET

———

LARGER IRISH CIRCULATION THAN ANY NATIVE PAPER

———

SUPPORT HOME TALENT

DUBLIN SPICE
IS JUST AS GOOD AS ANY IMPORTED FILTH

OUR LITERARY CORNER
A Novel with a Purpose.
"Blood and Fire," by B. S. T. Sellar. Charlatan & Co. 10s.

This gifted and popular author breaks new ground in his latest and greatest book. Is war right? Is there not something inequitable in the present unequal distribution of wealth? Is marriage what it might be? These are the startling questions which the trials and sufferings of the last few years have moved Mr. Sellar to ask. The author faces them courageously and without flinching. There is a new note of thought in this remarkable book, and if Mr. Sellar does not answer any of the great questions he raises, his message is perhaps all the more effective in consequence.

DUBLIN DISTRICT COURT
Percy MacGoldbags, 22, was summoned before Mr. Donkey yesterday on the charge of killing three children when motoring through Cuffe Street on the 15th inst. Constable Ryan testified that accused went down the street at a speed of one hundred miles an hour-twenty beyond the limit. Accused pleaded contributory negligence, and said that he had never driven a car before. Mr. Donkey, fining the young man five pounds, advised him to take lessons before again driving through crowded thoroughfares.

CENTRAL CRIMINAL COURT
The concluding stage of the trial of Bill Bungle, 40, bricklayer, for the murder of his wife, was heard yesterday. Prisoner read a statement in which he declared that his wife drank, and neglected the home and children. He had tried to get a divorce

by setting up a sham domicile in England, but the subterfuge had been discovered. After five minutes' consideration the jury returned a verdict of guilty, and prisoner was sentenced to be hanged.

———

PROVINCIAL NEWS

The Ballycatandog Urban District Council met yesterday to discuss the resolution forwarded by the Ballymess Council, condemning the proposal of the Government to establish the metric system in Ireland.

Mr. Brady, proposing the motion, said that it was the duty of every Irishman worthy of the name to denounce the most tyrannous piece of legislation ever introduced into a democratic country. The action of the Government made the deeds of Nero, Queen Elizabeth, and Oliver Cromwell look mild and benignant in comparison.

MR. GRADY: Where was your grandfather in 1916?

MR. THADY: Under the bed.

MR. BRADY: I defy any man here to say my grandfather was a funk.

MR. GRADY: The Bradys were always great heroes.

MR. BRADY: They're every bit as good as the Gradys anyhow.

MR. GRADY: You old fool.

THE CHAIRMAN: Order! Order!

Mr. Grady: Don't you start putting in your oar.

THE CHAIRMAN: I will if I like. And who has a better right? My grandfather was out in 1916.

MR. GRADY: Yes. Right out of it.

THE CHAIRMAN: No. That's where yours was.

MR. GRADY: Do you call my grandfather a funk?

The meeting broke up in disorder.

———

HOUSES TO LET

A five-roomed house to let. South suburbs.
Moderate rent. No children.

Cosy house. Two bedrooms, sitting-room, kitchen, bath.
£150 and taxes. No dogs. No children.

Delightful house. Five miles from city. Six bed., four reception
rooms. Billiard room, conservatory, stables, garage, kennels,
garden and kitchen garden. No children.

Fine house, beautifully situated in own ground ten miles from
city. Children objected.

Gate lodge to let. Five rooms. No dogs, no poultry, no
children. Suit married couple.

Perfect house. Situated in own grounds. Beautiful scenery.
Healthy climate. Five bedrooms, four reception. Day and night
nursery. School-room. Large Bower garden. Playing field, with
goal-posts., etc. Tennis-court. Suit married couple. No children.

Pigstye to let. 10s. weekly. Suit large family.

Victorian mansion. Beyond repair. Situated in formerly
fashionable quarter in heart of city. Reasonable rent. No objection
to dogs, cats, poultry, canaries, tortoises, goldfish, axolotls, or
even children.

––––

LATEST NEWS
Micronetta shelled
Strong action of Nervolini.

Micronetta has been shelled by the Wolfian Fleet. The first
shell struck an infant school in the centre of the town, killing the
teacher and eleven children. The white Flag was at once hoisted.
The Wolfian admiral, landing soon afterwards, fainted with relief
on learning that no British or American citizens were among the
casualties. All lightermen in the town have been Bogged and
boiled in oil.

CHAPTER V

How Cuanduine was mobbed by a Bevy of Damsels

AT THIS LAST NEWS Cuanduine cast down the paper in a rage, being too concerned with the fate of the Lambians to bother about the remaining ten pages, though they were close packed with racing news and tipsters' chit-chat.

"Here's work to hand for me," said he to the Philosopher. "I must stop this war."

"Nonsense, lad," said the Philosopher. "You must first try your hand at a lighter task. Depend upon it, the Lambians will surrender before they suffer further hurt, and you can right their wrongs in your own good time. Let us begin our work now at the beginning. Come out with me into the street and see man as he is."

Cuanduine, seeing the wisdom of this advice, went out with the Philosopher to explore the city as his father had done before him. This likewise was unchanged since those days, only that the people and the buildings were grown shabbier, and the sky-signs more progressive. Also there were great numbers of men to be seen in the uniform of King Goshawk digging up daisies and dandelions in the public parks and among the ruins of houses.

When they had emerged from those regions of the city where the people are too occupied with work and their sufferings to notice anything else, and had come amongst the shoppers and strollers in the brighter districts, the girls came running from all sides to look at Cuanduine and to catch his eye: for, indeed, he was the most beautiful creature that had ever been seen upon the earth. The whole street was soon a swishing sea of petticoats, sparkling with smiles; and tinkling with girlish voices, in the midst of which Cuanduine and the Philosopher kept their feet with difficulty, like stranded mariners on a bank in a rising tide. Cuanduine, who, from what he had heard, was not prepared to find the earth such a pleasant place, nevertheless quickly recovered from his surprise, and gave smile for smile and chat for chat, even pressing a hand or two that succeeded in finding his. There were red lips too, ripe for kissing; but in so rich a harvest he knew not where to begin his reaping. While they were thus merrily sporting, there arose a cry of alarm from the outskirts of the bevy, and a squadron of Censors with their lily-shaped truncheons came ploughing like battleships through the frothy sea of femininity, which fled before them like the tide through a narrow channel. Most of the damsels got away in safety, but a few were clubbed about the head and brought before the magistrates, charged with unmaidenly behaviour, for which they were sentenced to terms of imprisonment ranging from three weeks to one year, according to the incomes of their fathers.

Cuanduine stood looking after their heels, transfixed with amazement; and the Philosopher was also overcome, having received one very amorous caress by mistake. From the stupefaction thus induced he was awakened by a glance at Cuanduine, which sent him straightway into a laughing fit; for all the pockets of the hero's garments, not only the side and breast pockets of his coat, but his trouser pockets, his waistcoat pockets, and even his ticket pocket, were distended and swollen up to the size of so many footballs. Cuanduine, putting a hand to one of them to find what the stuffing was, drew out a fistful of little screwed-up bits of paper, some tied with pink and blue ribbon, but for the most part merely folded up tight; which, when he opened them, proved to be hasty but tender billets-doux, inviting him to the homes of these bold-faced hussies, or to other trysting places, the next day or the day after.

"By heaven," said the Philosopher, "it is the devil's own luck that you are so handsome! There will be broken hearts over this."

"Not a whit," said Cuanduine. "I will keep these assignations."

"What? All of them?" cried the Philosopher.

"Of course," said Cuanduine.

"Your father's son speaks again," said the Philosopher. "Have sense, lad. What if some of them fall in love with you?"

"I hope," said Cuanduine, "they will all fall in love with me, as I have with them."

"But surely," said the Philosopher, "you must see that that will bring torment and heartbreak among them? "

"No, faith," said Cuanduine; "for I will deny myself to none of them."

"Now God help your seraphic innocence," said the Philosopher. "Have you never heard of jealousy among the stars?"

"Why should they be jealous?" asked Cuanduine. "Not one shall have a jot more of me than her neighbour; nor a jot less."

"Bless your innocence again," said the Philosopher. "That will not be enough for them. Each will want you altogether to herself."

"O gluttony!" said Cuanduine. "Are the fools then as jealous of the sun's rays, of the greenness of grass, of the corn and wine?"

"So much so," said the Philosopher, "that, if you waste any time keeping those assignations, you may find that someone has bought the sun before you can redeem the birds or the flowers. Come: you have dragons to kill."

CHAPTER VI

How Cuanduine was Docketed, Injected, and Psychalysed; and how he came to the Gateway of the Fortunate Fields

"BUT FIRST," SAID THE Philosopher, "we must get you a docket." Cuanduine asked what that might be. "Everybody must have a docket," explained the Philosopher, "to identify him; else he is liable to arrest as a vagrant."

Going on at once, they came to a stationer's shop, where the Philosopher purchased a blank form; after a scrutiny of which he led Cuanduine to a photographer, and affixed the version of his face so obtained in the space provided. Next he took him to a doctor, who injected him with a variety of preparations as listed hereunder:

> With cowpox, to preserve him from smallpox;
> With chickenpox, to preserve him from thrush;
> With roserash, to preserve him from nettlerash;
> With ringworm, to preserve him from tapeworm;
> With lockjaw, to preserve him from phossyjaw;
> With German measles, to preserve him from Russian cholera;
> With housemaid's knee, to preserve him from woolsorters' disease;
> With catalepsy, to preserve him from dogbite;
> With lobster, to preserve him from cancer.

All these particulars he entered in the spaces provided on the docket. O the wonders of Science! O the providence of Government! Between them they preserve us from every ill, both corporal and spiritual, that afflicts our effete and sinful natures: that is, at least, the preventable ills, and such as are with in their province. And if any puling sentimental crank shall tell you that the proper cure for these evils is sunshine, soap, eggs, and butter, you can answer him that there is not enough of these to go round—not, at least, without an undue interference with the order of nature and the structure of society—and that cow's pus is plentiful enough to save us this latter inconvenience. Tell him also to consider what a difficult task it would be to distribute these eggs and things so broadly, the burdens it would heap on capital, the grave abuses it would lead to. How easy, on the other hand, to induce a little baby (which can scream, indeed, and struggle a bit, perhaps—though not so much as to hurt you) to undergo this salutary operation. A prick or two, a little gentle scraping of the cuticle, then in with the pus, and all is over except the sequelae. So praise we Science, and the priests of Science, who taught us to scald the germs off our babies' rattles, and clap them in so beneficially under the skin.

The Philosopher next took Cuanduine to a Psychanalyst; who, after surveying his left ear gravely for an hour or so (for he: dared not look into his eyes), asked him had he been troubled with any dreams lately: to which Cuanduine answered Yes, that he had been disturbed the previous night by a very strange dream indeed: namely, that he had found himself in a public street without his trousers; that after an anxious search under the mocking gaze of the multitude, he had at length caught sight of them lying on the ground not far off; but when he stooped to pick them up, they had turned into a black cat, which immediately ran away, leaving its tail in his hand.

"It is clear," said the Psychanalyst, "that you are suffering from a repressed. desire to kill your great-aunt's solicitor in order that you may enjoy her yourself."

This also was recorded on the docket.

"And now," said the Philosopher, when they had left the Psychanalyst, "what lie shall we put down for your birth and parentage?"

"Why not put down the truth?" asked Cuanduine.

"Tush!" said the Philosopher. "No one would believe it. I will set it down that you are my natural son, begotten on a passionate holiday in Hawaii, whence you are lately arrived." This he did, and presented the docket at the Registry Office, where it was duly countersigned and stamped with the arms of the Republic.

These formalities completed, they were free to continue their explorations of the city. But first by the Philosopher's instruction, Cuanduine smutched his face with dirt here and there in order to escape the attentions of the girls. Then they sallied forth again and climbed to the top of a tramcar. The Philosopher pointed out the different features of the city to Cuanduine as they sped through it. First there were the ruins of Sackville Street and Westmoreland Street, almost covered over with huts and small houses. Then came the two great mounds of rubble where the Bank of Ireland and Trinity College had once stood. Then the vast slum area of Grafton Street, Stephen's Green, Rathmines, Rathgar, Terenure, and Rathfarnham. After that there was something of improvement, the tram running for a mile and a half along a straight street of sober little red brick houses, containing perhaps five rooms apiece, with a neat patch of garden: the residences of artists, doctors, engineers, university professors and lecturers, scientists, librarians, civil servants, and others of the respectable poor. This was followed by a pleasant and comfortable-looking suburb, with large handsome houses and well-cared grounds, where dwelt the moderately rich: small shopkeepers, cabinet ministers, generals, admirals, and so forth. Then came the great mansions of the larger shop-keepers, importers, and bookmakers, extending for half a mile along a broad boulevard lined with statues, fountains, plane trees, and bandstands. Right at the end of this vista Cuanduine could see an immense triple-arched gateway, surpassing in its proportions even the greatest triumphal arches of the Romans and the French. It was the gateway to the domain of the Millionaires.

Leaving the tramcar, Cuanduine and the Philosopher approached this mighty portal. Upon its blockish summit flew a huge white banner, bearing in its centre a closed fist gules; and large on its entablature was carved and gilded the inscription: WHAT WE HAVE WE HOLD. The pillars of the central arch were supported by two gigantic figures in bronze. That on the left represented a woman, naked, laughing with empty eyes. Her breasts were small and shrunken; her feet trampled upon a mead of flowers; and in her hands she held a cornucopia, spilling its treasures upon the winds of the world. That on the right was of an aged man, blind and dumb, clad in a thick and sombre garment, his feet immersed in a clinging mire. It was well for the artist, said the Philosopher, that his employers had not understood his symbolism; and well also for those within the gate that those without could not understand it either.

The gates themselves were of hammered bronze, with bosses of gold and spikes of silver. They were open: but Cuanduine and the Philosopher did not go through that day. Instead they turned and went home, by the way they had come, to Stoneybatter.

CHAPTER VII

How the MacWhelahan held Court at Bohernabreena

HAVING SEEN DUBLIN, IT was now necessary for Cuanduine to look upon the rest of the world. The Philosopher explained that the easiest and quickest way to do so would be to charter an aircar; but that, as he had not sufficient money for this, and as he could not borrow any owing to his lack of credit—

"What?" interrupted Cuanduine. "Are you not an honest man?"

The Philosopher answered that he would wish to be thought so; but that a man's credit was dependent not upon his honesty, but upon the sufficiency of his means.

"That is to say," said Cuanduine, "that to borrow money one must have it already: so that those only can borrow it who have least need of it. I verily believe you might search Berenice's Hair for a stranger world than this."

"Be that as it may," said the Philosopher. "Our need is still money. In this world nothing can be done without it. A church can be built without God, but not without money—But I was going to tell you how I propose to get some. Amongst our millionaires there are some who are pleased to be regarded as patrons of art, learning, religion, and so forth; and some who think it good policy to keep other people's minds distracted with such toys from the real business of life. This afternoon we will go to such a one, tell him you have a mission to preach the word of God to mankind, and see if he will not paper our pockets as liberally as Croesus gilded the Delphic pythoness."

In the afternoon, therefore, the two of them took tram again to the Millionaires' quarter. They passed through the great gateway, and, walking between sumptuous gardens and plantations, came presently in sight of a castle of white granite, with towers and battlements, wall and moat, portcullis and drawbridge flanked with brass flame throwers and gas ejectors.

"Yonder," said the Philosopher, "is the house of Padraig MacWhelahan, who holds the wheat resources of Ireland as tributary to King Goshawk. As the nearest of his fraternity, he shall be the first to endure our importunity."

Approaching the castle they saw that the drawbridge was down, and that a sentry was on guard, clad in a gorgeous uniform of purple and gold, with white gaiters, brass helmet, and horsehair plume. Within the courtyard other soldiers could be seen, dressed in like fashion, which was the livery of their master. The sentry let the Philosopher and Cuanduine pass after formal challenge, but in the courtyard they were stopped and searched by the Sergeant of the Guard before they were allowed to proceed. In the hall they were met by a servitor, who, having learnt their business, told them that the MacWhelahan had but just descended to the audience chamber, and conducted them there forthwith.

After passing through many corridors and ante-rooms Cuanduine and the Philosopher found themselves presently in a chamber of moderate size, hung with blue satin and lit with a hundred softly shaded lamps of fretted silver. There was a dais at the far end. On it was a silver chair studded with sapphires and upholstered with peach-coloured velvet, in which sat a little old bald-headed man clad in a Paisley dressing-gown. Behind him stood nineteen prosperous looking attendants of varying ages, in plainly cut suits of purple with gold braid. These were the MacWhelahan's doctors, by whose constant ministrations the ancient financier, who was close to his hundred and sixth birthday, maintained a precarious hold on human existence.

On his right hand stood the MacWhelahan's seven solicitors (one for every day of the week), and on his left, his seneschal, his private secretary, and the magnificently uniformed Captain of the Guard. There were besides in dutiful attendance on their lord an obsequious multitude of stewards, valets, sutlers, hat-holders, coat-offerers, cigar-buyers, wine tasters, chefs, chauffeurs, hairdressers, masseurs, physiculturists, chiropodists, chiromancers, coueists, soothsayers, scientists, sophists, psychanalysts, weather clerks, journalists, art experts, stamp experts, encyclopaedists, archeologists, bric-a-brac hunters, epigrammatists, horse-trainers, grooms, jockeys, airmen, skippers, sporting advisers, dog fanciers, golf professionals, tipsters, swashbucklers, informers, procurers, apologists, idea merchants, bailiffs, agents, rent collectors, income-tax recoverers, shorthand typists, publicity agents, priests, parsons, poets, and political advisers. All these stood meekly in the background behind the nineteen doctors. Soldiers, motionless as statues, with bayonets fixed, lined the chamber walls.

In front of the dais stood the little group of clients or suppliants, half-a-dozen in all, humble folk, utterly dumfounded and overawed by their surroundings. The private secretary having tapped a gong for silence (though indeed there was silence enough already) the seneschal came forward, and in a loud voice announced:

"The audience will now begin. Greeting to the MacWhelahan, master of millions!"

At these words the private secretary and the Captain of the Guard, the nineteen doctors and the seven solicitors, and the whole congregation of stewards, sutlers, hat holders, chiropodists, horse trainers, bailiffs, and publicity agents; along with the bric-a-brac hunters, dog fanciers, and others of the fraternity listed as aforesaid; suddenly flopped upon their bended knees, making loyal obeisance to their lord and master, while the soldiers presented arms, the call of a hundred bugles

sounded from twenty towers, and a peal of ordnance was shot
off on the battlements. At that the unpractised clients and
suppliants made shift to imitate their betters, tumbling to their
knees with more humility than grace. Cuanduine and the Philosopher, however, remained upon
their legs; perceiving which the seneschal, who, by reason of
the gout and of a portly presence, had not yet completed his
prostration, straightened himself up and called out to them:
"Unmannered dogs! Down on your knees!" whereat a wave of
curiosity swept over the assembly. A hundred necks uncrooked
themselves. The nineteen doctors opened wide their eyes in
horror; the seven solicitors swooned one on top of another; and
the whole multitude of stewards, chefs, chauffeurs, cigar buyers,
soothsayers, and sporting advisers trembled like a pantryful of
jellies in a draught. Cuanduine and the Philosopher, however,
were by no means impressed; neither, when the seneschal
repeated his command, did they make any move. Thereupon
the MacWhelahan, who till now had remained sunk half
comatose in his chair like a deflated balloon, suddenly sat up
and took notice. At sight of the two unbent ones he uttered a
wheeze of astonishment, which the loyal and dutiful assembly of
hairdressers, art experts, journalists, and other varlets felt boded
ill to the presumptuous pair. Therefore they kissed the floor with
more than usual unction, and rose hastily to their feet to hear
the sentence of doom. There was none, however, forthcoming;
for the seneschal, looking into the eyes of Cuanduine, was so
troubled by what he saw in the depths of them, that he deemed
it wise to overlook the offence of their owner, to which effect
also he advised his lord. Then, tapping on the silver gong, he
invited all who had boons to beg or communications to make
to the MacWhelahan to present themselves at the foot of the
throne.

Thereafter came a string of suppliants: an employé asking
permission to marry; a tenant begging for a roof to his shanty;

a widow claiming compensation for her husband, killed by
one of the MacWhelahan's motors; and others of similar sort;
some of whom received favourable answers, but the most went
empty away. Lastly came a little man, very old and bent, and
wearing spectacles of such immense thickness as to distort and
magnify his eyes to the size and appearance of those of a cow
with goitre; who, speaking in tones tremulous with age, haste,
and excitement, cried: "My lord! My lord! I have found the
great secret."

At that the Millionaire almost leaped to his feet in astonishment; but in the act his heart failed him, and he would
have died then and there but for the instant attention of the
nineteen doctors, by whose united efforts he was presently
brought to. Then, gasping for breath, "I was nearly gone that
time, my friends," said he. "And you," he said to the ancient
suppliant, "came near to making the secret useless to me by
your manner of announcing it. Let us hope that you have really
found it, or I shall scarcely be able to pardon you."

"I have certainly found it, my lord," piped the suppliant;
whereat the nineteen doctors uttered one united guffaw of
professional scepticism: for they knew the fellow to be some
unscrupulous quack hole-in-corner experimenter with an
alleged corrective to Fuhzler's Elixir, the search for which
was now being abandoned by reputable scientists. But the
millionaire turned angrily on the scoffers, ordering them to
be silent. Then he very graciously gave his hand to the aged
suppliant to kiss, afterwards commending him to the care of a
steward, and promising to go further into the matter later on
in private.

There being no other suppliants left, Cuanduine now came
forward, and standing erect before the throne, said: "Son of
Earth, I have come here neither to beg nor to complain, but to
give. Is there anything you want?"

"Nothing," said the Millionaire coldly.

"Think again, Son of Earth," said Cuanduine.

"I want nothing," repeated the Millionaire.

"Think again, Mr. MacWhelahan," interposed the Philosopher. "Look down deep into your soul and see if there be not some assurance lacking, the possession of which might make you sleep easier of nights."

The Millionaire thought a moment: then, clapping his withered hands, he signified to the seneschal and the seven solicitors and the nineteen doctors and the whole assembly of chiropodists, horse-trainers, poets, *et hoc genus omne*, that he wished them to withdraw; which they did most reluctantly. As soon as they were gone the MacWhelahan spoke thus:

"You have come to tell me—?"

"The Truth," said the Philosopher.

"Nay, nay," said Cuanduine. "No man living could bear to hear the Truth. Besides I do not know it yet, having attained no higher than the Fourth Heaven. I will tell you some of the Truth."

"Did you say you've come from heaven?" asked the MacWhelahan.

"I did," replied Cuanduine.

"He will not believe that," said the Philosopher, "unless you give him a sign: work him a miracle, I mean."

"The most effective miracle," said Cuanduine, "will be to make him believe."

He looked into the Millionaire's eyes, and MacWhelahan believed.

"Now," said Cuanduine, "ask me what you will, and I will tell you the truth."

"Is there such a thing as hell?" asked the Millionaire.

"What do you mean by hell?" asked Cuanduine.

"I mean a place where we suffer eternal torment for the wrong we've done here."

"No," said Cuanduine.

"Not even mental torment?"

"No," said Cuanduine.

"Say, mister," said the Millionaire, with keen interest, "is this a sure thing?"

"I have said it," said Cuanduine.

"I wish to God I'd known it before," said the Millionaire. "When I think of all the things I might have done—It's not true either, is it, that a rich man cannot enter the kingdom of heaven?"

"Yes," said Cuanduine. "That is true."

"Oh, well, who wants to enter the kingdom of heaven anyway?—so long as the other place isn't the alternative, I mean. You know, prophet, I wish I'd met you a bit earlier. When I think of all the money I've wasted on charities, churches, schools, convents, and the lord knows what—to say nothing of the business opportunities I've let slip on account of conscientious scruples—well, it pretty well gets my goat."

Here the old gentleman, whose voice had begun to slither somewhat at the end of this speech, rang for a doctor, who injected him with some stimulant, and again withdrew.

"Now, see here, prophet," resumed the MacWhelahan, with more vigour, "I'm tremendously obliged to you for this information, and I won't forget it to you. Trust me. But this thing's got to be kept a secret between us three."

"Not so," Cuanduine interrupted. "The message I bear is not for one, but for the general ear."

"My dear sir," said the Millionaire, "you don't know what you're talking about. How am I to benefit if you destroy scruples all round? And what price can you expect for a secret that is to be shared by everybody?"

"I do not understand this language," said Cuanduine to the Philosopher. "Speak you to the fellow."

"Sir," said the Philosopher, "you have just been granted a very precious gift, namely, the power to believe that here before you is a messenger from heaven."

"Oh yes. I believe that all right," said the Millionaire. "But what's the good of it if I'm not to make anything out of it?"

"He who has the truth has all things," said the Philosopher. "But to you has been granted over and above the privilege of being asked to help in giving the truth to others."

"Now, see here, you two greenhorns," said the MacWhelahan. "Let's cut the cackle and get down to brass tacks. You don't seem to realise that you've dished yourselves: handed over the bally goods before you'd seen the colour of my money. I've got your secret. I know that hell is what I'd long guessed it to be: a priests' yarn, got up to squeeze Peter pence out of a world of mutts. Well, knowing that, I'm the strongest man on this planet, and can do anything I blame well choose. As for you two: keep out of my path, or you'll find yourselves cooling your ardour for truth down in one of my oubliettes."

Said the Philosopher: "God forgive me that I should bandy threat for threat; but the faith that came by miracle can be taken away by miracle."

The Millionaire smiled uneasily, knowing no parry to the thrust; but bethinking him that it would be a long time before the new truth could be generally established, and that meanwhile he had a considerable start of all other converts; and reasoning also that the diversion of the public mind to questions of religious controversy would be good for business, he dissembled with much skill and spoke his visitors fair, declaring that what he had said was but to test their sincerity and firmness of purpose. "For we Lords of Industry have big responsibilities on our shoulders," he explained. "What are we but the Trustees of the national inheritance? and in that capacity is it not our duty to be cautious of innovation—especially of innovations which may alter the whole trend of human development? If this truth of yours were to be given to the world without due preparation, precaution, reservation, or qualification, who can foretell what the consequences might be? There might even be revolution; and in revolution, as you know, there is danger of all religion being overthrown. I see, however, that you are staid, sober, and trustworthy pastors of your sect; and as earnest of my conversion to your views, I hope you will permit me to give a small donation to the General Purposes Fund of the new Faith."

Having thus spoken, he summoned his secretary, and wrote them a cheque for ten thousand pounds; telling himself when they had gone that the information they had given him was cheap at the price.

CHAPTER VIII

Which might have been the Longest in the Book, but shall prove to be one of the Shortest

I CRAVE PARDON HERE, my friends—whether you belong to the humble many that read for entertainment and not instruction, or to the arrogant few that demand Art and not Propaganda (which amounts, when all's said, to much the same thing)—for allowing the intrusion at this point of some regrettably grave and disturbing matter into the even flow of my hitherto frolicsome, adventurous, and, I hope, artistically constructed narrative. Believe me that I do so with no intention of harrowing your feelings or pricking your consciences: which is a liberty I should be the very last to venture on. If the impending episodes of the adventures of the Philosopher and Cuanduine could be omitted without impairing the sense and sequence (and therewith the value both as literature and entertainment) of their story, I should certainly omit them. But since that is impossible, I beg you to make the best of it; brace yourselves, like December bathers to the plunge; take a long breath; and away with you, hard as you can crawl, to the opposite bank. If your speed is but good enough you shall be out of it before the chill reaches your bones.

Know then that the Philosopher and Cuanduine went the round tour of the world by airplane, visiting cities, villages, ploughlands, and deserts in their course, not forgetting the steppes, prairies, pampas, etc., the limit of floating ice, the Region of Mosses and Lichens, and other interesting spots that you may look for on the map. Everywhere they went they saw things at which Cuanduine wondered exceedingly; as, for instance,

children working for a living, and adults with nothing better
to do than dance, flirt, play ball, and ride-a-cockhorse; children starving, and adults shortening their lives with overeating;
middle-aged women doctoring their complexions by bathing
in cream, and children fed on the skim; millionaires, sick with
idleness and high living, ordered holidays and change of air by
their doctors, and broken-down clerks, sick with undernourish-
ment and overwork, dosed with coloured stuff out of bottles;
millionaires' wives, surfeited with pleasure, recuperating on
tropic beaches, and poor men's wives hard at work a week after
childbirth; mansions and vast estates inhabited by idle sterile
couples, and teeming families crammed into a single room; a
millionaire buried in a silver coffin, and children stifled in the
womb for lack of the money to bring them into the world. They
saw also poets and artists drudging at desk and counter while
their fancies went unrecorded; and brainless fools whiling away
their endless leisure killing foxes and kissing women. They saw
racehorses housed in splendour and richly fed, with servants
to wait on them and clean up their dung; and they saw dogs
and guineapigs tortured by learned men in search of a cure for
Richman's Bellyrot. They saw men who coined gold out of the
necessities of the poor honoured by priests, dined by judges, and
saluted by policemen; and they saw the hungry man that stole
such a one's cigarette case sent to lie in a gaol. These and a thousand more such follies they saw; and they saw men that asked
for a better and a wiser world scorned as madmen or locked
up as dangerous. Such indeed was the wickedness and folly of
the world at this time that you would have deemed it fortunate
that the Lord had made a covenant with man not to visit him
with a second Deluge: for I take it that it was not harlotries nor
idolatries that called down upon our forbears the wrath of the
most High, but that the generation which it repented him that
he had made was in its ways of thought and living very much
like our own.

CHAPTER IX

The Beginning of Cuanduine's Campaign

WHEN THEIR TRAVELS WERE completed, Cuanduine and the Philosopher returned to Dublin. They found the city in the throes of a by-election; which Cuanduine deemed fortunate, thinking that the concourse of people so occasioned would be fertile soil for his own message. The Philosopher thought otherwise, but allowed himself to be overruled. The two accordingly repaired to College Green, where Blathero, the Greenyallo candidate, was addressing the multitude.

"Up to this," he was saying, "I have spoken mainly of principles—of the basic, fundamental ideals upon which the whole fabric of Greenyalloism, the mainspring and inspiration for which our fathers faced the rack, the gallows, the gibbet, and the gaol, is founded firm as upon a rock. But, gentlemen, you will ask—indeed an interrupter has already asked—what is our policy in the immediate situation. That is a fair question: a question that I will go so far as to say that any candidate who would not be prepared to give a frank and full answer to such a question would be unworthy to receive a single vote from the truehearted voters of the Muckandirt Division. (*Cheers.*) Not, gentlemen, that I do not set a high value on principles and ideals. On the contrary, the Greenyallo party has ever had Principle for its watchword and Idealism embroidered on its banners. How different from the vile Yallogreens, who have trampled every principle dear to the hearts of Irishmen in the mud, cast ideals into the gutter, and exalted base opportunism and vile materialism in their places. But, as I have said before, principles and ideals are not everything. It is on our practical policy that we appeal for your votes; and in defence of that policy I am ready now to hear any questions that you may put to me, and to answer them to the best of my ability."

At this invitation a ringing voice called out from the fringe of the crowd: "When will the Government get us back our song-birds from the grip of Goshawk?"

It was Cuanduine, as you may guess.

"Throw that man out," thundered Blathero. "The Government welcomes constructive criticism, but vulgar abuse is another thing. Throw him out."

A hundred stalwart fellows moved to do his bidding: but, at sight of Cuanduine's build and the dangerous gleam in his eye, they backed away from him, so that he passed from the meeting, along with the Philosopher, without mishandling. Walking a little farther, the two came presently to another gathering, which was being addressed by Blithero, the Yallogreen candidate.

"Well, fellahs," he was saying, "I've tole yez enough about our ideels an' princibles, which is the same our fathers was executed and went to gaol for. Yez'll want to know next what we're reelly up to. In fact that interrupter yez pegged out just now was asking as much. Well, that's fair enough, and yez ud be bigger fools than I think yez if yez ud vote for a man that wouldn't answer that question fair and square. Of course us Yallogreens puts ideels and princibles first, not like them Greenyallos that has betrayed all the princibles and ideels that th' Irish people has shed their blood for. But practical policy has its place too, and if anybody wants to know what ours is, he's only got to ask, and here I stand to answer him."

Cuanduine accepted the invitation as before, calling out from the background : "If you come into power will you get us back our birds from Goshawk?"

"Peg that fellah out," yelled Blithero in a fury. "We'll have none of the Gover'ment's paid interrupters and hooligans here. Peg him out."

A chosen gang of toughs turned to obey this suggestion; but Cuanduine repulsed them as before, and retired with the Philosopher to their room in Stoneybatter, where they awaited in patience the end of the election.

On the day of the declaration, they went down to see the results, which were posted up as follows:

Victor: BLATHERO 28,439
Moral Victor: BLITHERO 121

"What does that mean?" asked Cuanduine of the Philosopher.

"In the old days," said the Philosopher, "it was the custom after an election for the defeated party to claim a moral victory, and on the strength of it to commence a civil war. To obviate this we have arranged that there shall be no defeated party in an election. The candidate who gets most votes gets the seat and the salary, the other gets the moral victory and the glory."

At this moment the two candidates came out on to the balcony. After the cheering had subsided, Mr. Blithero addressed the crowd.

"Fellahs," he said, "in proposing a vote of thanks to the Sheriff, I must congratulate Mr. Blathero on the most tremendous victory ever won in the history of Europe. Judging from the mere figures he has scored a splendid material triumph, and I for one don't grudge it to him." (*Cheers.*)

"Gentlemen," rejoined Mr. Blathero, "in seconding this vote of thanks to the Sheriff, I extend my cordial congratulations to Mr. Blithero on achieving the most stupendous moral victory in the history of the world. The figures speak for themselves, and I bow to their verdict."

You should have heard the applause that greeted this magnanimous oration. It would have done your heart good, it was so warm hearted and appreciative. Alas that there should be any dissentient voice in such rare agreement and general jubilation; but so it was.

"Fools!" Cuanduine to two men who were yelling their throats sore beside him. "With a tithe of this energy you could win back your wild flowers."

"Bah!" said one of the men. "Who cares about a few old weeds."

"We got a good bargain for them, anyhow," said the other. Then all who were in the neighbourhood, both men and women, began to give their opinions of Cuanduine.

"He's a crank," said one. "Mad," said another.

"Maybe he has some sugar shares," hinted a third.

"He's a Greenyallo!" cried a fourth. "He's a Yallogreen!" shouted a fifth.

"If he's so keen on flowers," said a sixth, "can't he pay for a sniff like everybody else?"

"And if we had the flowers back," said another, "he'd be wanting the birds next.

There's no satisfying some people. Give them an inch and they take an ell."

A wild-eyed girl turned directly on the hero, saying: "You are a base materialist to pursue such sordid practical aims instead of sacrificing yourself for ideals and principles."

"You are a wild visionary," said an older woman, "to chase after impossible dreams instead of trying to do some practical good in the world."

"Sure, he's only a damned fool!" cried several other voices in chorus.

Then a gallant young fellow, emboldened by Cuanduine's unpopularity, smote him with his clenched fist from behind: but he burst all his knuckles against the hard tough muscle of the hero's back, and dislocated his wrist and elbow joint, so that his arm and hand were never much use to him afterwards. Moved by this object-lesson, the crowd made way respectfully for Cuanduine and the Philosopher to pass out.

CHAPTER X

The Continuation of Cuanduine's Campaign

THE NEXT DAY CUANDUINE was walking by himself along a crowded street, saddened by his many failures, but still planning for the future, when he saw a funeral procession coming towards him. It was a most extensive funeral: fifty mourning coaches followed the hearse, and a meadow of flowers had been slaughtered to enliven the coffin. Several men doffed their hats reverently during its transit; whereat Cuanduine, who had seen more than a dozen perambulators pass without receiving any such tribute, was so amazed that he stopped to expostulate with one of them, who looked shocked, and turned down his eyes.

Anger came on Cuanduine at that; and stepping forth, he seized the leading horse by the bridle, and sprang on its back, where he stood upright, facing the multitude.

"People of Eirinn," he said. "Cease this folly. Let the dead bury the dead."

Then the people of Eirinn raised a great shout around Cuanduine, and the windows of the fifty mourning coaches were opened, and a hundred heads popped out interrogatively. The coachman of the hearse took his whip, and would have slashed at Cuanduine with it, but the hero gave him a look so fierce that it dropped from his nerveless fingers, and he had much ado not to follow it himself. At that same look also the people in the street, who had gathered in a threatening circle around the hearse, fell back apace, and the hundred interrogative heads vanished into their coaches.

"People of Eirinn," said Cuanduine. "What evil have I

spoken that you look. on me so wrathfully?"

"Blasphemy and balderdash!" yelled a man in the crowd; and the words were taken up by a thousand throats.

"I thought you were Christians," said Cuanduine in astonishment.

"So we are!" said the people stoutly.

"It is a pity then that you do not know your founder's precepts," said Cuanduine.

"We do!" cried the people.

"Then," said Cuanduine, "it is a pity you do not practise them."

At that there was such an uproar as had not assailed his ears even in the stormy days of the elections. "Who says we don't practise our bloody religion?" yelled the people of Eirinn. "We're the best bloody Christians in the world!" howled the sons of the Gael. "Tear his eyes out!" screeched the daughters of Banba. Then these fair damosels strove to push their way to the front, but they could not prevail against the crowd, which was backing in terror from before the face of Cuanduine: for the hero-light was beginning to shine about his head, and the Bocanachs and Bananachs and Witches of the Valley were gathering upon the winds. Now there was on the outskirts of the crowd a quiet man that had not joined in the uproar: on him, therefore—as one that had shown tacit approval of the blasphemy and treason that had been spoken—the maidens of Innisfail turned their wrath and their finger-nails, ripping and rending him until he ran home almost naked, and it was much if he had half his skin on his back, or a dozen hairs left on his head.

Then Cuanduine spoke again, and the thunder of his voice sounded above the clamour of the swirling multitude like a fog-horn over the howling of wind and waves.

"Fools," said Cuanduine. "Have you not read that you cannot serve God and Mammon? Yet you cringe before God on bended knee on Sundays, and serve Mammon so faithfully the rest of the week that some of you can scarcely carry your bellies, and cannot breathe without the help of a doctor, or think without the help of a solicitor, while the rest of you are so ignorant, stupid, dirty, diseased, and ugly; so shiftless and lecherous, cowardly and dishonourable, slavish and vindictive; so meanly proud and so weakly stubborn that pity for your condition is dried up with disgust of what it has made of you."

At that the people were moved to such a fury of inexpressible anger that they danced upon the pavement, foaming at mouth, beating their heads with clenched fists, and howling demoniac imprecations. The women, in particular, were so carried away that they flung themselves on the ground, tearing the stones with their nails, and shrieking till their throats gushed blood. Then some of those that were behind Cuanduine, and therefore beyond the influence of his eye, made a murderous rush upon him; whereat he gave his salmon-leap, and alighted on the roof of the nearest house, whence he made his way homeward to Stoneybatter. The people, however, fell upon the horses of the hearse and tore them limb from limb, afterwards fighting among themselves for the pieces, many being slain and more crippled, of whom the numbers have not yet been accurately computed, so that the place is called Sraid an Air, that is to say, Slaughter Street, to this day.

These events formed the principal topic in the Dublin newspapers the following morning, and were also the subject of editorial comment.

"Decent Irishmen of all creeds and politics," said the *West Briton*, "will be unanimous in condemning the outrageous conduct of an as yet anonymous street preacher who has recently shown himself in our midst. The justifiable, though perhaps too violently expressed, resentment of the citizens has precluded the possibility of obtaining any very accurate report of his doctrines, but from the little that has been gleaned we judge them to be as narrow and bigoted as his methods of disseminating them are vulgar and blatant. The preacher, though misguided, is doubtless sincere: we therefore suggest to him that the cause of true religion will not be served by a too rigid insistence on the strict letter of Christian precept. . . . Thoughtful Irishmen of all sects and classes will deplore this alarming recurrence of religious fanaticism in an island which by earnest and sustained effort was beginning to be regarded as truly non-political and unsectarian. . . . For the present, however, we would advise Unionists that there is no cause for undue alarm. Only in the very last resort would we counsel them to reconsider their attitude to the Republic and call for the intervention of Great Britain."

Under the caption "Bestial Libels" the *National Sheet* held forth as follows:

"Once more a foul and underhand attempt has been made to pour filthy calumnies on the Irish Race. The principal figure in yesterday's revolting display of bigotry and bad taste declared that the Irish People are dirty and ignorant. We spit the reeking lie back in his loathsome face."

Thus did Press and Public receive Cuanduine's message.

CHAPTER XI

How the Universities received the New Evangel

CUANDUINE, HOWEVER, NOT YET despairing of his countrymen, and feeling that perhaps something of unpremeditation and of haphazard in his choice of a pulpit might have been a contributing cause of their unwillingness to hearken to his message, by the advice of the Philosopher made announcement in the press and by placard that he would address a public meeting the following Sunday in the Phoenix Park. Thither, accordingly, just before the appointed hour, the pair of them made their way, and having set up a board and trestles as a platform, awaited the arrival of the populace.

Now, when word of the meeting had been brought to the two Universities, namely, the National University of Ireland and the College of the Holy and Undivided Trinity near Dublin, it had been resolved by the students of each that the occasion called for action on their part which would be consonant with the character and traditions of those seats of learning. They assembled, therefore, after Divine Service at their respective headquarters, each supplied with ammunition according to his taste: the men of Trinity carrying bad eggs, stink bombs, and slap-bangs; the Nationals having stones, lumps of lead, and rolls of lavatory paper. Marching to the Park Gate the two magnificent bodies of young men met face to face and halted of one accord. Of one accord also the two leaders, George Face, Sen. Mod., B.A., of the Holy and Undivided Trinity, and Patrick Mohone, B.A., of the Sea-divided Gaels, stepped forward and shook hands. It was an historic moment. Mr. Mohone, speaking

in a voice that trembled with manly emotion, said that at last
the longed for day had arrived, and two noble colleges, hitherto
estranged, stood united in a cause worthy of both. Mr. Face said:
"Not at all, old chap. Trinity has always been ready to patronise
you fellows if you'd only have given us the chance." Cheers and
embraces followed. Then the whole mass of enthusiastic youth
advanced gallantly towards the scene of action.

Cuanduine, sighting them from afar, questioned the
Philosopher; and on being informed of their identity was at first
inclined to rejoice that the vanguard of his audience should be
the alumni of two such venerable seats of religion and learning:
but on their nearer approach, discerning the wickedness and
folly of their hearts, as also their immediate intention of evil,
he was moved to anger that flamed forth immediately from his
splendid eyes. At that the further progress of the students was
manifestly retarded, in so much that in half a minute they had
receded more than two hundred yards. As to the actual sequence
of events: whether the holy and undivided men of Trinity, who
were in front, were first seized with panic and swept away the
sea-divided Gaels in their flight; or whether the latter fled first
and the men of Trinity, demoralised by finding themselves
without supports, fled after them: on these points historians
are divided according to the source from which they draw their
salaries. The fact, however, which is beyond dispute is that the
students of both seats of learning fled with equal celerity and lack
of ceremony, overthrowing and trampling upon one another
in their youthful impetuosity, and scrambling over hedges,
ditches, stone walls, and barbed wire fences (whereby many
limbs and necks were broken and many trousers ripped beyond
repair) until they came at length to a place called Malahide,
nine miles away, where they were held up by an arm of the
sea; into which several in their blind haste were precipitated
and perished miserably: in whose regard some historians say
that they were men of the National, maintaining that, as these

were in the rear of the advance, they must have been in the van of the retreat; while others assert that they were men of Trinity, arguing that these, being in the front at the beginning, must have been the first to take alarm, and had broken clean through the National ranks before the latter were aware of what was happening. Many historians, however, of undoubted repute dismiss both versions, and declare that those who were drowned did not belong to either university, but were only natives of Malahide whom the students threw into the water for scoffing at their plight.

CHAPTER XII

How the People of Dublin received the New Evangel

SOON AFTER THE FLIGHT of the Boy Troop, the people of Dublin began to come upon the scene. In thousands and tens of thousands they swarmed around the platform. Some came for amusement; some to see what the others came for; and some to sell oranges. When all were assembled Cuanduine arose to speak.

"People of Eirinn," he said. "The occasions which I formerly took to address you seem to have been ill-chosen, and my words hasty and ill-considered. You also were unprepared to receive them, being ignorant who I am and whence I have come. Know, therefore, that I am Cuanduine, son of Cuchulain of Muirthemne, son of Lugh of the Long Hand; and that I am come from the heavens to set you free, to tell you the truth, and to show you the way of wisdom."

At these words there burst from the multitude a great roar of laughter: such laughter as had not been heard in Eirinn since Goshawk got his grip on the wheat. Every lung in those thousands of bosoms did now bellow with merriment. To what shall that hilarious orgy be compared? Some shrieked like cockatoos; some yelped like hyaenas; others brayed like donkeys, bleated like goats, or yowled like amorous cats in the small hours. Some roared and stamped their feet. Some whooped and threw up their caps. Some screamed and held their sides as though to save them from splitting. Kindred of a jest, man turned to man in joyous accord, slapping each other on the chest, elbow digging each other's ribs, thumping each other between the shoulders, kicking each other's backsides in very ecstasy of mirth. "Did y'ever hear the like? Split my kidneys, but that's a good one! Heaven, be jabbers! what next? What did he call himself? Galong! True as I'm standing here. Well, that bangs Banagher! O my stars! 'tis the best ever. Slap my back: I'm choking. Holy God, 'tis as good as a play. When I think of it! God, I wouldn't have missed this for a thousand. Boys-o-boys! Ha! Ha! Haaaah!! It's too good altogether. Well I never! Blast my eyeballs! Give us a chance! If he goes on I'll burst." Thus spoke those who had breath for utterance. Others flung themselves upon the ground, purple in the face and speechless, gasping for breath in helpless paroxysms of laughter. Many went skipping and leaping across country until they fainted from exhaustion. Not a few went clean out of their wits and became maniacal. Great numbers of women, between fits of swooning, danced and capered around in Bacchic measure, screeching like hysterical locomotives. Pandemonium thus reigned a full half-hour; by the end of which time the whole vast assemblage had either run away or lay sobbing helplessly on the grass.

At that Cuanduine and the Philosopher went home, trundling their planks and trestles in wheelbarrows before them.

BOOK III

THE TRAVELS OF CUANDUINE

CHAPTER I

The Lord Mammoth and the Lord Cumbersome

THESE EVENTS IN IRELAND were recorded in one half of the English newspapers as follows:

Renewed political and sectarian strife appears to be breaking out in Ireland as a result of the speeches of a man named Cooney, evidently a Bolshevik, who claims descent from some legendary hero. Our readers will recollect that the island passed out of British control some twenty or thirty years ago. England is fortunate in having rid herself of these turbulent subjects.

The other half of the newspapers reported the matter in these terms:

Claiming descent from the old Celtic divinities, a Bolshevik agitator named Considine has been creating fresh religious and political discord in the Emerald Isle. British intervention appears to be called for.

One half of the Press of England was in those days owned by Lord Mammoth, and the other half by Lord Cumbersome. These two potentates had bought up all their smaller rivals, and would have bought up one another if they could: for though both were staunch upholders of the principles of competitive civilisation, they knew better than to allow any competition against themselves if they could help it. Being unable to buy each other up, they hated each other with notable intensity, and directed their newspapers to take opposite standpoints on all topics. Thus a Government which happened to be supported

by Lord Mammoth's papers was certain to be denounced
collectively and individually by Lord Cumbersome's as the
most incompetent cabal that had ever guided the Empire to
destruction; if Lord Cumbersome were to advocate a policy
of peace and retrenchment, Lord Mammoth's organs would
brand as a traitor anybody who might suggest that England's
safety could be secured without the immediate conquest of the
whole world; and if Lord Mammoth proposed the remission
of a penny from the milk tax, Lord Cumbersome would insist
that without the imposition of another two pence the Budget
could not be balanced. A very bitter controversy raged one time
between one of Lord Cumbersome's pet scientists who wrote
that vegetables should be very lightly cooked in order to preserve
their vitamines, and one of Lord Mammoth's special hygienic
experts who argued that they should be given a prolonged
boiling in acid to destroy the germs that infest them. Nay
more, Lord Mammoth's humourists could not make a harmless
jest about mothers-in-law, without the Cumbersome satirists
denouncing the bad taste and pointlessness of such allusions,
and maintaining that in jokes about bad cheese alone could
the good old Anglo-Saxon type of humour be preserved as the
precious heritage of their imperial race.

The question of greatest moment in England at this time
was whether London should be rebuilt or whether a new city
should be erected upon a fresh site. For London, like most of
the world's cities, had been largely laid in ruins in the great
wars. The problem was a thorny one; and as the organs of Lord
Cumbersome and of Lord Mammoth had thrown themselves
into the fray on opposite sides, and were bandying arguments
with even more than their wonted ferocity, they had little space
to spare for the doings of a prophet across the water. Hence the
meagre space allotted to the matter.

It happened, however, that Lord Mammoth, who had a drop
or two of Irish blood in his arteries, reading the report in his

most important organ, the *Daily Record*, felt some slight stir of interest; which was quickened when he turned to the account given by Lord Cumbersome's *Morning Journal*. The noble newsmonger was taking breakfast at the time in a sunny parlour of his castle in Epping Forest (which, like the region of Tallaght and Bohernabreena near Dublin, was enclosed as a ghetto for millionaires). The breakfast was a fine one and a récherché, calculated to put anybody in good fettle and adventurous mood: under which influence Lord Mammoth ordered that an airplane should be at once dispatched to London to fetch for his inspection the original wire from Dublin which had been compressed into the paragraph aforesaid.

It was brought to him half an hour later as he sat in his garden smoking a cigar. It ran to about a thousand words, and he read it through carefully twice, chewing his cigar as the cinema had taught all strong characters to do. This impressed the valets, secretaries, runners, and others who were standing about, but he did not like the taste, so presently he threw the cigar away with a gesture of decision, and desired to be carried indoors. He had really come to no decision at all, but later on in the day he did; and the result was that next morning he flew to Dublin with but a single attendant, a junior valet who had been deaf and dumb from birth.

So perfect, however, was the intelligence department of his rival, so resourceful and daring were his spies, that within half an hour his flight, and within two hours the reason of it, were known at Castle Cumbersome. The Lord Cumbersome was not so energetic a person as his fellow prestidigitator, his eliminating organs being somewhat overcharged with the by-products of rotten goose-liver, which was his staple diet; neither had he any Irish blood or interests; nevertheless, he knew the laws of competitive economics better than to leave the field to the enemy. Summoning therefore an airplane and two eunuchs he set off in hot pursuit.

CHAPTER II

How the Two Lords made Propositions to Cuanduine

IT WAS THREE DAYS before the Lord Mammoth was able to find out where Cuanduine dwelt. When the information was brought to him, discarding his gorgeous raiment—for the making of which a hundred furry creatures had writhed in the cold steel jaws of traps—he donned a simple suit of plain grey tweed, and, accompanied by his faithful valet, took tram to Stoneybatter. He found the Philosopher alone in his room; for Cuanduine was out, walking gloomily on Merrion Strand by its sluggish waters.

"Good day, sir," said the Lord Mammoth.

"Good day," said the Philosopher.

"I had better introduce myself," said the newsmonger. "I am Lord Mammoth."

"And the other gentleman?" inquired the Philosopher, indicating the deaf and dumb valet who stood modestly behind.

"My attendant," said Lord Mammoth. "I—"

"I meant his name," said the Philosopher. "His name? Ha, ha, ha," laughed Lord

Mammoth. "Don't think I know it, now that I come to think of it. However, that's not what I came about. You're Mr. Cooney, I suppose?"

Before the Philosopher could answer, the door opened, and the prosperous figure of Lord Cumbersome came breezing in, almost upsetting the deaf and dumb valet, and completely ignoring Lord Mammoth, swept up to the Philosopher, clasped him warmly by both hands, and with radiant smile and treacly voice said: "My dear Mr. Considine, how do you do? I

hardly expected to find you in. Pray excuse my enthusiasm"—
shaking his hand with a fervour which the Philosopher found
as embarrassing as it was uncomfortable—"but having read
of your interesting discourses in the newspapers, I have been
unable to rest until I should see you in the flesh."

Here he was interrupted by the cold stern voice of Lord
Mammoth: "I don't know where you learnt your manners,
Cumbersome, but I was engaged in conversation with Mr.
Cooney when you came butting in."

"My dear Mammoth, a thousand pardons," said Lord
Cumbersome, as with a start of surprise. "I entirely overlooked
you. I apologise sincerely, and can only excuse myself on the
ground that in the presence of such a man as Mr. Considine—"

"Gentlemen," interrupted the Philosopher, "this is some
strange mistake. My name is not Considine."

"Cooney," suggested Lord Mammoth.

"No," said the Philosopher. "Murphy."

"Then I owe you a most hearty apology," said Lord
Cumbersome winningly. "But is there not a man called
Considine or some such name—a street preacher or something,
with a mission of sorts—living somewhere near here?"

"The name is Cooney," said Lord Mammoth sourly.

"If you mean Cuanduine," said the Philosopher, "he lives
here. But he is out at present, walking on Merrion Strand, with
the weight of the world's sorrow upon his shoulders."

"I shall await his return," said Lord Cumbersome, ap-
propriating the only comfortable chair in the room.

"So shall I," said Lord Mammoth, planting himself firmly
on his own two legs.

"You've no objection, I hope," said Lord Cumbersome
pleasantly to the Philosopher; but the Philosopher did not hear
him, being already reabsorbed in contemplation.

"Funny old bird," observed Lord Cumbersome, but Lord
Mammoth made no answer. Tired of standing, he directed

his deaf and dumb valet to go down on hands and knees on the floor, and then sat on him. Lord Cumbersome's eunuch presently made obeisance to his master, and began fanning him with a handbuzzer of platinum and ivory; for the air of the Stoneybatter back street was oppressive.

Thus Cuanduine found them on his return. At his entry the Philosopher came out of his meditation; Lord Mammoth eagerly arose from the small of his underling's back; and Lord Cumbersome followed suit from his chair. The Philosopher introduced them: "Lord Mammoth and Lord Cumbersome, news-purveyors Cuanduine."

"Delighted to meet you, sir," said Lords Mammoth and Cumbersome in a breath.

"Why?" asked Cuanduine.

Lord Mammoth was taken aback, but Lord Cumbersome spoke suavely: "O come, sir. Can you ask such a question?"

"I have asked it," said Cuanduine.

Here the Philosopher laughed, saying: "You see, gentlemen, it is no use offering polite commonplaces to Cuanduine. Answer his question and have done with it."

"What question?" asked Lord Cumbersome.

"Why," said the Philosopher.

"Why what?" said Lord Cumbersome.

"Better leave it at that," the Philosopher said to Cuanduine. "These people's memories are rather short, and their words often meaningless. And now, gentlemen,"—turning to the paper merchants—"if you have anything to say, say it. If not, begone. Open your mouths wide, and speak distinctly."

Now in all their lives these two lords of the linotype had never been spoken to in such terms as these, being used only to the baited breath of menials, and the oleaginous murmur of suppliants. Therefore, the choleric Mammoth flushed with anger, and even the courteous Cumbersome was perceptibly annoyed; yet owing to the lack of experience aforesaid, they had no words for the occasion, so that near two minutes went by in silence while the flush faded from Lord Mammoth's countenance, and the ruffling of Lord Cumbersome's serenity sank into smoothness.

"Well—hm! hm!—quite so—yes," said Lord Cumbersome. "Well, Mammoth, you were here first, and I'm in no hurry anyway, so I give place to you with the greatest pleasure in the world. Go ahead."

"Thank you, Cumbersome," said Lord Mammoth. "No doubt it would suit you excellently that I should make my offer first, and give you a chance to go one better: but I'm not having any. As far as I know, the side that wins the toss doesn't have to go in first if it doesn't like: it gets the option; and my option is to field until the wicket hardens."

"How little you know me, Mammoth, and how little you know yourself," sighed Lord Cumbersome. "I can wait here quite comfortably all day, and all night if necessary, whereas you must speak out or burst. Better do it now, and get it over," and the languid forest-pulper reseated himself with a yawn.

Intolerably goaded, his rival addressed the waiting hero: "See here, Mr. Coondinner. Is this fair? I come here at a great deal of trouble and expense to make you an offer for our mutual advantage, and this fellow Cumbersome sets out to double-cross me. Well, he's wasting his time. I'll put my proposition now, and we can come to terms later. Meanwhile, whatever he offers, you can take it I'll go ten per cent better, penny for penny. Is that clear?"

"Do you mean that you have come to offer me money?" asked Cuanduine. "Exactly," said Lord Mammoth.

"Then believe me, sir, I am deeply beholden to you, but I have some already."

The Lord Mammoth was so astounded to see any one so receive an offer of money, that for full fifty seconds he was without breath for utterance. At last he said: "But good heavens, man, wouldn't you like some more?"

"Why should I?" asked Cuanduine. "I have enough for my wants."

"Now look here, young man," expostulated Lord Mammoth, "you don't know what you're turning down. I'm putting anything from fifty to a hundred quid a week in your way. Just listen here. You come over to London with me tomorrow, and I'll put you on our magazine staff right away. You'll have an office all to yourself, and all you'll have to do is to turn out three or four articles a day—say two to four hundred words apiece— just plain straightforward religious stuff, you know, with a bit of snap in it—nothing very deep, of course—look, here's a sample of what I mean"—unfolding a copy of the *Daily Record*. "This is our special feature page. Snappy articles on all subjects, from Women to Religion. 'Why Flappers Flirt,' 'The Habits of the Dandelion,' 'Love Jesus and Obey your Employer': now that last is no good. It's the effect we're aiming at, of course, but it's laid on too thick altogether. That's because the fellow who's doing it doesn't really believe in it, and writes with his tongue in his cheek. Now you're different. When I read that speech of yours at that funeral the other day, I saw that you'd got what few people have Nowadays—Faith. You'll write with conviction: and when I see a thing as rare as conviction on the market, I go for it straight and buy it, regardless of cost. Now this fellow I've got on the job has no convictions, and he doesn't seem to know the difference between snap and blasphemy, so I want you to take his place. You've only got to write straight ahead exactly as you feel, provided of course that you keep within certain lines which I'll mark out for you—'Be not solicitous what you shall eat or what you shall be paid,' 'Never mind the housing shortage: heaven is our home,' 'Render to Caesar the things that are Caesar's,' 'Blessed are the poor in spirit,' 'The poor you have always with you,' 'Whatever may be said about the slums, the Son of Man had nowhere to lay his head,' and so on—the sort of thing to cheer and elevate the poor, and generally comfort everybody. If you like to question the reality of Hell, do so by all means. I understand the latest notion is that it's merely a sort of sense of spiritual loss. If you like to write that up, so much the better. Now what do you say to twenty quid a week for a start with your chances, of course?"

"What an insufferably vulgar person you are, Mammoth," drawled Lord Cumbersome, smothering a yawn. "Gentlemen, pray do not take this gentleman as representative of the newspaper world. Remember he wasn't born to great wealth, but started as a reporter on four pounds a week."

"The first Lord Cumbersome started as a printer's devil," snapped Lord Mammoth.

"True," admitted Lord Cumbersome, smiling. "But the second and third were born Cumbersome. It only takes an accolade to make a peer, Mammoth; but it takes at least three generations to make a gentleman."

"Never mind Cumbersome, gentlemen," said Lord Mammoth. "He's a wash-out. He hasn't a third of my circulation—blue blood doesn't flow as fast as red, you know. Ha! ha! Got you there, Cumbersome, didn't I? That joke, gentlemen, is appearing in all my papers to-morrow, and the cream of it is that it was made by Cumbersome's best humorist a few weeks before I bought him over. But let's get back to business. What do you say to my offer, Mr. Cooney?"

"What does he want?" asked Cuanduine of the Philosopher.

"He wants you to write pious-sounding trash to keep people quiet while he makes money; and he'll pay you twenty pounds a week for doing it."

The danger star glowed in Cuanduine's eye at that, and the whirr of the gathering of the Bosnich's and Bananachs sounded in the distance like the first whisper of a coming storm. The Philosopher, mindful of how they used to treat Cuchulain in such crises, threw over him a jugful of water. I will not say that it boiled as it fell from his body (though indeed it did), for you would not believe me; but we have Lord Mammoth's testimony that a splash of it scalded him through his trousers, and certain it is that two jugs more were needed to reduce the hero's temperature to normal.

"You had better make no more such offers," said the Philosopher to Lord Mammoth, "or the Water Trust will raise my rates." But the Lord Mammoth was so awed by the miracle he had seen, and withal so dumfounded by the reception accorded, for the first time in his experience, to an offer of money, that there was no need for the warning. In fact, it was only by strenuous application to the smelling salts supplied to him by his deaf and dumb valet that he was enabled during the next five minutes to breathe at all.

Taking advantage of his silence, Lord Cumbersome arose from his chair and spoke.

"Gentlemen, I have not come here—to in his own eloquent and memorable phrase double cross a brother journalist in the speculative enterprise that has led him to the Emerald Isle. My sole object is to obtain for England the help and advice of one whom I unhesitatingly acclaim as a profound thinker and a legitimate claimant to the title of a truly Great Man. England, gentlemen, stands to-day on the brink of a volcano. All her most cherished ideals are in the melting-pot. Discontent is rampant among the lower classes—"

"Discontent with what?" asked Cuanduine.

"Goodness only knows," said Lord Cumbersome. "Of course there's the housing shortage, and the high cost of living, and the unemployment question, and the increased tax on milk, and so on-the usual, and I may say inevitable, concomitants of industrial civilisation: but, after all, when have we been without such troubles? Possibly the real cause is American dollars, as Lord Mammoth's papers suggest; more possibly it is Japanese yen, as my own assert; or, for all I know, it may be Tcheko-

Slovakian thingumabobs. But these are mere questions of academic interest. We are concerned to find a remedy rather than a cause; and that task I feel, sir, lies with you. Let me then, as an Englishman, who cannot watch unmoved the slow drift of his country to destruction, beg of you to come—amongst us and apply your saving doctrines to our desperate case. Do not fear a repetition of the treatment has been meted out to you here: you know a prophet is never honoured in his own country. Moreover, if I may say it without offence, Ireland has ever been intolerant of criticism. Now we English, though we cannot boast the dazzling qualities that distinguish Irishmen throughout the world, have certain solid characteristics which you admittedly lack. We are broadminded, tolerant, open to conviction. We are always ready to listen to new ideas, particularly when expounded by countrymen of your own. Did not our ancestors welcome the great Shaw to our midst, and though his every word was like a sharp stone flung at our vitals, did they not flock to his plays like sheep until they made him a millionaire, and praise and lionise him until he nearly burst with conceit? Mr. Coondinner, if you come to England, I can promise you that you will be received not with jeers and volleys of stones, but with rapt attention and showers of roses."

"I will consider this," said Cuanduine.

"Do so. And I will add one word more. I would not presume to ask you to become a paid contributor to my organs. But, to forward the good cause, they shall be always at your service. They have not the enormous circulation enjoyed by those controlled by Lord Mammoth; but they are papers of weight and standing, preserving the best traditions of English journalism, and read by the solid common-sense elements that are the backbone of the community. And now, sir," concluded Lord Cumbersome, taking his hat from his eunuch, "I will not try to hurry you to a decision, but will take my leave, confident that the cry of England's bewildered millions will not fall on deaf ears. Good day, gentlemen."

He withdrew. After a decent interval the Lord Mammoth crept out also, followed by his deaf and dumb valet; whom later he cast into an oubliette, lest his affliction should not suffice to deter him from revealing the humiliation of his master which he had witnessed. As for Cuanduine, when the two Lords had left, he lay on his back on the floor and howled with laughter. What a shallow, flippant fellow he was to be so affected by the conversation of such shining examples of the successful life. Nevertheless, he followed them soon after to England.

CHAPTER III

Cuanduine comes to London

THIS IS THE WAY London was when Cuanduine came to look upon it. All that portion of the city that lay south of the Thames was in ruins, as was also a broad belt stretching from Buckingham Palace to Shoreditch, with large isolated areas at Paddington, Hendon, and Hackney. Besides, there was scarcely any region that had not some scar to show. In the middle of Chelsea there was a crater a third of a mile in diameter and over two hundred feet deep; there was another in Maida Vale, not quite so wide, but deeper; and there were two smaller ones between Euston and Regent's Park. Kensington Gardens and Hyde Park were a blasted wilderness; the great block of buildings between Leadenhall Street and Fenchurch Street was a mass of pounded wreckage; and most of the bridges crossing the Thames were shattered, with wooden structures spanning the gaps. On a broken arch of London Bridge dozens of young artists from New Zealand were always to be seen, sketching the ruins of St. Paul's.

The population, of course, had greatly declined. For motives of economy no census had been taken for nearly twenty years; but it was estimated that about three million people still clung to their desolated city, fully half of whom were living, like the Dublin people, in patched-up ruins or temporary huts.

Yet in the midst of this desolation the spirit that made old England great was still alive. In the National Arsenal, which had once been the British Museum, mighty guns capable of throwing a twenty-four-inch shell two hundred miles were being turned out at a rate of a dozen a week; and in the secret

laboratories of the London University grey-headed men of science were ransacking the labyrinths of chemistry for weapons
that would render them obsolete.

Now, as every Irishman knows, the people of England are in
every way inferior to the people of Ireland, being materialists,
whereas we are idealists. This they show most particularly in
their politics; for their principles are in nature so mundane and
trivial, and held with such lukewarm conviction, that men of
opposite parties do not regard each other as traitors, cowards,
or tyrants, but even salute each other in the street, and, with
characteristic hypocrisy, maintain as friendly relations as if there
were nothing to divide them: all which they justify with a mean
and time-serving proverb to the effect that "opinions differ."
The most momentous national problems are by these people
invariably decided by vote, and since the seventeenth century
all their controversies have been settled without violence. Ever
unready to sacrifice anything on the altar of principle, they
would no more think of burning an opponent's house than they
would of shooting him in the street. An Englishman will not
even defame the character of a man he disagrees with; nor does
he hold any ideal high enough to impel him to rob a bank. By
this timidity and love of compromise the English are deprived
of that ennobling inspiration which we draw from our martyrs,
and they lose also what we have aptly named the suffrage of the
dead. The reincarnation of thousands of deceased patriots to
outvote the living would be impossible in an English election.
The English, in fact, have scant reverence for the dead, which
they express in another base: and cowardly proverb: "A live ass
is better than a dead lion"—a final proof of their inferiority to
ourselves, who believe that there is nothing so wise and noble
as a dead ass.

You may count it then, my friends, as a vice in these English
that they welcomed Cuanduine most cordially to their shores.
They did not believe in his celestial origin, nor did they pretend

to; neither did they argue about it, but politely disregarded it, as if it mattered nothing one way or the other; an attitude which, if it did not please Cuanduine very much, left him without grounds of complaint. This policy was initiated by the Cumbersome Press, which, while joyfully heralding him as a "distinguished and brilliant intellect," a "master mind," a "thinker of unusual depth and seriousness, whose lessons Englishmen could not afford to ignore," was most discreetly allusive as to his origin, maintaining always a tone which was neither incautiously credulous nor discourteously skeptical.

On the day when his arrival was expected there was gathered at Hendon by the aerodrome a bevy of bright reporters and enterprising photographers, and not a few also of the general public. The instant the hero's foot touched the soil of England a hundred and eighty camera shutters snapped together like a clap of thunder (only not so loud nor so deep nor so rumbling, if truth be admissible in descriptive writing); and as he strode forth from the drome, escorted by an equerry in the livery of Lord Cumbersome, they kept on snapping like a battery of machine-guns in action. Cuanduine and the equerry then motored to a hotel, where a suite of rooms had been reserved for the hero at the Lord Cumbersome's order. Here also were reporters and photographers, enough to overawe even the heart of him that had faced undaunted the howling mobs of Baile Atha Cliath. For these reporters had their way of him and interviewed him, harrying him with questions as hereunder set forth, namely:

What would win the Derby?
Was the modern girl maligned?
Had the short skirt come to stay?
Did men prefer clever girls or stupid?
Who would win the Little Perkington Election?
How long would the side-creased trouser remain in vogue?

Had he learnt how to play Jim-jam?
Did he believe in love at first sight?
Did he believe it possible to love more than once?
How long did love last?
Did business girls make good wives?
Should engaged couples hold hands in public?
Should the Parks be purified?
Should a girl marry for money?
What was the best way to get rich quickly?
What should be done about profiteering?
What should be done about unemployment?
Did he think the song "Blue Bananas" likely to be immortal?
Were there really men in Mars?
Should girls wear pyjamas?
What sort of undies did the ladies wear in Tir na nOg?

—to all of which Cuanduine made such responses as his bewilderment allowed, which need not be recorded here, as they were duly misreported in the papers of the time.

The hero's photograph also appeared in all these sheets, so that he was soon a familiar figure in the eyes of the English people. They saw him

Setting his first foot on British soil,
Setting his second foot on British soil,
Steadying his hat in the first puff of the British wind,
Smiling,
Chatting with his equerry,
Chatting with reporters,
Blinking in the sunshine,
Putting up his umbrella,
Walking in Piccadilly,
Walking in another part of Piccadilly,
Walking in the Strand,

Walking in Fleet Street,
Walking,
Sitting down,
Standing up,
Sitting down again,
Sitting on a chair,
Sitting on a seat,
With arms folded, smiling,
With arms folded, grave,
With arms at his side, grave,
With arms at his side, smiling,
With a friend,
With two friends,
With a dog,
Without a dog,

—in short, in a thousand and one poses, conditions, accompaniments, occupations, and predicaments. Never had anybody been so photographed in England, unless it might be some royal personages or the leading beauties of the cinema.

To escape this constant persecution, Cuanduine left his hotel and took him a house at Richmond.

CHAPTER IV

What Cuanduine saw in Westminster Abbey

WHEN THE PUBLIC INTEREST was somewhat abated—that is to say, when he had been close upon a week in London—there was appointed to Cuanduine a bright young reporter, named Robinson, of the staff of the *Morning Journal*, to guide him around the city and show him the sights; who, after a comprehensive tour embracing the rubble heap that had once been the Tower, the shell of St. Paul's Cathedral, the remains of the Bank of England, the smithereens of Buckingham Palace, and the traditional site of Selfridge's, led him presently to the still undamaged Westminster Abbey; in the solemn twilight of whose stately aisles he looked upon the many memorials to England's mighty dead. Chief amongst these were the statues of the famous generals who had led the men of England to victory in the different wars which had glorified the century. I wish I could remember their illustrious names; but I cannot, both because of the strangeness of the names themselves, and because of the eccentricities of their spelling and pronunciation. For the English language is still in that primitive stage wherein neither of these is dependent upon the other, so that words spelt the same may be pronounced differently, and words differently spelt may be pronounced the same. For instance, the words "bough" (meaning "carob") and "bow" ("umhlu") are both pronounced *babh*, whilst the word "bow", when pronounced *bó*, means "bógha."

But to our Generals. There was one of these whose name I may yet recall, for there were not more than thirty letters to it, and he was, besides, the very last of the line, having won the greatest and the sublimest, the ultimate and the final War to End All Wars that Ever Were. The grim old warrior was represented in a characteristic attitude, sitting at his table in the War Office, doctoring up a report of a defeat to make it look like a victory. His name was gravening on the pedestal—but, indeed, I cannot remember it.

And now Cuanduine turned his gaze towards another statue that stood dominant over all lesser memorials. It was the statue of a woman in white marble, and on the front of its pedestal was inscribed her name:

SAINT PROGRESSA

and underneath it the text:

Woe to Them that are with Child and that Give Suck.

I will now tell you the story of Saint Progressa, as abridged from the hagiographers.

CHAPTER V

The Legend of Saint Progressa

PROGRESSA WAS A HOLY woman in her time, by whose intercession the world was redeemed from the greatest plague that ever threatened it: namely, a plague of babies. In those days all who came together in love (unless man or maid were blessed with the precious gift of sterility) would commonly reproduce their kind: which was a grave inconvenience both in marriage and out of it. Progressa held this to be a most unjust accompaniment to the joys of love; for, as the maiden says in Theocritus:

ἀλλὰ τεκεῖυ τρομέω, μὴ καὶ χρόα καλὸυ ὀλέσσω,

nor was it any consolation to her to be told, as *ibidem*:

ἤν δὲ τέκῃς φίλα τέκνα, νέον ᾦάος ὄψεαι υἶας.

Besides, child-bearing interferes with the Higher Development of Woman, especially in the provinces of dancing, hunting, and voting at elections. And why should mules and jennets have privileges denied to the Lords (and Ladies) of Creation? Moreover, as she was a serious-minded young person and addicted to the study of social problems, walking once through a city slum in a time of stress, she noticed that those workers who had large families suffered more than those with small ones; for which evil she saw that there could be but one remedy: to increase their incomes? No, by Procrustes (whom she would as soon have asked to enlarge his bedsteads): to cut down their families,

154

of course.

Now you must know that before this time there were many enlightened persons who had learnt how to be provident in this respect, but, alas, the world was for the most part inhabited with ignorant, unfit, narrow-minded, old-fashioned, out-of-date, prejudiced, and unprogressive people who held all such practices in superstitious abhorrence, calling them evil sounding names, such as race-suicide, and in other ways retarding the march of emancipation. The good Progressa in her hermit cell wept many tears, and fasted and prayed in atonement for this perversity, and vowed that she would not wear flannelette nor eat strawberries without cream until they were gathered to the fold. Thereafter the Lord appeared to her in a vision, saying: "Progressa, Progressa." Progressa answered: "Here I am." "Tell mankind," said the Lord, "that I did not really mean what I said when I bade them increase and multiply. I was young and unpractised in those days, and had not made a study of political economy. This is the new Gospel: 'Dwindle and Diminish. Henceforward my blessing shall be upon the barren, and the fruitful shall have no part in me.'" Heartened by this vision, Progressa contested a seat in Parliament as an Anticonceptions, haranguing the constituency in speeches that have ever since been the Testament of the new religion. That you may appreciate its nature, and the beautiful and logical mind of its prophet, I will quote you bits of them.

"The natural desire of the sexes, formerly regarded as a survival of the animal in man, is now known to be a purely spiritual attraction. When love looks into the eyes of love, soul rushes to soul, and both are interblent in spiritual ecstasy so intense as to transcend the mere bodily union which accompanies it. It is in that moment that each soul achieves its highest spiritual potentiality, and in the repetition of such moments it grows in power and nobility . . . .

"Conjugation is no longer regarded as a mere episode in the phenomenon of procreation. Modern reasoning, in fact, tends to show that its connection with procreation is purely incidental. Doubtless with the broadening of up-to-date thought even this connection will be found to be fallacious . . . .

"Let us face facts. On the one hand, the most elementary knowledge of Nature makes it clear that the male's powers of self-restraint are limited. A superficial observation of the habits of cats, dogs, and barn-door fowl will make that plain to the most ignorant. It is therefore unreasonable to expect prolonged continence from the average man. On the other hand, it is equally unreasonable to expect a modern woman to be a mere breeding animal like a cow. Woman has a higher destiny . . . .

"Besides, Contraception does not really prevent conception at all . . . ."

Mindful of the old proverb, "Give a dog a bad name and hang him," which being reversed might read: "Give a viper a good name and he will be fed on butter," she called the new gospel "Babylove."

A Limited Company was formed forthwith to acquire a monopoly of the necessary appliances. Yet in spite of millions spent on advertising there were few purchasers. Those who were already of the faith were too few to be profitable; those who were not were still deterred by superstitious objections, or even, incredible though it may seem, by a depraved taste for offspring. This was especially true of the poor, whose pleasures were not so plentiful that they were ready to sacrifice any of them. Here was a cause of deep searching of heart among Progressa's disciples, since it must lead to the multiplication of the least desirable elements of the community—of the idle, the thriftless, the vicious, and the unfit at the expense of the hard-working, provident, and virtuous rich. What a prospect was this for the future of the race: an infamous thing, not to be endured, said the Directors of the Company. These were no puling sentimentalists nor wicked subversives to think that the race could be saved by tampering with the laws of economics, which are as old as the laws of the Medes and Persians, and like them do not change. The rights of property are sacrosanct; but the babe unborn has no rights: therefore a decree went out from the new Conclave that there should be no more babies—or at any rate as few as possible.

O Spirit of Liberty, thou art mighty yet. Now were the most comfortable in the land intoxicated with thy breath, and came pouring in well-dressed multitudes to hear the perfervid oratory of the Revolutionists. What warlike banners of emancipation now floated on the breeze, defying the tyranny of ages with such daring mottoes as, "No More Babies!" "Extirpate the Embryo!" "Abolish the Brats," and "Down with Babies! Up with the Race!" Now did many of the most brilliant of the subversive writers of the day see the error of their ways and turn from the preaching of licence to the preaching of true liberty. But alas! Revolutions were ever the work not of the many, but of the few with clear vision; nor was this Revolution an exception. Dissident voices were occasionally heard at meetings. Once, for instance, when an orator declared that during the Great War if the population of England had been any larger they would have been starved into surrender, an aged General interrupted to point out that if their army had been any smaller it would have been beaten in the field. He was very properly thrown out, and only his grey hairs, great reputation, and obviously failing intelligence saved him from a well-deserved lynching. On another occasion an interrupter asked: "Why not legalise abortion, or revive the old Roman custom of exposure?" The fellow was expelled from all the best clubs for this display of bad taste. The general multitude, besides, living in hovels unfit for pigs, remained indifferent to the new gospel and went on producing babies as mischievously as ever.

Then arose one of the Progressives, an ecclesiastic of austere countenance, and said: "The balance can be righted in this way. Let the Government decide that not more than three children in each family of the lower orders shall be educated at the public expense, and that a stiff fee be charged for any beyond that number; and let the more desirable classes be encouraged to breed by exempting from income tax all that a man expends on education."

A Bill to this effect was presently promoted in Parliament by the interests concerned, and rapidly found its way to the Statute Book. This measure did for Babylove what the Edict of Constantine did for Christianity. It was the Charter of the New Liberty. True, it had to be repealed twenty years later, when it was found that the growing numbers of illiterates were a menace to industrial efficiency. But it was immediately followed by the Limitation of Families Act, under which the number of children permitted to a couple was graded as in schedule:

```
Millionaires . . . . . . . . . . . . . . . . . ad lib.
Income £100,000 and over . . . . . . . . 10 children
   "        50,000     "  . . . . . . . . . . 9   "
   "        20,000     "  . . . . . . . . . . 8   "
   "        10,000     "  . . . . . . . . . . 6   "
   "         5,000     "  . . . . . . . . . . 5   "
   "         1,000     "  . . . . . . . . . . 4   "
   "           500     "  . . . . . . . . . . 3   "
   "           250     "  . . . . . . . . . . 2   "
   "           100     "  . . . . . . . . . . 1 child
   "       under £100 . . . . . . . . . . . . nil
```

The penalties for breach of these regulations were extremely

severe, ranging from one year's imprisonment for a first offence
to penal servitude for life in flagrant cases. A stringent social
code reinforced the law most efficaciously; a woman who
"exceeded"—as the polite phrase went—being treated with the
same opprobrium meted out in a less enlightened age to the
mother of a bastard. 'Sdeath, you should have seen with what
virtuous disdain a sterile dame would pluck her petticoats out
of contact with one of these fallen sisters.

The pious Progressa, now in a green old age, thus saw her
life's work brought to the threshold of triumph. Had she lived
a little longer she would have seen all her girlhood's dreams
come true. She would have seen the whole face of England
swarming with ancient Spinsters busily instructing children of
ten in sex knowledge and contraception. She would have seen
the passage of an Act of Parliament forbidding the publication
of anticontraceptive literature, and of another disfranchising
all persons convicted of infringements of the Limitation of
Families Act. She would have seen priests imprisoned under
the Blasphemy laws for preaching against contraception. She
would have seen Trade Unionists striking in protest against
being asked to work alongside parents of more than the
statutory number of children. Finally—triumph of triumphs—
she would have seen the commencement of a steady decline in
the population of England which soon reached the satisfactory
quota of one million per decade. But Providence seldom
permits the pioneers to enter the Promised Land. Before this
happy consummation Progressa had passed away in the odour
of success, while monopolists and financial magnates crowded
round her bedside to hear the last words of the dying saint. Her
final moments were rejoiced by the news that Contraception
had been defined as a dogma by the Sacred Congregation of
Advanced Thinkers, which is infallible. Ten years later the case
for her Beatification was laid before the General Consensus of
Modern Thought, which is more infallible still. So obviously

heroic were her virtues, and so astounding her miracles (for, if it be a miracle to raise the dead, is it not a greater miracle to erase the embryonic?) that it was decided to waive all preliminary formalities and enroll her at once among the Saints.

CHAPTER VI

Cuanduine meets divers strange Persons

HAVING SHAKEN OFF HIS guide, Cuanduine passed out of the city and came presently to a grove not far off, wherein an army of workmen had just finished erecting a huge pyre of logs over tar-barrels. A hundred and fifty feet square it was at the base, and forty feet high, and it was overtopped by an earthen ramp over a mile in length. Just as Cuanduine arrived torches were put to the tar, and flames two hundred feet high shot up into the sky. Then up the ramp came a motor lorry heavily laden, which, when it reached the summit, was tilted back until there tumbled upon the flaming pyre an avalanche of hams and gammons of bacon, to the amount of nearly three and a half tons. What a sizzling there was as the flames fastened on this succulent feast, and what a divine odour. It was as if a fifteen-acre rasher were being fried for the breakfast of Zeus Olympicus, which, had he smelt it, would have provoked his mouth to watering the world with a second deluge. Then came a second lorry and emptied into the fire ten thousand or so long hundreds of eggs. But that sent forth a different savour, not quite so appetising: indeed, you would have thought the Plutonian cook was brewing a hell-broth of asafoetida for the supper of the legions of the damned. This was followed straight by other lorries, more than I can count, which shovelled on to the leaping flames a goodly holocaust of meat, butter, vegetables, groceries, wheat, oats, barley, flour, fruit (both fresh and preserved), fish, poultry, game, sweetmeats, biscuits, cheeses, and a thousand other sorts of provender, some packed in bales and boxes, but much of it loose and *au naturel*, until the mixture of smells was so foul that the stomach of Cuanduine could stand no more of it, and he was about to withdraw in search of a more salubrious climate, when he noticed a workman standing near, whom he approached and asked the meaning of this incineration.

"This is the Regional Destructor, sir," said the workman, "where we destroy the surplus food, sir, to keep the prices up."

"Why do you keep the prices up?" asked Cuanduine.

The workman took a handbook from his pocket and read: "Low prices depend on mass production. Mass production depends on unlimited capital. Capital requires a reasonable return for its outlay. Therefore the prices must be kept up. Q.E.D. Socialism is an economic fallacy."

"This," said Cuanduine, "seems to me the very sublimate of criminal folly."

The workman gave him a look of incredulity not unmingled with horror. "What, sir?" said the honest fellow. "Do you speak like that of the inevitable laws of political economy?—you who are so well fed. Look at me. My children are all crippled with rickets because I cannot afford to give them butter, yet I see all this butter burnt without complaint. Why? Because I know that if it wasn't for the good Capitalists there'd be no food, nor money, nor nothing. Besides, this destructor gives employment to hundreds of men who would otherwise have none." So saying the honest fellow picked up a firkin of butter that happened to have fallen from one of the lorries, and hove it into the fire. Then, "Thank God," said he, "I have done my duty," and walked away, whistling very resolutely the tune of "Blue Bananas." Soon afterwards men came with eighty big hosepipes and quenched the embers of the fire with a deluge of milk.

Cuanduine then went his way. A little farther he came to a glade, where he found a profiteer tied to a stake upon a pile of brushwood. The unfortunate man had rashly gone for a walk unescorted, and now his captors, a dozen or so of hungry, wolfish men, were quarrelling as to who should have the honour and pleasure of applying the torch to him. Perceiving Cuanduine's approach, they surrounded him with supplications to adjudicate between them.

"It is a pity," said Cuanduine, "that you do not read your scriptures more closely. Let him that has never profiteered apply the torch."

When the men had departed Cuanduine loosed the bonds of the profiteer, who went forthwith to lodge information with the police. Cuanduine now began to retrace his steps homeward, but soon lost his way among unfamiliar roads. Presently, however, he accosted a labouring man whom he met, a flat-faced fellow with humped shoulders and vacant eyes, and asked him how many miles it might be to London.

"Ninety-nine," said the man.

"Nay," said Cuanduine, "that cannot be, for I left it no more than three hours ago. Do you mean perches?"

"Ninety-nine," said the man.

"Then pray tell me by which of these roads in front I should proceed."

"Ninety-nine," said the man.

"You are fooling me, sir," said Cuanduine. "There are but three roads yonder. If you know which of them is mine, please you to say so: if not, why, say so too, and we'll end the matter. Now, which is it?"

"Ninety-nine," said the man.

"Have you no other word in your language but ninety-nine?" asked Cuanduine.

"Ninety-nine," said the man.

"That is not a large stock," said Cuanduine. "Pray, name me some."

"Ninety-nine," said the man.

"I marvel you are so bold to keep on answering me so," said

Cuanduine. "Are there none that hold you dear?"

"Ninety-nine," said the man.

"A wife, doubtless?"

"Ninety-nine."

"And children?"

"Ninety-nine."

"One to each wife? It is a moderate allowance, like your vocabulary."

Here Mr. Robinson came up the road, looking rather hot and dusty. "How on earth did you give me the slip?" said he. "I've had the devil's own job to find you."

"See this excellent fellow here," said Cuanduine, presenting the workman. "I wish you would hold converse with him. He seems to have but one word, Ninety-nine, and I would like to know what he means by it."

"That is easily explained," said Mr. Robinson. "He is probably a worker in one of Goshawk's factories, and has been making Part Ninety-nine all his life."

"Part Ninety-nine of what?" asked Cuanduine.

"Oh, goodness only knows: I'm sure he doesn't know himself. It might be anything from a sparking plug to a screw for a watch. Whatever it is, he's been making it ever since he was a kid. He can make it to perfection, but he can make nothing else. By this time, he probably can think of nothing else. That's Goshawk's policy: one man one job, and get it Right. He's hardly got it going properly in this country yet; but, by Jove, you should see how it works in America. They've whole towns out there that can only say one word, like our friend here. Think of that! A whole town in which every blessed man, woman, and child is making, or being trained to make, Part Umpty-um of some blamed thing they've never seen entire, or even heard the name of. There's progress for you. That's what has America where she is."

"Where is she?" asked Cuanduine.

"On our necks, my boy, and don't you forget it. I suppose our boss seems pretty big to you—coming from a backward place like Ireland, I mean. Well, Cumbersome's big enough, as big men go in Europe. But I tell you this. He only owns what he does own by Goshawk's permission."

"Ninety-nine," said the workman.

"Quite right, old chap," said Mr. Robinson. "We mustn't talk treason, eh? Come, Mr. Coondinner, let's be getting home. There's an aerodrome just round the corner."

CHAPTER VII

Cuanduine meets an Author of "Blue Bananas"

ANOTHER DAY CUANDUINE AND Mr. Robinson, strolling in the Green Park, saw an old gentleman of remarkable appearance come sauntering towards them. He wore a frock coat and silk hat, with a pair of carpet slippers. His shoulders were humped; his hands, clasped behind his back, were twined in the ends of his flowing hair; and his pensive eye gazed upon the ground.

"'Tis a poet composing a song," said Cuanduine.

"Calculating profits, more likely," said Mr. Robinson. "But he's a poet all right. Most go-ahead poet in London, too. Holds his own even in America. That's Larky Giggleswick. He and six others wrote the words of that song, 'Blue Bananas,' and between them they made a cool million out of it."

Cuanduine, who had heard but stray snatches of the song, desired now to be made better acquainted with it.

"I can scarcely do justice to it without a band," said Mr. Robinson modestly, "for the tune is a syncopated version of Beethoven's Sonate Pathetique. However, here goes."

These are the words of "Blue Bananas":

> Blue Bananas!   Blue Bananas!
> Clickety-clickety-clack!
> Blue Bananas!
>   Banana-nananas!
> Whoop!
>   Yah!!
>   Whack!!!

"Is it not a noble song?" demanded Mr. Robinson, wiping his brow. "I don't claim to be much of an authority on music; but that song just gets me. A great song! A splendid song! And, by God, sir, a successful song! That song has given pleasure to the weariest business men on Broadway The funny thing is that it didn't take on when it first came out. Then one day a Boston hardware merchant took an action against a music shop for selling him the book of the words under false pretences. He said that the man behind the counter had assured him that there was no meaning in it; but the shopman swore that what he had said was that there was no more meaning in it than a tired business man could understand; and he called in a dozen tired business men to prove it. The case was dismissed with costs, and the song at once began to sell like hot cakes. It turned out afterwards that the whole thing was a publicity stunt got up by Giggleswick. Oh, there are no flies on Larky. Snooty's the word for that poet. I hear, by the way, that he's negotiating for the exclusive syncopation rights for Handel: he has Beethoven, Bach, and Mozart already, you know. One of these days, I imagine, there'll be a *coup d'etat*, and Giggleswick will proclaim himself Song King."

Thus far Mr. Robinson's discourse on the poetry of the period. 'Tis unfortunate that Cuanduine's answer is not reported in the chronicles.

CHAPTER VIII

How they celebrated the Shaw Centenary

ANOTHER DAY CUANDUINE WAS invited, with all the Wealth, Blood, and Intellect of England, to attend a great dinner in celebration of the Centenary of Bernard Shaw. No less than five millionaires, with a choice collection of politicians, soldiers, archbishops of all denominations, vivisectionists and other scientists, a couple of the leading sportsmen of the day, and a sprinkling of fashionable novelists, had all assembled to do honour to the memory of this great Artist and Moral Teacher. The menu consisted of dishes mentioned in his immortal works, *foie gras*, veal, capons, and plum-pudding being the most important. When all this was tucked away, great speeches were made over the cigars and wine. The chairman, Sir Hawtrey Cutpurse, the well-known financier, said that no words of his were necessary to ensure the lasting, nay, the undying fame of a writer whose works were an imperishable monument to Britain's glory. He, Sir Hawtrey, did not claim to be a man of any literary taste, but he had read Shaw when he was at school, and he had found at least one sentence there that went home to him: "The first duty of every citizen is to make money." That had been an inspiration to him all his life and made him the man he was. (*Prolonged applause.*) He was not, however, as he had already said, a man of any literary discrimination. Nor was he ashamed of the fact. He would therefore leave to others better qualified the task of appraising the great dramatist whose festival they were celebrating that night. It was his duty, however, as chairman to announce that he had received some letters in explanation of some of the vacant chairs that should have been at the table. The Prime Minister (*applause*) was the first. That great statesman (*applause*), putting, as usual, duty before pleasure (*renewed applause*), was at his post in the House of Commons, where he was at the moment moving the third reading of the Government's measure to defend their liberties against the menace of Socialism. (*Loud and prolonged cheering.*) Lord Mammoth (*cheers*) had also written, saying that he was prevented from attending to pay his homage to the Great Thinker by a Trust meeting at which his presence was vital. (*Cheers.*) Finally, the Lord Chamberlain had telegraphed at the last moment: "Busy censoring plays. Please excuse. Best wishes. Bonehead." (*Applause.*) Having called upon the next speaker, the chairman sat down. (*Prolonged applause.*)

The other four millionaires having spoken, Professor Treacle, Litt.D. (Oxon.), said that in these days of polemical art it was refreshing to take up such a classic as *Mrs. Warren's Profession* or *Getting Married*, and give oneself to the pure enjoyment of Shaw's delightful human creations, untroubled by the cloven hoof of the propagandist, so commonly obtruded in the so-called plays of the present generation. It was customary among modern youth to jeer at Shaw as a back number. But the most brilliant writers of the present day were mere temporary flashes beside the great Luminary. They were but the cult of the few, and for a period only, whereas Shaw was for all men and for all time. (*Applause.*)

Mr. Pusher, the rising young politician, said that Shaw was an imperial asset.

Mr. Halfpenny, the fashionable novelist, spoke of the rush of incident in the plays of classic writers like Shaw and Ibsen. Modern plays were all talk. (*Hear, hear.*)

The Archbishop of Coddington said that there was a morbid tone about the modern theatre and a tendency to choose unpleasant subjects, which made one sigh for the good old days when the kindly human sentiment of Ibsen and the innocent gaiety of Shaw gave clean healthy entertainment to young and old. Shaw was not only a great dramatist: he was England's greatest moral teacher. Quotations from his works were in every mouth, and were the inspiration of all that was best in the British character. What British schoolboy did not know the line: "Do not do unto others as you would they should do unto you: their incomes may be different." What an inspiration, this, in the battle against Socialism. Another quotation leaped to his memory: "If you beat your child, be sure you do not beat it in anger." What deep, what sublime wisdom was here! Again: "Marriage must be for life. It would not be marriage at all if it were not for life"—a useful lesson, that, for their modern moralists—or rather immoralists. But if he were to begin quoting from Shaw he would never be able to leave off. As the old lady said in the familiar anecdote: "Shaw's plays are full of quotations!" (*Laughter.*)

Lord Buncombe said that Mr. Pusher had said that Shaw was an imperial asset. That was quite true. (*Applause.*) The works of Shaw were one of the Empire's most precious possessions. Shaw was above all else a patriot.

(*Cheers.*) The noble tribute to the English people, which he had put into the mouth of Napoleon, was no doubt familiar to all of them: "The Englishman does everything on principle." In that phrase was summed up all that was best in the British character. It was the inspiration of every Briton all over that Empire on which the sun never set. That was all he had to say, and he would now sit down.

Mr. Borax, the coming milk monopolist, said that a great patriot like Shaw would have been deeply distressed by the present condition of British trade. (*Hear, hear.*) That condition, continued Mr. Borax, smoothing his well-filled corporation, was entirely due to the refusal of the workers to accept a lower standard of living (*grunts of agreement*), and would continue so long as the British workman insisted on two meals a day, while his American rival was content with one. (*Groans.*)

The Bishop of Cheddar agreed entirely with the previous speaker. If any one doubted that the working classes were overpaid, let him go and watch the queues. outside the picture houses on a Saturday evening. Many workers undoubtedly went to the pictures as often as once a week. What would an apostle of work and efficiency like Shaw have thought of that? He himself had recently been compelled, from motives of economy, to dismiss his fourth under-gardener's fifth assistant; yet he knew of a case in which a working man had once taken his whole family to the seaside for three whole days. How foreign was such indulgence to the spirit of Christianity, whose founder—divine or otherwise—had repeatedly counselled his disciples to deny themslves. But, alas, the Christianity of the lower classes was rapidly being swamped under waves of debauchery and hedonism. (Here the pious prelate sat down, carefully concealing his emotion with a handkerchief of purple silk.)

General Puncher said that like a previous speaker he had no pretensions to literary taste, but in the distant parts of the Empire he also had taken a wrinkle or two from Shaw. In one of his plays a character had said: "Men are not governed by justice. They have to be governed by force." He thought that applied just as well at home as in the Colonies. (*Applause.*)

Dr. Putter, Professor of Literature, Cambridge, said that sufficient stress had not been laid on Shaw's position as a poet. Nothing in English poesy could equal the mighty lines of the Admirable Bashville, and who could ever forget the tender lyric:

> I met thee first in Whitsun Week,
> Louisa! Louisa!

or the passionate patriotic hymn:

Tell England I'll forget her never,
O wind that blows across the sea.

Mr. Twinkler, the popular actor-manager, now stood up and said that this was an opportune moment to broach a subject he had long had in mind. England, alone among civilised nations, had no National Theatre. He had taken the liberty of writing a circular letter to the papers on the subject, and he would now pass it round for the inspection and signature of that distinguished company. So sponsored, the proposal would carry a weight which could never have attached to his own humble sign manual.

This suggestion was unanimously complied with, and, having sung the National Anthem, the party rolled home.

CHAPTER IX

How the People of England received the New Evangel

W<small>HILE</small> C<small>UANDUINE WAS THUS</small> engaged in studying the life of old England, the Cumbersome papers were busy boosting him in vast write-ups and intimate personal pars, of which I will give a few samples.

Any lingering doubts which Englishmen may feel of the utter abomination of Socialism should be dispelled on Monday next when our Special Correspondent in Ireland, Mr. Coondinner, will relate at the Albert Hall a horrifying tale of the horrors it has given birth to in that unhappy land.—*Morning Journal*

Mr. Coondinner, who is to deliver an address at the Albert Hall on Monday, is Irish by birth, and speaks Erse fluently. He is said to have remarkable psychic powers, and claims to have visited some of the planets by airship.—*Daily Proser*: Notes of the Day.

It is not generally known that the real name of Mr. Quandine, who is to address a meeting at the Albert Hall on Monday, is Cuhoolin. Quandine is only a pseudonym; and even the name of Cuhoolin was only recently adopted by the family, whose true cognomen is Setanta. The story of how the change of name occurred is interesting, and reveals some quaint Irish customs. An ancestor of Mr. Quandine's, when quite a small boy, was sent on a message to a friend of his father named Hoolin. This gentleman kept a particularly ferocious watch-dog, which happened to be unleashed when young Setanta arrived, and immediately attacked him. Nothing daunted, the little lad seized the brute by the throat and strangled it. Mr. Hoolin later sent in a bill for damages to Mr. Setanta, who not unnaturally declined to pay it. The youngster, seeing that a quarrel was imminent, ran round at once to Mr. Hoolin's house. "Never mind, Mr. Hoolin," he said. "I will be your watchdog in future." From this he was called Cu Hoolin, Cu being Gaelic for dog.—*Daily Blitherer*: Notes by the Way.

Heard an amusing story from Mr. Coondinner, the young Irish wit who is to give an exhibition of his native humour at the Albert Hall on Monday. Mr. Coondinner's father, who is a noted athlete, is very punctual in keeping appointments. Some time ago he and his wife were invited to dine at the house of a friend named Brickyew, and Mrs. Coondinner—as is the way of the fair sex—was so long in putting the finishing touches to her attire that her hubby started without her. She followed as soon as she could, but by the time she reached Mr. Brickyew's residence the company were already sitting down to dinner. Her husband saw her through the window, and in order to avoid the delays necessitated by ringing at the door, etc., broke down the wall of the dining-room so as to admit her at once. The dinner, as it happened, was not expedited at all by this ingenious device, for Mr. Brickyew insisted that his herculean guest must restore the wall before the meal was served.—Mr. Tittletattle in the *Daily Lookinglass*.

I met the famous Mr. Coondine in Hyde Park yesterday. He has such a pleasant smile and such lovely hair. His complexion too is a marvel, and that's such a rare thing in a man, isn't it? Mr. Coondine is to address a gathering in the Albert Hall on Monday.—Mrs. Twaddler in *Home Tosh*.

FLOSSIE.—I dare say Mr. Coondine would sign your autograph album if you sent it to him privately, c/o Lord Cumbersome. You Could scarcely hope to get near him at the Albert Hall Meeting on Monday. He is not married.—*Woman's Mush*: Answers to Correspondents.

By these means the public was stimulated to such interest in Cuanduine that whereas it would ordinarily be a difficult thing to fill a moderate sized aining-room for a lecture, or to fill a pantry for a lecture on an important subject, yet for this lecture, which was to be called "Mankind in the Unmaking", there was such a rush for tickets that you would have thought it an exclusive appearance of a superfilm star.

Very distinguished was the gathering upon the platform when the great night came. The Lord Cumbersome himself was in the chair. On his right hand were the Prime Minister and the leader of the Opposition, and on his left a couple of vassal peers. Eight Cabinet Ministers and the Archbishop of Canterbury were in the background. The Lord Cumbersome, with a few well-chosen words (say the papers), introduced the speaker, who came to the front of the platform, and spoke as follows:

"People of England, I know not whether this be the wickedest world in the universe; for who has seen the horror of the Hyades? and who can tell what things are done in Betelgeuse, or plumb the unfathomable mystery of Fomalhaut? But this I know, that there is not in all the universe a world so curious and comical."

This is as much of the speech as can be given verbatim, for it is all that appeared so in the newspapers of the time, the rest being reported in *oratio obliqua* that is beyond my powers to straighten, and with lacunae that would baffle the ingenuity of a German commentator. But if we take as evidence the litany of descriptive phrases used by the reporters, namely:

Brilliant,

Dazzlingly brilliant,
Brilliantly witty,
Scintillating wit,
Sheer brilliance,
Keen satire,
Biting satire,
Whimsical satire,
Mordant satire,
Daring paradox,
Brilliant paradox,
Brilliantly paradoxical,
Scintillating epigrams,
Original, if occasionally perverse, outlook on life,
Keen analysis,
Trenchant criticism,
Comments which, however impracticable, cannot be ignored,
Remorseless exposure of human weaknesses,
Deliberately topsy-turvy viewpoint,
Almost inhuman detachment,
Intellect unwarmed with human sympathy,
Clear-cut intelligence devoid of soul.

Taking these as evidence we may well believe that what Canduine said of mankind and his works that evening was not very different in substance or intent from what has been set down in their books by the great satirists of the world: by Lucian, by Juvenal, by Martial, by Rabelais, by Swift, by Voltaire, by Samuel Butler, by Bernard Shaw.

As for the audience they took the speech as only an English audience can; namely, with delighted appreciation of the barbed shafts of satire, with laughter for each stroke of wit, and with applause for the eloquence and vivacity of the whole. The speech was indeed a tremendous success, and reflected great glory on Lord Cumbersome. In face of the general enthusiasm even the Mammoth Press was overwhelmed, though it strove manfully to damn with faint praise.

"Truly the English are a great people," said Cuanduine next day to Mr. Robinson as they sat over their breakfast reading the various accounts. "How ready they are to acknowledge their own wickedness and laugh at their own folly; how eager to admit themselves in the wrong. I tell you, Mr. Robinson, this people will remake the world."

Such was the success of the inaugural meeting that Lord Cumbersome's agents arranged that the next should be held at the Wembley Stadium, and preparations to broadcast the speech were made on an unprecedented scale; for it was known that the very poorest classes—philosophers, artists, school teachers, and casual labourers—were making superhuman efforts to purchase listening sets for the occasion. Again Cuanduine spoke, pelting jagged stones of satire into the ethereal pond, ruffling its complacent surface with keen-crested waves. The vast audience at Wembley listened with a relish which did credit alike to its artistic discrimination and its broad spirit of tolerance; and the incalculable multitude of broadcatchers crouched so tensely at their instruments that silence reigned over the broad realm of England. From that night the name of Cuanduine, in its various mispronouncements, was a household word from Land's End to John o'Groats. No newspaper dared omit his photograph from its columns for a day; no revue or ragtime song was complete without a reference to him; and he was regularly invited to contribute to symposia in the magazines on such subjects as "Why are our Churches Empty?" or "Should a Woman tell?" or "How to bring Christianity up to date." *Punch* caricatured him once a week, besides mentioning him regularly in Charivaria. All the most renowned critics wrote appreciations of him. Novelists found it impossible to keep him out of their works. Moreover, cinema stars and litterateurs were always asking him to stand godfather to their children. He was ever being harassed to write testimonials for soaps, cigarettes, tonics, fountain-pens, shaving creams, safety-razors, arm-chairs, books on sex knowledge, and a hundred other articles; many of which were also named after him. He was eternally laying foundation stones, opening bazaars, launching ships, and going to dinners and garden-parties. Financiers and monopolists feted him; their wives and daughters offered him their love; women in humbler station took his photograph to bed with them. Cuanduine was indeed in great demand. England took him to her bosom, and hoped he would entertain her for ever. The Mammoth Press lay low, biding its time.

CHAPTER X

How Cuanduine began to Fall in England's Estimation

BY THE ESTEEM IN WHICH he was held, and by the feeling roused by his orations, Cuanduine judged that the time was now ripe to urge the immediate liberation of the song-birds and wild flowers from Goshawk's control: to which effect he spoke at his next meeting. To his surprise the suggestion was received with coldness, and the applause when he sat down was of the most perfunctory character, and intermingled with not a few hisses.

The Mammoth Press at once saw its opportunity, and next morning opened the campaign with characteristic headlines:

QUANDINE THROWS OFF THE MASK
UNDILUTED SOSH
BLACKBIRDS AND BUTTERCUPS FOR
EVERYBODY!!

The leading paper of the group said:

Mr. Quandine's latest effusion can only be described as a violent attack upon the rights of property and the freedom of the individual. It is nothing less than a proposal to tax the provident and efficient for the benefit of the thriftless and idle. Briefly, his policy is the forcible expropriation of the birds and wild flowers in private ownership and their transference to communal control, when their enjoyment will of course be permitted only on a dead level of equality. Mr. Quandine shows all the ignorance of human nature and indifference to the realities of life characteristic of the agitators' breed. He apparently forgets, or pretends to forget, that tastes differ: that to listen for an hour to a thrush's warbling might be torture to one man, and merely whet the appetite of another for more. Even leaving such extremes out of account, a regime under which every man, woman, and child would be compelled to listen to, say, three bird-songs, and smell, say, half-a-dozen wild flowers daily, would be absolutely intolerable in its appalling monotony.

Another said:

This anarchical proposal means the complete disorganisation of our whole social and economic system. What order or discipline is possible if the private is to have as many daisies as the colonel? if the man behind the counter is to enjoy the melody of the robin equally with his employer?

Another asked:

What incentive do we offer to industry and enterprise, if the financier or monopolist, at the end of a lifetime of toil, is to be allowed no more of melody and perfume than the tramp lying by the roadside?

And another cried:

If this wildcat scheme were put into practice it would drive capital out of this planet to Mars or Venus, or even out of the Solar System.

The Cumbersome Press was more mildly remonstrative. The *Morning Journal* said:

Mr. Cuanduine's poetic imagery and moving eloquence were never better displayed than last night. He drew a beautiful and touching picture of a world in which every man and woman, whatsoever their condition or income, should enjoy the song of the birds and the perfume of flowers to their heart's content. It was a delicate and tender fancy: but we must not mistake a poet's dream for a practical possibility.

The *Daily Sootherer* said:

Mr. Quandine's remarkable theories are interesting subjects for intellectual speculation; but they will not stand the test of practical application. How, for instance, is the distribution to be effected? Is every man, woman, and child, regardless of its age, capacities, and tastes, to be given, free, gratis, and for nothing, say three robins, two larks, and a dandelion? And how is this equality to be maintained? The very next day one person may lose one of his larks, another may want to sell his robins, a third will want to buy them. In a short time we should be back exactly where we are. The fact is that you cannot change human nature by act of Parliament; and few things are so deeply planted in human nature as the acquisitive instinct.

There were also two wretched little sheets which clung to a precarious independence outside the two great Combines. These, likewise, shot their bolts at Cuanduine. Said the *Daily Trumpeter*:

It is useless for elegant aristocrats like Mr. Coondine to talk academically about beauty and freedom. The time is gone by for palliative measures. Until all the birds and flowers are nationalised and managed by Government Departments, abuses like the present must continue.

And the *Red Bonnet* said:

The speeches of Mr. Quandine, though doubtless well intentioned, and not unfriendly to the toiling millions, only show how impossible it is for these dilettante artistic members of the bourgeoisie to grasp realities. The fundamental fact is that so long as there are birds and flowers at all they must inevitably accumulate in private hands, and the remedy is—Abolish them.

Cuanduine was filled with astonishment at this opposition, and overwhelmed by the arguments on which it was founded. Conceiving himself to be misunderstood, he delivered another speech in the same tenor, but using simpler language to explain his meaning, and replying exhaustively to each several criticism. He was listened to in obstinate silence; the applause was more formal than before, the hisses more distinguishable. The Mammoth papers redoubled the vigour of their attacks; whilst those of Lord Cumbersome, though they maintained stoutly that, judged purely as an artist, Cuanduine was one of the greatest men that England had ever produced, found it all the more necessary to outdo them in denunciation of his policy.

He spoke a third time to a half-empty theatre. With commendable patience he tried to answer a hundred silly or tipsy questioners. At the finish there was no applause at all.

Now amongst the multitude of his changing hearers there was one young woman that came to every meeting, and sat always in the front row, entranced by the beauty of his godlike countenance and by the grace and strength of his manly form. Her name was Ambrosine, a lovely and accomplished girl, that had been brought up on the intellectual novels and plays of the Edwardo-Georgian period—of course, in bootleggers' editions at ten guineas a copy. She sat on now in the darkened auditorium watching the figure of Cuanduine leaning, deject and weary, against the chairman's table on the deserted stage. Presently, rising from her seat, she went forward to the footlights and softly called his name.

Cuanduine looked up and saw her. "What?" said he. "Have I one listener left?" Then he leaped to the ground beside her, lightly as a cat. "Tell me," he said, "why are the people fled? But yesterday my voice was music in their ears; my words carried them to ethereal regions. Now they will not hear me, and they begin to hate me. What have I done?"

"You have become a bore, Cuanduine," replied the girl. "You have ceased to be an entertainer, and have become a man with a mission."

"But my mission is for their benefit. My one desire is to restore the beauty that has been stolen from their lives."

"A vain desire, Cuanduine. The people who are really robbed of the birds and flowers are too hungry and ill-clad to miss them. The others do not grudge the couple of shillings charged for entry to Goshawk's show places. They do not go very often, you see."

"And you?"

"I am rich, and go as often as I please. I spend most of my days there, feasting on melody and perfume, lost to the world, its sordidness and cruelty."

"That must be very bad for you," said Cuanduine.

"How so?"

"Beauty is no soothing drug. It is the salt of life. Taken otherwise it is a poison: it induces not sleep, but death."

"If that is so," said the girl, "I cannot help it. I cannot change the world: but neither can I live in it as it is."

"I have seen that sorrow in your face," said Cuanduine, "time after time, when you have sat in the front row at my meetings."

"What?" said the girl joyfully. "Did you really see me? Did you single me out—just me—amongst your thousands of hearers?"

"Yes. The footlights illuminated your face."

"Oh, don't spoil it," said Ambrosine. "Say that there was something you saw in me different from the rest: understanding, perhaps: sympathy, even. For I do understand and sympathise. Listen, Cuanduine, I am a woman of advanced views, and not afraid to speak what is in my mind. I love you, Cuanduine. I have loved you from the first moment I saw you."

"What has that to do with the advancement of your views?" asked Cuanduine.

"Why, this: I believe that love should be free and unfettered, and should admit no bar to its expression."

"Your ancestor, the Stonewoman, did not think that an advanced view," said Cuanduine.

"I do not understand you," replied Ambrosine.

"If you cannot understand that," said Cuanduine, "you should not trust any of your beliefs so far as to act on them. There was a gentle maiden once that had never seen a lion, and knew no more of its habits than she might have gleaned from a picture and a chance saying that it was a noble beast. One day she paid a visit to a menagerie, and, seeing a lion pent up in a cage, her heart was wrung with pity, in so much that she besought the keeper to set it free, saying that it was a shame that so fine and generous a creature should be so trammelled. Then, as the keeper stirred not, 'What, fellow,' says she, 'art thou a rude uncourteous boor, that thou refusest me this boon? or what fault dost find with my sentiments?' 'Nay, madam, 'tis not your sentiments are at fault,' quoth he,' but your zoology.'"

Ambrosine was fain to laugh, saying that Love was not a lion. "Nay, 'tis more dangerous," said Cuanduine, "and will not bear playing with. But shall I argue with Beauty? No! If a kiss will stead you, here's arms to leap to."

CHAPTER XI

A Drama of Love and Hatred

Now amongst the other women who loved Cuanduine (and whom, for the appeal in their eyes, he kissed, and then forgot) there was one Eulalia, fifth and eighth wife of Lord Waterfall, the milk monopolist. In the bloom of her youth this noble dame had been engaged to Goshawk, then a rising young financier not yet of royal rank, who had wooed her with a promise that when he should have come into his kingdom he would give her all the humming birds in the world to trim her hats with; but later jilted her for the more advantageous hand of a sugar princess. Eulalia was deeply chagrined by this perfidious behaviour (as she deemed it) of her fiance, nor can history altogether acquit the royal lover of a certain inconsiderateness in the matter. For her humiliation the maiden sought balm in a breach of promise action, by which she netted forty thousand pounds; and for her revenge she went hunting for a husband fit to contend with Goshawk in the moneymarket. Such a one she found at last in Tompkins, son of the Leather King; but that princelet had none of the qualities that had made his noble sire what he was, and, after a short struggle, beaten, broken, and bankrupted, she divorced him for business inefficiency, being thus the first person to reap the benefits of tbe Matrimonial Causes (Amendment, Extension, and Consolidation) Act, which had just become law.

Thereafter Eulalia took many husbands with the same intent, whom one by one Goshawk smashed and she divorced. By each victory the power of the conqueror was increased, and lustre added to his name; until at last, coming into his full estate, he bestowed all the humming birds in the world upon Guzzelinda, his Queen, who henceforward never appeared in public without a hatful of them on her head, and had a cloak also made for herself out of their breast feathers, some fifteen thousand of the creatures perishing to the purpose. What a heartscald and torment was it for Eulalia to see her birthright thus dissipated; and what briny floods did rawly channel her cheeks as she made her plaint at even to the moon and stars.

But if any one think that the age of chivalry was dead at this time, let him mark what follows. As Eulalia sat thus at her window one night, there comes into her garden a troubadour, singing:

> Lady, Lady, though your grief
> Lighter were than aspen leaf,
> Alone you could not bear it.
> But, be it ne'er so heavy weighted,
> As a nothing 'twill be rated
> If with one true love you share it,
> Lady, Lady.

Eulalia hearkened to the song; and "Lo!" says she. "Let him who would gain my hand, fetch me but one humming bird from Goshawk's forests." 'Twas a behest at which a faint-heart lover would have blenched, for the forest laws were stringent. But the lute player was none other than the Count O'Conor de Valois-Stuart-Plantagenet, who had the blood of four royal lines in his veins, though no more than you or I in his pocket.

A lady's lightest breath to him was a command. Therefore, returning to his lodging he furbishes up the old elephant gun with which his greatgrandfather was wont to go a-hunting in the days when Africa was dark, and at once books his passage by the liner *Stupendorificus* (for there were still ocean liners at that time, though they were only used by the poorer sort of passengers). After a long and tedious journey of two days he comes in sight of the Statue of Efficiency (with a time-check in her hand, and the light of salesmanship about her brow) and, after submitting to a careful inspection of his lungs, liver, and bankbook (which last did only barely pass muster) he lands in America, the Great, the Renowned, the Progressive, the Uplifted, to whom all nations bow.

> When U.S. first at Wealth's command
> Rose from the Red Man's wild domain,
> This was the audit of our land,
> And spirits of Progress sung the strain:

> Rule, Columbia! Columbia rules for sure!
> Yankees never never never shall be poor.

> Peoples without progressive itch
> Must in their turn as bankrupts fall,
> While ye shall flourish, great and rich,
> The dread and envy of them all.

> Rule, Columbia! Columbia rules for sure!
> Yankees never never never shall be poor.

But let me not be swept, by this gush of loyalty, away from my matter. The gallant Count shogs it afoot to the Goshawk forests, where, ensconcing himself in ambush, he cuts up one of the elephant bullets into slugs with his pocket knife, and so awaits his prey. Soon he pricks his ears at the sound of humming, and in a moment, with a whirr of tiny wings, the glade is alive with the splendid midgets, darting hither and thither in joy. The blood of kings is at once afire: the hunting blood, the hawking blood, not yet tamed by generations of straitened respectability. The Count raises the elephant gun, and fires.

Bang! You may guess what execution was done among the birdlings; and hard now was the task of the sportsman to find one carcass of them fit to grace a lady's hat. After a long search, however, he spied one that had been but stunned by the explosion, and was scarcely mutilated at all; but ere he could retrieve it the minions of Goshawk were upon him. Hup! Woosh! With the butt end of the elephant gun he dashes out the brains of one and the teeth of another, then backs up against a tree and stands at bay, ready to sell his life dearly. But there's no spirit in these base-born churls. Even at the odds of seven to one, they dare not close with the desperate patrician, but, turning their asphyxiators on him at long range, they stretch him, purplefaced and panting, upon the sward.

Next day, having been expeditiously tried and sentenced, the unhappy cavalier was imprisoned in an iron cage, in which he was hung, like a second Wallace, from the walls of Castle Goshawk in the Adirondacks; in which predicament, exposed to the parching suns of summer, the bitter winds of winter, and the cameras of pressmen, he passed the remainder of his natural life. You may be sure that Goshawk did not fail to send a photograph of her champion to Eulalia, who, though she had forgotten all about him in the meanwhile, was thus stung to even fiercer rage for vengeance. To this end she remarried Lord Waterfall, her third husband, who had somewhat recovered in prosperity since her divorce of him. But alas, Milk, though never so well watered, was but a weak weapon against the power of Wheat, and Eulalia was already contemplating a fresh divorce when Cuanduine came to London.

She went as often as was fashionable to the hero's lectures, and you may guess it pleased her well to hear him trounce King Goshawk. Moreover, she soon became enamoured of the handsome orator, and longed ardently to be his. Her Love thus marched with her Ambition, with Revenge in attendance: under whose triple prompting she accosted Cuanduine one day at a reception of Lady Cumbersome's, craving that, as a humble admirer of his talents and sharer of his views, she might be accorded an interview some day when he should be at leisure. "Madam," said Cuanduine, "I have no leisure by day. Those who desire private converse with me must content themselves with the night hours."

If the invitation sound bold to you, you may set it down to the hero's innocence. And though she was fain to blush, it displeased Eulalia not a whit. Nay, as soon as she could spare the time, she went down to Richmond to Cuanduine's house, choosing, as it happened, the very evening of his failure.

CHAPTER XII

A Comedy of Loves

A ROOM IN CUANDUINE'S house at Richmond. Looking at it as from the auditorium of a theatre, you see a large bow window which occupies almost the entire of the back wall. In the right-hand wall, well forward, is the door. There is no fireplace; but in the centre of the room is an electric stove fashioned like an ancient brazier. Near this is a fair-sized table. The furniture, what there is of it, is severely simple in style. It consists of about a dozen carved mahogany chairs and a couple of stands holding potted plants. There are neither books nor bookshelves; nor ornaments of any kind; and no armchairs.

It is dusk outside. An oldish man wanders into the room, dabbing at things vaguely with a duster; then draws the curtains, and switches on the electric light. He fidgets round a little more, and is just about to go out when some one appears at the door. It is Eulalia.

EULALIA. Is Mr. Cuanduine at home? I walked in because the door was open and I could find no bell. A nice way you look after your master's property.

THE OLD MAN. Our door is never shut; there is no need of a bell; and Cuanduine has no servant.

EULALIA. Oh, I beg pardon, I'm sure. Stupid mistake to have made.

THE OLD MAN. Not at all, madam. Quite natural. In any other household a servant is what I should be called, but Cuanduine is good enough to call me friend. I look after his creature comforts, which he hasn't time to attend to himself, and in return—well, I have the pleasure of living in this beautiful

190

house and hearing his conversation.

EULALIA. You must be a very devoted admirer of Mr. Cuanduine to serve him so contentedly without wages.

THE OLD MAN. Wages, ma'am? What do I want with wages? If I need anything, I've only to help myself.

EULALIA. Help yourself?

THE OLD MAN. Yes, ma'am. Like this. (*He opens a drawer in the table, takes out a bundle of notes, detaches one and puts it in his pocket, then replaces the bundle and shuts the drawer.*) Quite simple.

EULALIA. A most remarkable arrangement, though I fancy it must be rather more profitable to you than to your master. I hope you don't abuse the privilege.

THE OLD MAN. Lord, no, ma'am. The way money lies about in this house, you get to think nothing of it. Bundles of notes in convenient situations. A jar of small change on every window-sill. Why, it's like water with us.

EULALIA. I'm afraid a lot of it must go to waste.

THE OLD MAN. Oh no, ma'am. One doesn't waste much water, after all; and what we do waste is just what isn't worth the trouble of saving. Same with money.

EULALIA. Your master must be very wealthy, then?

THE OLD MAN (*non-commitally*). So-so. So-so. I've served in richer houses, but Cuanduine knows the value of money.

EULALIA (*smiling*). You mean he doesn't know it, I think.

THE OLD MAN (*with finality*). No, ma'am. (*Remembering his duties*) But won't you sit down while you're waiting, ma'am— or should I say My Lady?

EULALIA. I am Lady Waterfall.

THE OLD MAN. Chair, m'lady (*offering one, which she takes*). Cuanduine should be home any minute now, m'lady.

EULALIA. I'm afraid this must seem a very unusual hour for a call, but the fact is—

THE OLD MAN. Oh, not at all, m'lady. You see, Cuanduine

is never at home by day, so he keeps the night for private calls. Very busy man, Cuanduine. Public meetings all day; private conversations all night. Scarcely a minute he can call his own. No regular meals, and doesn't eat as much as would keep a canary.

EULALIA. Doesn't sleep much either, I suppose.

THE OLD MAN. Lord bless you, ma'am, he never sleeps.

EULALIA. What do you mean?

THE OLD MAN. Just what I say, m'lady. He never sleeps. Never even lies on a bed. Uncanny I call it.

EULALIA. But the thing's impossible. And how can you know?

THE OLD MAN. Well, for one thing, he never goes to bed. Hasn't even such a thing as a bedroom. And he spends most of the night chatting with visitors. Just listen to this, m'lady. I had a toothache about a week ago, and it kept me awake. About four o'clock in the morning I couldn't stand it any more, and came down here to get a little something for it. I expected to find the room empty, for the last visitor had gone about an hour before. But when I came in, there was Cuanduine standing at the open window looking out at the stars. When I told him what was wrong, he came over and looked into my eyes, and the pain vanished on the spot. However, that's neither here nor there. What I wanted to tell you was this. You'd expect a man who had been up all night—to say nothing of speechifying all day—to look a bit worn and pale: wouldn't you, m'lady? But Lord, no, not Cuanduine. He was looking straight into my eyes, and on my solemn oath he was as bright and fresh as a bride on her wedding morning. (*With a sudden and complete change of tone*) Do you think a man like that is going to fall for any tricks you can play, m'lady?

EULALIA (*startled into incoherence*). Howhow dare you talk to me like that? I'll report you to your master.

THE OLD MAN. If you dare. (*Cocking his ear*) That's his

step, so now's your chance.

He goes out. A moment later, Cuanduine comes in.

CUANDUINE. Good evening to you, madam.

EULALIA. Oh, Mr. Cuanduine, I thought you might be at home to-night.

CUANDUINE. You see that I am at home.

EULALIA. Er—yes. I hope I don't intrude. Perhaps you are busy.

CUANDUINE. Yes, I am busy. But it is not the custom of my people to turn the stranger from the door. If you are tired, rest. If you are thirsty, there is wine and coffee.

EULALIA. Oh, not at all. It's of no consequence. I—er-I suppose you must be wondering who I am to come disturbing you like this.

CUANDUINE. What should it matter to me who you are? There are thirty million people in England, whose names I could never remember, even if I could learn them.

EULALIA. No—er-of course not. However, I'm Lady Waterfall; wife of Lord Waterfall, you know.

CUANDUINE. Is that the man who lives by starving the London babies of milk? *(She retreats a step.)* Never mind: you are welcome none the less.

EULALIA. I've often told him his prices are too high. But then, you see, he has to pay his tribute to the Milk King before he can touch a penny himself. These Kings are such extortioners: such blood-suckers: such tyrants. Oh, Mr. Cuanduine, you don't know what a noble work you are doing in challenging their power. *(Takes off her wrap.)*

CUANDUINE. I know it well, madam.

EULALIA. Er—quite so. A great mind like yours would be above false modesty and the cant of self-depreciation. Oh, I know you are a great man, Cuanduine. I have sat at your feet, as it were, listening to your thundering denunciations of this dreadful world; and though I am only a weak, vain, worldly woman, living, as you have so frankly told me, by robbing the London babies of their natural fats, still I have been touched by your eloquence, my conscience has been stung by the lash of your satire, and my one desire now is to play some part in the work of creating a better state of things. Oh, Mr. Cuanduine, let me help you in your work. Let us pull down the Kings, and bring back the days of freedom and progress in business.

CUANDUINE. By God, woman, are you a fool, or do you take me for one, that you slaver me with such balderdash? Do you think I am going to destroy the Kings only to leave the monopolists a free hand? Go to.

EULALIA. I thought no such thing. But surely the Kings must go first? I know what it is, Cuanduine. You despise my help because I am a woman. But a time will come when you will need it. You are setting yourself to fight the world, alone and friendless Even if

your own strength is enough for the fighting, you will need comfort, you will need a heartening voice, you will need sympathy. Here are they all offered to you freely. Do not turn them away.

CUANDUINE. What do you want of me?

EULALIA (*shamming shyness*). Can't you guess?

CUANDUINE. It should be something shameful, by your giggling and blushing.

EULALIA. Only to conventional minds: but what have we to do with convention? Oh, you bashful boy, where are your eyes? Where is your cleverness? Can you not read a woman's heart?

CUANDUINE. Your heart is hidden from me, madam.

EULALIA. Then I'll be bold and show it. Cuanduine, I love you.

CUANDUINE. Therein you show some wisdom. I love you too.

EUALIA. Yes, with a gospelly sort of love. But I don't want to be loved according to the commandments, or philosophically.

I'm a woman. I wanted to be loved. Loved do you understand? Say you love me again: but put the warmth of the words into your voice. Say it. You are a poet, and should know how to love. Say it, boy.

CUANDUINE (*bewildered, and no longer quite master of himself*). How shall I say it?

EULALIA. Like this. (*She clasps her arms about him, wooing him with her body*) I love you—more than anything in the world —more than honour—more than life—more than wealth. Now, how do you love me?

CUANDUINE. I love you better than that.

EULALIA. Where is your poetry gone? There is no love in your voice. Are you shy? Dare you not kiss me? (*As he hesitates, she throws her arms around his neck, and pulls his head down to her lips.*) You certainly know how to kiss, Mr. Innocence. Again (*he kisses her*). Now don't you love me, dear? Let's put out the light, and sit in the window there, and watch the stars. (*He switches off the current, plunging the room in darkness. A moment later she draws back the curtain from one section of the window, letting in a flood of moonlight. They sit together on the cushioned window-ledge, hand in hand.*) What a night for love, Cuanduine. (*She sniffs the air.*) Ah, you have night-scented stock in your garden. There is no perfume like it.

CUANDUINE (*leaning out of the window, with one knee on the ledge, to show her*). See the little pale star-clusters, there under the trees.

EULALIA. How awfully pretty.

CUANDUINE (*speaking with the first sign of emotion, a slight catch of the voice*). Yes, they are very beautiful: but not more beautiful than you.

EULALIA (*smiling whimsically*). So you find me beautiful?

CUANDUINE. Beautiful as a dream-fancy of Tir na nOg. (*Physically intoxicated, and carried away by his own feelings*) Oh, my dear, how I love you.

EULALIA. Sounds like as if you'd only just discovered it. I was right, then. You were only fooling when you said you loved me the first time.

CUANDUINE. No. I loved you then-and better than you love me.

EULALIA. I don't see how you make that out: you, who stood there like an iceberg while I begged for a kiss. But no matter. You love me now at all events, don't you?

CUANDUINE. Yes.

EULALIA. What a nice shy boy it is. Come now. Sit here beside me. (*He complies.*) Close. (*He put his arms around her. She sighs contentedly.*)

CUANDUINE. Dear, you are too beautiful. I have let my soul slip from me all wittingly. Can I ever get it back?

EULALIA. It will come back to you in the morning full of poetry: poetry inspired by me. You must write it all down at once and bring it out in a limited edition, privately printed, and dedicated to me: won't you, dear? What was it you said I was like a few minutes ago? A vision of fairyland?

CUANDUINE. A dream-fancy of Tir na nOg.

EULALIA. Of course. Tir na nOg. I forgot that you're Irish. I suppose you spend a lot of time in Tir na nOg?

CUANDUINE. Not now. I left it, a long time ago, to fight this Goshawk.

EULALIA. Gave up poetry for politics, eh? Well, I can't say I'm sorry, especially as it has brought us together. (*She kisses him.*) Oh, what a night. (*She lies back in his arms, her head on his breast.*)

CUANDUINE. Eulalia—

EULALIA. What a nice voice you've got, my dear. I believe I could listen to it for ever. Go on. Tell me more about Tir na nOg. I must share all your thoughts now, you know. You must tell me all your dreams and fancies.

CUANDUINE (*shortly, loosing his clasp*). No. You want too

much. (*Startled, she sits upright, facing him.*) Besides, I have not the time. I expect another woman here at any minute.

EULALIA (*astonished*). What! (*She looks hard at him.*) You're joking.

CUANDUINE. I am not joking.

EULALIA. Another woman!

CUANDUINE. Do you think I am a beggar in love because I have spent some on you?

EULALIA. This is outrageous. (*She jumps to her feet.*) I'm not prudish or strait-laced myself, but two appointments on one night—well—(*She walks angrily away from him.*)

CUANDUINE. It was not at my invitation that you came, madam.

EULALIA (*reddening with mortification*). Just like you to rub that in. If you were any sort of a man of the world you'd have told your servants to keep me out at the beginning; or else (*watching him coyly as she drops the hint*) well—you'd tell them to keep her out now.

CUANDUINE. Do you think you can prevail on me to break my word?

EULALIA. Hm! She must be very beautiful, whoever she is. Who is she, by the way?

CUANDUINE. Her name is Ambrosine.

EULALIA. What? Not Ambrosine Overall, the poetess?

CUANDUINE I do not know what other names she may have, nor what her trade is.

EULALIA. Is she a tall slinky woman with black hair and eccentric clothes?

CUANDUINE. What are eccentric clothes?

EULALIA. Oh—like nothing on earth.

CUANDUINE. Yes. Her clothes are like nothing on earth.

EULALIA. Then it's the Overall woman for a cert. Well, I can't say I admire your taste.

CUANDUINE. She is more beautiful than you, and her

ways are tender.

EULALIA. Oh yes. She's tender all right. She's had so much practice, you know. *(She sees that he does not catch her meaning.)* Didn't you know that she goes in for Free Love?

CUANDUINE. Do not you do so?

EULALIA *(indignantly)*. What do you take me for? Oh, it's just like a man to think a woman a profligate because she breaks the old-fashioned conventions. Well, I'm no Free Lover, and the sooner you realise it the better. I'm a believer in reasonable marriage and divorce laws, not in anarchy. But this other woman—ugh!

Some one outside the window whistles the first bars of Osmino's Aria from "Ii Seraglio."

CUANDUINE. There she is, and before her time.

EULALIA *(resuming the siren tone, and adopting a manner coaxingly conspiratorial)*. Don't let her in.

CUANDUINE. I must. I will.

EULALIA *(suddenly resolute)*. Then I'm off. Keep her out for a minute while I dress. *(She runs to look for her wrap. The whistling is repeated closer.)* Oh, this is dreadful. Listen, Cuanduine, I'll hide behind this curtain. You take her to another room. Then I'll dress and slip away. *(She darts behind the window curtain.)*

Ambrosine's head and shoulders appear at the open window. Cuanduine goes to meet her.

AMBROSINE. My love! All alone in the darkness.

CUANDUINE. Ambrosine. *(He offers to take her hands to help her through the window.)*

AMBROSINE. No. Kiss me first. *(He does so.)* Doesn't that make it just like Romeo and Juliet, only the other way round? Help me up now.

CUANDUINE. Put your foot on the large flower-pot. *(This makes her visible to the waist. He helps her through the window.)*

AMBROSINE. My love! Another kiss.

CUANDUINE. No, Ambrosine. I have already had more

love to-night than I can stand.

AMBROSINE (*amused*). What! One kiss?

CUANDUINE. A hundred kisses.

AMBROSINE. What on earth do you mean? Have you been mobbed again by schoolgirls?

CUANDUINE. No. I had them all of one woman.

AMBROSINE. Do you mean to tell me that you've been dallying here with another woman while waiting for me?

CUANDUINE. Yes. I have told you that I am weary of kisses. Come now. Let us retire to another room and play some music, so that she may depart unseen.

AMBROSINE. Well! You certainly are a cool customer. Is she here still?

CUANDUINE. Yes.

AMBROSINE. Where?

CUANDUINE. In this room. (*Ambrosine looks around her quickly. Her eye falls on the curtain. She strides over and pulls it aside, revealing Eulalia in a state of shamed consternation.*)

AMBROSINE. Well! That's the last straw. A married woman! I wouldn't have believed it of you.

EULALIA (*firing up*). Who are you to come the virtuous over me?—you, a Free Lover.

AMBROSINE. Yes. I am a Free Lover. But if I were so foolish as to take vows I should keep them. Especially when I had taken them with my eyes open for the twentieth time.

EULALIA. You lie. I haven't had twenty husbands.

AMBROSINE. Pooh! What matters a dozen more or less? I dare say it was your misfortune rather than your fault.

CUANDUINE. Ladies—

AMBROSINE. Where's the switch? I want some light. (*She finds the switch and turns it on.*)

CUANDUINE. Ladies—

EULALIA (*putting on her wrap*). Oh, don't talk to me. I'm going.

AMBROSINE. So am I. Your conduct tonight, Mr. Cuanduine, has been nothing short of disgraceful. (*The two women make for the door.*)

CUANDUINE (*barring the way*). You shall hear me first. Eulalia, when you came to me, I did not quarrel with you about the men you would love after me. Neither, Ambrosine, did I quarrel with you about the men you had loved before me. Why, then—

AMBROSINE (*interrupting indignantly*). How dare you speak to me like that! I have never loved a man in my life.

EULALIA. Oh, come, Miss Overall! What about all that stuff you've been putting in your poems?

AMBROSINE (*with cool contempt*). Lady Waterfall, if you cannot understand that freedom from convention is not synonymous with slavery to appetite, the sooner you go back to the nursery the better. (*To Cuanduine*) It's true that I believe in Free Love: but I have yet to meet the man that I could give my love to.

CUANDUINE. It is no matter. I neither knew nor cared whether either of you had loved before or would love again. Why, then, could not you be equally forbearing with me?

AMBROSINE . Oh, come! I didn't inquire into *your* past or future for that matter. But this is different. To make appointments with two women for the same hour! There is a limit, you know.

EULALIA. You must draw the line somewhere.

CUANDUINE. Yes. But where?

EULALIA. I don't know, and I don't care. Wherever you draw it, a man who behaves as you have done to-night is an outsider.

CUANDUINE. You forget, madam, that it was not for my asking that you came here. (*Ambrosine starts, and shoots an inquiring glance at her rival.*)

EULALIA. Oh, you beast! To fling it in my face again. (*She bites off the last word sharply, and raises her voice desperately to cancel the admission.) It's a lie: a lie.* I won't stay another minute. Let me go, sir.

AMBROSINE. Don't be absurd, Mrs. Tompkins—Lady Waterfall, I mean. Why shouldn't you take the initiative if you wanted to? Really, you're behaving—we're both behaving—like a pair of ridiculous women of the twentieth century. I beg your pardon, Cuanduine, for making such a fool of myself. Let us sit down quietly, the three of us, and discuss this interesting question.

EULALIA. What interesting question?

AMBROSINE. Where the line should be drawn, of course.

EULALIA. You can sit here till Doomsday, if you like, but I'm going. (*She makes for the door. Cuanduine bows her out.*)

CUANDUINE (*returning to Ambrosine, who is sitting on a table, swinging her legs, quite at home*). She is not beautiful in her anger like you.

AMBROSINE. I'm sorry for making such an ass of myself. I didn't understand. Am I forgiven?

CUANDUINE (*indifferently*). There is nothing to forgive. Let us have some music.

AMBROSINE. That's not a nice way to forgive. Come, give me a kiss: just one. (*She slips from the table and stands invitingly. He kisses her without passion, but she puts her arms around him, holding him to her.*) That wasn't a kiss, darling. I want a real kiss. (*He complies with sudden ardour. Her head falls on his breast.*) My own dear love.

CUANDUINE (*carried away by a flood of tenderness*). Oh, my wonderful darling. (*He kisses her with reverent passion, murmuring over her*) There is no one like you in the world. When I hold you I have all the beauty of the universe in my arms, and the fragrance of all flowers in my nostrils. Another kiss. My love, my very own. One more. And another. How beautiful you are, my sweet. Your scented hair: your soft, warm body: and your eyes—how they gleam and soften, like deep pools of night under a starlit sky.

AMBROSINE (*smiling up at him*). Do they really seem like? It's you that make them so, you know. (*With the vigour of sudden purpose*) Oh, when we love like this, what do we care about anything else? What does the world matter with its crimes and follies? Let us fly from it and live for love alone. Love is the only thing that matters, isn't it, dear? There is nothing else but love.

CUANDUINE (*abruptly releasing her*). No. For your soul's sake don't believe that. For though I have been in Tir na nOg I have been in Tartarus also.

AMBROSINE. What! In Hell? But have you not told us a hundred times that there is no Hell?

CUANDUINE. Tartarus is the First Heaven—the lowest heaven—the heaven of Material Delights. There dwell all sinners against life, the Devil's own children, with Mammon for their God, and Procrustes his prophet: that is to say, all hunters after wealth; all puritans and teetotalers by conviction; all devotees of art and beauty; all enemies of the light; all who wrest the living to the services of the inanimate. There dwell the great lovers who lived for love alone. Paris and Helen, Naoise and Deirdre, Paolo and Francesca, Tristan and Isolde: there they remain, locked in each other's arms, languishing in unspeakable boredom, yet incapable of holding any other desire: there they will linger until in the knowledge of their own futility they wither away.

There is silence for a moment. Ambrosine, who has listened intently to this speech, gives a short laugh and sits up again on the table.

AMBROSINE. How wise you are in some things, and how innocent in others. Who are you, Cuanduine?

CUANDUINE. The Hound of Man: the messenger of Life: the laughter of God. Do you know what Life is?

AMBROSINE. What is it?

CUANDUINE. A flame in a dark place full of rushing winds. Who can tell how difficult is the way of life? how powerful its enemies? It is a little thing, a feeble thing, though it fights so valiantly, feeding upon itself to produce energy and to renew itself: and all around it the implacable night, that needs neither energy nor rest nor renewal, waiting and watching, watching and waiting. The tale of life is told in every weed that grows in the crack of a wall. Why, even the mighty stars are but sparks of fire in the devouring immensity of nothingness. Look. (*He leads her to the window and parts the curtains.*)

AMBROSINE. The moon outshines your stars to-night.

CUANDUINE. So does your gospel of love and beauty outshine the truth of life.

> Desolate stars, and cold
> > Black eons of night,
> What of the feud of old?
> > What of the ancient fight?
> Provident Death that reaps,
> > Life that must sow and spend,
> Which shall possess the deeps?
> > Which shall win in the end?

AMBROSINE. Which?

CUANDUINE. Who can tell? Life survives only by sheer prodigality: prodigality in seed, prodigality in sowing. Like the sower, he scatters his seed broadcast on the wind: it is Death, the reaper, that conserves. And now the Devil has whispered the noblest of God's creatures that he must be provident: he has wrapped the red story of life in a pale romance of love and beauty, as the flaming stars are veiled by the light of the moon; and man stands listening, bewitched, while Mammon and Death and the Devil await his abdication. The first of living creatures, shall he be the first to fail in the fight?

AMBROSINE. Oh no, no, no!

CUANDUINE. You say No. Yet you would poison me with a barren love, and drug me with the kisses of your mouth.

AMBROSINE. No. I am sick of the very name of love. What shall we do if life is to survive?

CUANDUINE (*with sudden energy*). Work. Let us turn to the work in hand. I have dragons to fight. I have Goshawk to overthrow: for Mammon and Death and the Devil are one. Tell me, Ambrosine, what have my speeches lacked that they win applause but do not stir to action?

AMBROSINE. Nothing. You have said all that can be said. Like the great satirists of the past, you have moved the people to laugh at their follies, but not to renounce them. To achieve that you must stop talking and Do something: something big and striking to fire their imaginations: something to show them that you are a man to whom they can resign their wills, and whom they can follow blindly. Oh! (*struck by an idea*) I've got it. Next Thursday is Gold Cup Day at Ascot Races. All the world's great ones will be there, and swarms of England's little ones as well. You must go down there, and in face of them all confront King Goshawk in his box. (*With enthusiasm, as a picture of the scene passes before her mind's eye*) Oh, I can imagine the whole thing: the proud shallow fools in the Enclosure, and the humble fools outside admiring their dresses; the splendid horses fretting at the tape; the obscene figure of Goshawk in his royal seat. Then down swoops my splendid Cuanduine into the midst of the course, mounted on a milk-white steed, his glorious eyes flashing, a picture of grace and strength. Oh, the confusion among the worldlings; the rapturous joy of the people at the sight of their deliverer; the cowering terror of the tyrant. What do you say to it, Cuanduine?

CUANDUINE. I will do it.

AMBROSINE. Good. I will be there, watching you. No, I never could stand the atmosphere of the race-course. I will wait here to welcome you when you return in triumph. I can see the rest on the movies next day.

CHAPTER XIII

How Cuanduine put his Foot in it

YOU WILL BE RELIEVED, virtuous reader, if from these wicked
and licentious scenes I conduct you to the chamber within
whose chaste seclusion the Lady Cumbersome is being habited
for Ascot by her tirewomen. Five deft and tactful damsels were
these. First they put on her a marvellous fine chemise of triple
ninon, soft and pink as rose petals, and edged with lace. Then
they drew over her noble thighs a pair of knickers of the same
texture. Very fair and costly were these garments: a common
fellow like you or me could keep himself and his family for a
month on the price of them. Next they packed my Lady's noble
figure into a goodly corset, and on her legs they put stockings of
smooth spun silk. Poet never got as much for a lyric as the hosier
got for those stockings. Afterwards they put on her a petticoat of
swishing taffety that a worker might toil six weeks to pay for, and
shoes on her feet that would keep him in comfort for a fortnight.
Over all they put her gown, which I will not describe further
than to say that I could live for two years on the money she paid
for it, and so could any but the Devil's children. Come, let us
drink, not forgetting that this excellent liquor, this Guinness,
that warms the heart with the love of both God and man, is yet
cheaper than my Lady's shoelace.

Forth then steps my Lady thus elegantly caparisoned, with
a jewel or two added, and a hat proportionate to her frock; and
is conveyed to Ascot, there to coruscate with others as richly
apparelled under the benison of a June-day sun. The newspapers
of the time say it was an historic Ascot, and the scene in the

Royal Enclosure the most brilliant on record. There sat King Goshawk on his royal seat, and Queen Guzzelinda beside him. The two Oil Kings were there, the Banana King, a Tea King, and a Cotton King, each with his family; the King of England and his family; above three hundred and fifty monopolists; and a few determined members of the aristocracy—these, for the most part, carrying what little was left of their estates on their backs. Very dazzling was the play of colour, and bizarre and striking the shapes of frock and hat and parasol that were there on view. There was but one feature to mar the general radiance. "It was observed," said the newspapers next day, "that the Queen of England wore a dress that had already done duty on a previous occasion, and this breach of etiquette did not escape the notice of the Wheat Queen. Queen Lindy is unbending in all matters of decorum, and nobody will be surprised if the Englands' name does not appear on next year's invitation list to the enclosure."

But in the general brilliance Queen Henrietta's unfortunate gown was but as a fly-blow on the crystal mirror of a millionairess; and the papers all agreed that it was the most brilliant Ascot on record. The Less Rich, from their part of the course, watched all this grandeur through their field-glasses, with the thin acid saliva of envy dribbling on to their waistcoats and blouses. In like manner the Merely Rich stared at the Less Rich; and on the other side of the course the ordinary folk gave anxious ear to the tipsters advising them, for a consideration, how to Become Rich.

At last came the moment for the great event of the day, the race for the Gold Cup, and the stewards went around examining each horse (as had been the custom ever since that infamous and historic Derby) to see that none of them was a rejuvenescence of the Fuhzler process. While they were engaged in this scrutiny, a swelling murmur and a cry broke from the crowd, as a great black horse, with Cuanduine on its back, came trotting over the heath, and leaped the railings on to the course. Some of the people, and a policeman here and there, made essay to stop him, but fell back blasted by the light in the hero's eyes. Urging his horse to a gallop, he thundered along the course to where King Goshawk sat somnolent beside his Queen in the Royal Stand. Then, reining in, he stood erect in his stirrups, and cried out in a loud voice that was heard by every ear in the vast multitude that was now swarming to the rails and over them to see what was towards:

"Goshawk, give us back our birds and flowers."

You would have thought that at this war-cry a shout would have pealed from ten thousand throats, and that the tyrant would have cowered at the sight of Liberty in her Red Cap sprung full grown from the breasts of the people of England: at least I, a barbarous Irishman, would have thought so. But what fools we Gaels do be. There was no shout: only an embarrassed silence. Then the three hundred and fifty monopolists and their wives in the Royal Enclosure sniffed contemptuously in unison, and immediately afterwards the democracy outside called out in one voice:

"Cheese it, Paddy. Get off the course."

Cuanduine looked at King Goshawk, who was too full of lunch to move; then at the monopolists and their ladies, who smiled uppishly; then at the democracy, who repeated their request; then at the police, who were advancing towards him, but were brought to a stand by his gaze. Then he gave another look at Goshawk, and "Long life to your Majesty," said he, and rode from the field, shouting with laughter.

You may guess that Cuanduine's goose was well cooked from that hour. Was he not a bounder and a low fellow and a spoil-sport and a kill-joy and no gentleman and no sportsman and a rotter and a cad and a general outsider to introduce politics and things like that into a race meeting? That sort of thing isn't done, you know. There was nothing for it but to cut the fellow.

In the then unsatisfactory state of the law there was no statute under which he could be indicted, as it had not yet been made treason to annoy a millionaire. But social practice was as usual in advance of constitutional forms. Cuanduine was frozen out of England.

CHAPTER XIV

Cuanduine Desponds

AFTER THIS DISCOMFITURE CUANDUINE returned to Ireland to seek advice from the Philosopher as to which of the other nations of the world would be likely to listen to his message.

"None," said the Philosopher. "You have failed with the two that are most tolerant: you will scarcely succeed with any others."

"The Americans?" suggested Cuanduine. "The American Government would take you for an atheist and refuse to let you open your mouth; and the American people would probably hang you from a lamp-post."

"The French?" said Cuanduine.

"The French would take you for a Christian and expel you from the country."

"The Germans?" said Cuanduine.

"The Germans would write ponderous books to explain what you didn't mean, and even read some of them. But they would not follow you."

"The Russians, then?"

"The Russians have abolished property, but they have not abolished tyranny. They might execute you, and then the rest of the world might make it a pretext to declare war on them."

"Then let us try the Japanese," said Cuanduine.

"The West will not follow the East," said the Philosopher.

"Oh, I am a man of no account," said Cuanduine. "I have failed in all the tasks I have set myself. I have not freed the songbirds nor the wild flowers; I have not taught men the wisdom of Charity; I have not taught them the folly of fighting."

"You may yet teach them how to fight decently," said the Philosopher. "Read this now," and he handed him a newspaper.

CHAPTER XV

How Cuanduine settled the Wolfo-Lambian Dispute

DURING ALL THIS TIME Cuanduine had been too busy to read the newspapers, so that he was unaware of the course of the dispute between Wolfia and Lambia of whose beginnings he had read at his first arrival on this remarkable planet. After the bombardment of Micronetta the Lambians had asked for and obtained a truce, during which an embassy was sent to Wolfopolis offering to pay double the indemnity demanded in return for the withdrawal of Point Six of the Wolfian demands. This Nervolini peremptorily refused, dismissing the delegation with the now historic phrase: "Omnia vincit vis a tergo!" As a last resort the Lambians now appealed to the League of Nations. Nervolini promptly lodged an objection that, as Lambia would shortly be a portion of the Wolfian Empire, the matter was a domestic one for the Wolfian Government, and outside the jurisdiction of the League. The League, however, had already replied to the Lambian appeal that the points at issue were so delicate, complicated, and obscure that it could come to no decision without impairing its reputation for impartiality. It is a curious and noteworthy feature of international politics that the rights of a dispute are invariably more difficult to determine when one of the contestants is considerably more powerful than the other. The Lambian statesmen were well aware of this, and had only lodged their appeal in order to gain time while their citizens were strengthening their fortifications and tightening their belts. Nervolini, however, was not to be stayed by such mean and treacherous devices. As soon as the League of Nations had despatched its judicious reply to the Lambian appeal, the Wolfian navy and air-fleet had been ordered to resume operations. The whole territory of Lambia was at once subjected to the most terrific bombardment ever known in the history of the world. Every town and village was raked with explosives and scoured with poison gas. The homes of the Lambians and the temples and monuments of their ancestors were shattered to fragments; hills were obliterated; fertile plains turned into desolate valleys; men, women, and babies were slaughtered and mutilated by men who a few hours earlier had taken a fond farewell of parents, children, wives, sweethearts, and all they held dear.

Cuanduine read of all this as he sat, gloomy and disappointed, in the Philosopher's room in Stoneybatter. Then his eye kindled, and, rising to his feet, he said: "I will go to Lambia."

Meanwhile the Lambians turned in their distress to Heaven, as it is the way of men to remember the Almighty only when all else fails them, and with a certain shamed reluctance the Government ordered public prayers for deliverance from the national peril. Assembling, therefore, in their ruined churches, in squares and market-places, the people of Lambia made what supplication they could amid the thunder of explosives and the fumes of smoke and gasses, scarcely hoping, however, that in such a furor their voices would be heard above those of the more influential Wolfians who, in the serenity of their own land, were praying for victory. But even as the whole population of Lambia had its eyes raised to where it conceived the Throne of Justice should stand, out of the northern sky came Cuanduine's airplane closely pursued by a squadron of the enemy. The foremost of these greatly harassed the hero with a stream of lead from its machine-gun. Cuanduine, having no gun, turned suddenly, and, giving his salmon-leap, landed upon the plane of this one with the lightness of a swallow. Then he took pilot and gunner, one in each hand, wrung their necks, and hurled them earthward with a message written: "Cuanduine to the People of Lambia." The remaining enemy machines held off aghast at this feat, and Cuanduine landed easily in the market-place of Micropolis.

"I will be your leader," said Cuanduine, and at that the people raised a great shout about him, and, leading him to their ruined Parliament House, they put all the symbols of power into his hands. Thereafter they offered him a gun; but Cuanduine would have none of it, and asked for a sword. Now there were no swords used in the world at that time; but in one of their museums they found an ancient weapon and brought it to him. Harder it was than any sword forged of mortal men, and it had a golden hilt ornamented with silver. Cuanduine knew it at once for his father's sword, the Cruaidin Cailidcheann, that he had lost on Baile's Strand the time the druids set him to fight the waves of the sea in atonement for killing his son Conlaoch; and the sea threw it up years afterwards on the coast of Lambia. Now Cuanduine took the sword in his hand, and he shook great circles of light that dazzled even the sailors of the Wolfian fleet and filled them with forebodings of doom. Again he shook the sword, and the people raised another shout that was heard above the clamour of the Wolfian guns. A third time he shook the sword, and the people fell silent, and Cuanduine made this song:

> The sword of the soldier
> It cleaves to my hand:
> The valiant, the strong one,
> The weapon of man.

> With the passing of steel,
> With the coming of lead,
> Passed the power of the people,
> Came the triumph of wealth.

With sword of his owning
Marched the freeman to battle.
But the gun and its holder
Are numbered like cattle.
The sword in his passion

Drinks blood and makes peace.
But lead in his interests
Beareth false witness,
Crushes and smashes
Strong and weak ruthlessly;
Cowardly in conquest,
Shrieks for security,
Trampling the fallen
Under his feet.

The sword's in my hand now,
The sword from the sea.
Who is for battle?
Who's for the steel?

Another shout went up from the men of Lambia, and they clamoured for Cuanduine to lead them against the foe, fully believing, as men do at such moments, that he was sent from Heaven in answer to their prayer. But Cuanduine said: "Let us first try to make peace." This suggestion was not so pleasing to the people; who, being rendered somewhat uppish by finding themselves in the special favour of Heaven, now looked forward to meting out some of their own measure to the Wolfians, and even perhaps to erecting a Lambian Empire on the ruins of Nervolini's. Cuanduine, however, dissuaded them, and, a truce having been made, he flew with three attendants to the Wolfian flagship. On the quarter-deck stood the Wolfian Admiral, impassively awaiting the surrender; to whom Cuanduine addressing himself said: "Sir, I am come to offer you fresh terms." "Sir," replied the Admiral, "you might have spared yourself the trouble. My instructions are to accept nothing but unconditional surrender."

"Nevertheless," said Cuanduine, "you shall hear me. These are my terms: that you shall choose twenty of the best men of your forces to meet me with twenty of mine, sword in hand, at any suitable spot that you may name. If we prevail, you shall withdraw your fleets and pay for the damage you have done; if you prevail, we shall pay for the repainting of the ship scraped by our lighterman."

"Have the Lambians chosen a lunatic for their spokesman?" asked the Wolfian Admiral. "Do you not know that we have you at our mercy, and that it is in our power to blot out your miserable people from the face of the earth? What terms are these to offer to a Wolfian Admiral?"

"Just terms," said Cuanduine.

At that the Admiral and his staff burst into roars of laughter. "Bundle the fool back into his airplane," said the Admiral, "and let the cannonade resume."

"Not so," said Cuanduine angrily. "Touch me at your peril, dogs, and keep your guns well muzzled until I have spoken with Nervolini. For I swear by the oath of my people that if a hair of any Lambian's head is injured from this moment, I will take satisfaction a hundredfold from the men of Wolfia." So saying he shook his sword in their faces; and as he did so the Morrigu appeared above his head in the form of a black eagle, whereat the Admiral and his staff were paralysed with fear, and made no further attempt to stay him.

Then Cuanduine mounted his airplane, and flew swiftly to Wolfopolis, to the Palace; and entering by a window he went straight to the apartments of the Dictator, whom he found reclining on a couch of swansdown being ministered to by female attendants. These were all greatly flustered at sight of

Cuanduine as he strode up the long room, dressed in airman's costume, with the Cruaidin Cailidcheann gleaming in his hand; nor was Nervolini himself much more comfortable, though he knew that there were guards within call, until Cuanduine, saluting, addressed him courteously: "Nervolini."

"Whence come you?" asked Nervolini.

"From Lambia, Signor." Nervolini's lip curled; said he: "If you have come to beg easier terms, you may save your breath for your instant return. For I will not abate one jot of them, and above all must Number Six be rigidly complied with."

"Sir," said Cuanduine, "only relinquish this, and perhaps we may come to a just agreement."

"I desire no agreement, just or otherwise," said Nervolini. "Go, tell the Lambians that they must pay for their defiance in full."

"Then you must fight me, son of a dog," said Cuanduine, handing him a sword which he took from one of his followers. Nervolini durst not but accept it, though he cast one longing look towards the door beyond which his guards were. "Defend yourself," cried Cuanduine at that, "for I would not kill you from behind." Nervolini therefore crossed his blade with the Cruaidin Cailidcheann, but in an instant it was sent flying from his grasp, and he dropped on his knees before Cuanduine. "I give you best in swordsmanship, young sir," said he, putting as good a face on his predicament as he could muster. "You have fairly won from me what you have asked. We will wipe Number Six from the peace terms."

"Nay," said Cuanduine. "The shadow of that clause has lain very heavy upon Lambia. Let us see whether we cannot lighten it."

Here, laying aside the Cruaidin Cailidcheann, he advanced upon Nervolini, and, taking him by the scruff of the neck, he bent him across his knee and slippered him very soundly, as provided in the Annex. Then indeed Nervolini did yell like a two-year-old, so that all the chamberlains, courtiers, soldiers, servants, and others of the Palace came running in hot haste to see what was the matter. When they arrived they saw Cuanduine sitting in very lordly fashion upon the couch of swansdown, and Nervolini, who was too sore and stiff to bend his hams, standing in posture of abjection before him; whereupon the Dictator, conscious that this was not a picture to impress the proletariat, motioned them away with as imperial a gesture as he could manage in the circumstances. In this his pride conquered his wisdom, to his immediate downfall: for now Cuanduine caught him up by the middle and carried him out, just as he was, to that very balcony on which the final humiliation of the Lambians was designed to have been staged for the delectation of the conquerors. There he gave forth his hero cry, and at the sound of it the citizens of Wolfopolis came flocking from all parts into the square beneath, thinking by its note of triumph that it was a signal from Nervolini to announce their victory over the hated Lambians. By thousands and tens of thousands they came pouring in, and so tight were they packed that you could have driven a motor-car over their heads and have felt not a jolt if it had been well sprung. But what a sight met their eyes when they looked up to the balcony. There stood Cuanduine leaning over the marble balustrade, and balanced upon one hand was their revered and worshipped lord, Nervolini the Fifth, the Great, the Earthshaker. There he dangled with his breeches down, as red as the setting sun of Wolfia's glory. For a moment the great people of Wolfia were in stupefaction; then they did what a great people could only do in the circumstances: they burst into a roar of laughter that shattered every pane of glass in the windows of Wolfopolis, and reverberated from the encircling hills over the waters of the sea to the Lambian coasts beyond.

After that there was peace between the Wolfians and the Lambians, and the Wolfians rebuilt the cities and villages they had destroyed: which moved the Lambians to cancel the arms they had devised for themselves in commemoration of their deliverance, namely, a pair of breeches descendant under a slipper rampant.

From this episode we learn a lesson of humility and brotherhood which I commend to all tyrants, war-mongers, and money-grabbers, and to all disbelievers in the equality of man: for the best and the worst of us, and the greatest and the smallest of us could be put to the blush in this matter as easily as Nervolini.

Thus far the account of the Wolfo-Lambian war; and here endeth the first part of the ancient epic tale of the deeds of Cuanduine.

EIMAR O'DUFFY (1893-1935) was born in Dublin. Both a participant in and, beginning with the publication of his first novel in 1919, a critic of the Irish nationalist movement in the first decades of the twentieth century, O'Duffy devoted much of his prolific body of work to the satirizing of modern Irish culture.

MICHAL AJVAZ, *The Golden Age.*
The Other City.

PIERRE ALBERT-BIROT, *Grabinoulor.*

YUZ ALESHKOVSKY, *Kangaroo.*

FELIPE ALFAU, *Chromos.*
Locos.

JOE AMATO, *Samuel Taylor's Last Night.*

IVAN ÂNGELO, *The Celebration.*
The Tower of Glass.

ANTÓNIO LOBO ANTUNES, *Knowledge of Hell.*
The Splendor of Portugal.

ALAIN ARIAS-MISSON, *Theatre of Incest.*

JOHN ASHBERY & JAMES SCHUYLER, *A Nest of Ninnies.*

ROBERT ASHLEY, *Perfect Lives.*

GABRIELA AVIGUR-ROTEM, *Heatwave and Crazy Birds.*

DJUNA BARNES, *Ladies Almanack.*
Ryder.

JOHN BARTH, *Letters.*
Sabbatical.

DONALD BARTHELME, *The King.*
Paradise.

SVETISLAV BASARA, *Chinese Letter.*

MIQUEL BAUÇÀ, *The Siege in the Room.*

RENÉ BELLETTO, *Dying.*

MAREK BIENCZYK, *Transparency.*

ANDREI BITOV, *Pushkin House.*

ANDREJ BLATNIK, *You Do Understand.*
Law of Desire.

LOUIS PAUL BOON, *Chapel Road.*
My Little War.
Summer in Termuren.

ROGER BOYLAN, *Killoyle.*

IGNÁCIO DE LOYOLA BRANDÃO, *Anonymous Celebrity.*
Zero.

BONNIE BREMSER, *Troia: Mexican Memoirs.*

CHRISTINE BROOKE-ROSE, *Amalgamemnon.*

BRIGID BROPHY, *In Transit.*
The Prancing Novelist.

GERALD L. BRUNS, *Modern Poetry and the Idea of Language.*

GABRIELLE BURTON, *Heartbreak Hotel.*

MICHEL BUTOR, *Degrees.*
Mobile.

G. CABRERA INFANTE, *Infante's Inferno.*
Three Trapped Tigers.

JULIETA CAMPOS, *The Fear of Losing Eurydice.*

ANNE CARSON, *Eros the Bittersweet.*

ORLY CASTEL-BLOOM, *Dolly City.*

LOUIS-FERDINAND CÉLINE, *North.*
Conversations with Professor Y.
London Bridge.

MARIE CHAIX, *The Laurels of Lake Constance.*

HUGO CHARTERIS, *The Tide Is Right.*

ERIC CHEVILLARD, *Demolishing Nisard.*
The Author and Me.

MARC CHOLODENKO, *Mordechai Schamz.*

JOSHUA COHEN, *Witz.*

EMILY HOLMES COLEMAN, *The Shutter of Snow.*

ERIC CHEVILLARD, *The Author and Me.*

ROBERT COOVER, *A Night at the Movies.*

STANLEY CRAWFORD, *Log of the S.S.*
The Mrs Unguentine.
Some Instructions to My Wife.

RENÉ CREVEL, *Putting My Foot in It.*

RALPH CUSACK, *Cadenza.*

NICHOLAS DELBANCO, *Sherbrookes.*
The Count of Concord.

NIGEL DENNIS, *Cards of Identity.*

PETER DIMOCK, *A Short Rhetoric for Leaving the Family.*

ARIEL DORFMAN, *Konfidenz.*

COLEMAN DOWELL, *Island People.*
Too Much Flesh and Jabez.

ARKADII DRAGOMOSHCHENKO, *Dust.*

RIKKI DUCORNET, *Phosphor in Dreamland.*
The Complete Butcher's Tales.

RIKKI DUCORNET (cont.), *The Jade Cabinet.*
The Fountains of Neptune.
WILLIAM EASTLAKE, *The Bamboo Bed.*
Castle Keep.
Lyric of the Circle Heart.
JEAN ECHENOZ, *Chopin's Move.*
STANLEY ELKIN, *A Bad Man.*
Criers and Kibitzers, Kibitzers and Criers.
The Dick Gibson Show.
The Franchiser.
The Living End.
Mrs. Ted Bliss.
FRANÇOIS EMMANUEL, *Invitation to a Voyage.*
PAUL EMOND, *The Dance of a Sham.*
SALVADOR ESPRIU, *Ariadne in the Grotesque Labyrinth.*
LESLIE A. FIEDLER, *Love and Death in the American Novel.*
JUAN FILLOY, *Op Oloop.*
ANDY FITCH, *Pop Poetics.*
GUSTAVE FLAUBERT, *Bouvard and Pécuchet.*
KASS FLEISHER, *Talking out of School.*
JON FOSSE, *Aliss at the Fire.*
Melancholy.
FORD MADOX FORD, *The March of Literature.*
MAX FRISCH, *I'm Not Stiller.*
Man in the Holocene.
CARLOS FUENTES, *Christopher Unborn.*
Distant Relations.
Terra Nostra.
Where the Air Is Clear.
TAKEHIKO FUKUNAGA, *Flowers of Grass.*
WILLIAM GADDIS, JR., *The Recognitions.*
JANICE GALLOWAY, *Foreign Parts.*
The Trick Is to Keep Breathing.
WILLIAM H. GASS, *Life Sentences.*
The Tunnel.
The World Within the Word.
Willie Masters' Lonesome Wife.
GÉRARD GAVARRY, *Hoppla! 1 2 3.*

ETIENNE GILSON, *The Arts of the Beautiful.*
Forms and Substances in the Arts.
C. S. GISCOMBE, *Giscome Road.*
Here.
DOUGLAS GLOVER, *Bad News of the Heart.*
WITOLD GOMBROWICZ, *A Kind of Testament.*
PAULO EMÍLIO SALES GOMES, *P's Three Women.*
GEORGI GOSPODINOV, *Natural Novel.*
JUAN GOYTISOLO, *Count Julian.*
Juan the Landless.
Makbara.
Marks of Identity.
HENRY GREEN, *Blindness.*
Concluding.
Doting.
Nothing.
JACK GREEN, *Fire the Bastards!*
JIŘÍ GRUŠA, *The Questionnaire.*
MELA HARTWIG, *Am I a Redundant Human Being?*
JOHN HAWKES, *The Passion Artist.*
Whistlejacket.
ELIZABETH HEIGHWAY, ED., *Contemporary Georgian Fiction.*
AIDAN HIGGINS, *Balcony of Europe.*
Blind Man's Bluff.
Bornholm Night-Ferry.
Langrishe, Go Down.
Scenes from a Receding Past.
KEIZO HINO, *Isle of Dreams.*
KAZUSHI HOSAKA, *Plainsong.*
ALDOUS HUXLEY, *Antic Hay.*
Point Counter Point.
Those Barren Leaves.
Time Must Have a Stop.
NAOYUKI II, *The Shadow of a Blue Cat.*
DRAGO JANČAR, *The Tree with No Name.*
MIKHEIL JAVAKHISHVILI, *Kvachi.*
GERT JONKE, *The Distant Sound.*
Homage to Czerny.
The System of Vienna.

JACQUES JOUET, *Mountain R.*
Savage.
Upstaged.
MIEKO KANAI, *The Word Book.*
YORAM KANIUK, *Life on Sandpaper.*
ZURAB KARUMIDZE, *Dagny.*
JOHN KELLY, *From Out of the City.*
HUGH KENNER, *Flaubert, Joyce and Beckett: The Stoic Comedians.*
Joyce's Voices.
DANILO KIŠ, *The Attic.*
The Lute and the Scars.
Psalm 44.
A Tomb for Boris Davidovich.
ANITA KONKKA, *A Fool's Paradise.*
GEORGE KONRÁD, *The City Builder.*
TADEUSZ KONWICKI, *A Minor Apocalypse.*
The Polish Complex.
ANNA KORDZAIA-SAMADASHVILI, *Me, Margarita.*
MENIS KOUMANDAREAS, *Koula.*
ELAINE KRAF, *The Princess of 72nd Street.*
JIM KRUSOE, *Iceland.*
AYSE KULIN, *Farewell: A Mansion in Occupied Istanbul.*
EMILIO LASCANO TEGUI, *On Elegance While Sleeping.*
ERIC LAURRENT, *Do Not Touch.*
VIOLETTE LEDUC, *La Bâtarde.*
EDOUARD LEVÉ, *Autoportrait.*
Newspaper.
Suicide.
Works.
MARIO LEVI, *Istanbul Was a Fairy Tale.*
DEBORAH LEVY, *Billy and Girl.*
JOSÉ LEZAMA LIMA, *Paradiso.*
ROSA LIKSOM, *Dark Paradise.*
OSMAN LINS, *Avalovara.*
The Queen of the Prisons of Greece.
FLORIAN LIPUŠ, *The Errors of Young Tjaž.*
GORDON LISH, *Peru.*
ALF MACLOCHLAINN, *Out of Focus.*
Past Habitual.

The Corpus in the Library.
RON LOEWINSOHN, *Magnetic Field(s).*
YURI LOTMAN, *Non-Memoirs.*
D. KEITH MANO, *Take Five.*
MINA LOY, *Stories and Essays of Mina Loy.*
MICHELINE AHARONIAN MARCOM, *A Brief History of Yes.*
The Mirror in the Well.
BEN MARCUS, *The Age of Wire and String.*
WALLACE MARKFIELD, *Teitlebaum's Window.*
DAVID MARKSON, *Reader's Block.*
Wittgenstein's Mistress.
CAROLE MASO, *AVA.*
HISAKI MATSUURA, *Triangle.*
LADISLAV MATEJKA & KRYSTYNA POMORSKA, EDS., *Readings in Russian Poetics: Formalist & Structuralist Views.*
HARRY MATHEWS, *Cigarettes.*
The Conversions.
The Human Country.
The Journalist.
My Life in CIA.
Singular Pleasures.
The Sinking of the Odradek.
Stadium.
Tlooth.
HISAKI MATSUURA, *Triangle.*
DONAL MCLAUGHLIN, *beheading the virgin mary, and other stories.*
JOSEPH MCELROY, *Night Soul and Other Stories.*
ABDELWAHAB MEDDEB, *Talismano.*
GERHARD MEIER, *Isle of the Dead.*
HERMAN MELVILLE, *The Confidence-Man.*
AMANDA MICHALOPOULOU, *I'd Like.*
STEVEN MILLHAUSER, *The Barnum Museum.*
In the Penny Arcade.
RALPH J. MILLS, JR., *Essays on Poetry.*
MOMUS, *The Book of Jokes.*
CHRISTINE MONTALBETTI, *The Origin of Man.*
Western.

NICHOLAS MOSLEY, *Accident.*
Assassins.
Catastrophe Practice.
A Garden of Trees.
Hopeful Monsters.
Imago Bird.
Inventing God.
Look at the Dark.
Metamorphosis.
Natalie Natalia.
Serpent.
WARREN MOTTE, *Fables of the Novel:*
French Fiction since 1990.
Fiction Now: The French Novel in the
21st Century.
Mirror Gazing.
Oulipo: A Primer of Potential Literature.
GERALD MURNANE, *Barley Patch.*
Inland.
YVES NAVARRE, *Our Share of Time.*
Sweet Tooth.
DOROTHY NELSON, *In Night's City.*
Tar and Feathers.
ESHKOL NEVO, *Homesick.*
WILFRIDO D. NOLLEDO, *But for*
the Lovers.
BORIS A. NOVAK, *The Master of*
Insomnia.
FLANN O'BRIEN, *At Swim-Two-Birds.*
The Best of Myles.
The Dalkey Archive.
The Hard Life.
The Poor Mouth.
The Third Policeman.
CLAUDE OLLIER, *The Mise-en-Scène.*
Wert and the Life Without End.
PATRIK OUŘEDNÍK, *Europeana.*
The Opportune Moment, 1855.
BORIS PAHOR, *Necropolis.*
FERNANDO DEL PASO, *News from*
the Empire.
Palinuro of Mexico.
ROBERT PINGET, *The Inquisitory.*
Mahu or The Material.
Trio.
MANUEL PUIG, *Betrayed by Rita*
Hayworth.

The Buenos Aires Affair.
Heartbreak Tango.
RAYMOND QUENEAU, *The Last Days.*
Odile.
Pierrot Mon Ami.
Saint Glinglin.
ANN QUIN, *Berg.*
Passages.
Three.
Tripticks.
ISHMAEL REED, *The Free-Lance*
Pallbearers.
The Last Days of Louisiana Red.
Ishmael Reed: The Plays.
Juice!
The Terrible Threes.
The Terrible Twos.
Yellow Back Radio Broke-Down.
JASIA REICHARDT, *15 Journeys Warsaw*
to London.
JOÃO UBALDO RIBEIRO, *House of the*
Fortunate Buddhas.
JEAN RICARDOU, *Place Names.*
RAINER MARIA RILKE,
The Notebooks of Malte Laurids Brigge.
JULIÁN RÍOS, *The House of Ulysses.*
Larva: A Midsummer Night's Babel.
Poundemonium.
ALAIN ROBBE-GRILLET, *Project for a*
Revolution in New York.
A Sentimental Novel.
AUGUSTO ROA BASTOS, *I the Supreme.*
DANIËL ROBBERECHTS, *Arriving in*
Avignon.
JEAN ROLIN, *The Explosion of the*
Radiator Hose.
OLIVIER ROLIN, *Hotel Crystal.*
ALIX CLEO ROUBAUD, *Alix's Journal.*
JACQUES ROUBAUD, *The Form of*
a City Changes Faster, Alas, Than the
Human Heart.
The Great Fire of London.
Hortense in Exile.
Hortense Is Abducted.
Mathematics: The Plurality of Worlds of
Lewis.
Some Thing Black.

RAYMOND ROUSSEL, *Impressions of Africa.*

VEDRANA RUDAN, *Night.*

PABLO M. RUIZ, *Four Cold Chapters on the Possibility of Literature.*

GERMAN SADULAEV, *The Maya Pill.*

TOMAŽ ŠALAMUN, *Soy Realidad.*

LYDIE SALVAYRE, *The Company of Ghosts.*
The Lecture.
The Power of Flies.

LUIS RAFAEL SÁNCHEZ, *Macho Camacho's Beat.*

SEVERO SARDUY, *Cobra & Maitreya.*

NATHALIE SARRAUTE, *Do You Hear Them?*
Martereau.
The Planetarium.

STIG SÆTERBAKKEN, *Siamese.*
Self-Control.
Through the Night.

ARNO SCHMIDT, *Collected Novellas.*
Collected Stories.
Nobodaddy's Children.
Two Novels.

ASAF SCHURR, *Motti.*

GAIL SCOTT, *My Paris.*

DAMION SEARLS, *What We Were Doing and Where We Were Going.*

JUNE AKERS SEESE,
Is This What Other Women Feel Too?

BERNARD SHARE, *Inish.*
Transit.

VIKTOR SHKLOVSKY, *Bowstring.*
Literature and Cinematography.
Theory of Prose.
Third Factory.
Zoo, or Letters Not about Love.

PIERRE SINIAC, *The Collaborators.*

KJERSTI A. SKOMSVOLD,
The Faster I Walk, the Smaller I Am.

JOSEF ŠKVORECKÝ, *The Engineer of Human Souls.*

GILBERT SORRENTINO, *Aberration of Starlight.*
Blue Pastoral.
Crystal Vision.

Imaginative Qualities of Actual Things.
Mulligan Stew. Red the Fiend.
Steelwork.
Under the Shadow.

MARKO SOSIČ, *Ballerina, Ballerina.*

ANDRZEJ STASIUK, *Dukla.*
Fado.

GERTRUDE STEIN, *The Making of Americans.*
A Novel of Thank You.

LARS SVENDSEN, *A Philosophy of Evil.*

PIOTR SZEWC, *Annihilation.*

GONÇALO M. TAVARES, *A Man: Klaus Klump.*
Jerusalem.
Learning to Pray in the Age of Technique.

LUCIAN DAN TEODOROVICI,
Our Circus Presents . . .

NIKANOR TERATOLOGEN, *Assisted Living.*

STEFAN THEMERSON, *Hobson's Island.*
The Mystery of the Sardine.
Tom Harris.

TAEKO TOMIOKA, *Building Waves.*

JOHN TOOMEY, *Sleepwalker.*

DUMITRU TSEPENEAG, *Hotel Europa.*
The Necessary Marriage.
Pigeon Post.
Vain Art of the Fugue.

ESTHER TUSQUETS, *Stranded.*

DUBRAVKA UGRESIC, *Lend Me Your Character.*
Thank You for Not Reading.

TOR ULVEN, *Replacement.*

MATI UNT, *Brecht at Night.*
Diary of a Blood Donor.
Things in the Night.

ÁLVARO URIBE & OLIVIA SEARS, EDS.,
Best of Contemporary Mexican Fiction.

ELOY URROZ, *Friction.*
The Obstacles.

LUISA VALENZUELA, *Dark Desires and the Others.*
He Who Searches.

PAUL VERHAEGHEN, *Omega Minor.*

BORIS VIAN, *Heartsnatcher.*

LLORENÇ VILLALONGA, *The Dolls'
Room.*

TOOMAS VINT, *An Unending Landscape.*

ORNELA VORPSI, *The Country Where No
One Ever Dies.*

AUSTRYN WAINHOUSE, *Hedyphagetica.*

CURTIS WHITE, *America's Magic
Mountain.*
The Idea of Home.
Memories of My Father Watching TV.
Requiem.

DIANE WILLIAMS,
Excitability: Selected Stories.
Romancer Erector.

DOUGLAS WOOLF, *Wall to Wall.*
Ya! & John-Juan.

JAY WRIGHT, *Polynomials and Pollen.*
The Presentable Art of Reading Absence.

PHILIP WYLIE, *Generation of Vipers.*

MARGUERITE YOUNG, *Angel in the
Forest.*
Miss MacIntosh, My Darling.

REYOUNG, *Unbabbling.*

VLADO ŽABOT, *The Succubus.*

ZORAN ŽIVKOVIĆ , *Hidden Camera.*

LOUIS ZUKOFSKY, *Collected Fiction.*

VITOMIL ZUPAN, *Minuet for Guitar.*

SCOTT ZWIREN, *God Head.*

AND MORE . . .